ANA ATANASKOVIĆ

MY LOVE NIKOLA TESLA

2022 YU Biblioteka Paper Edition

ISBN 979-8-218-06632-1

Translated by Vesna Savic
Book design by Hristina Radovic
Translated from Serbian by Vesna Savić

Dedicated to my father, Stanimir Atanasković, who died a few months before this novel was finished. My interest in science, metascience, the natural and supernatural, all originate from him. I was a very young girl when I first started reading about women who used to love Nikola Tesla in his Galaksija (Galaxy) magazine.

I know he must be proud of me now, wherever he may be.

Table of Contents

AIR

FEBRUARY

I got this leather notebook from Mr. Robert Underwood Johnson, whom I first met back in January. He returned to New York after having paid a visit to his family in Washington. Yesterday he told me something daring before his journey: this is a gift for you to take note of your heart's secrets.

§

A big lamp is hissing in my bedroom: it is already dark outside. I love fantasizing.

Mr. Johnson went away, promising to frequently write to me. I, Katharine McMahon, had drawn his special attention. He is 22 years old, born in Washington D.C., in Capitol Hill, just like me. He is three years older than me, and I find his company quite pleasant. He comes from a well-known family. His great-grandfather, after whom he got his name, was one of the first Washington settlers, and a recognized mathematician. His grandfather, John, is remembered for his honesty. His late father was a judge in Little Centerville, Indiana, where Robert had spent his childhood (both of our fathers died in our early childhood). He graduated from the Earlham College in Richmond when he was 18.

He is very venturesome and hardworking: he used to work in Chicago, first as an officer at Scribner Educational Publishers. Soon after that, he was promoted to a *Scribner's Monthly's* Editorial Team member, which is published in New York. He told me he is also writes poems! Tennyson, Shelley, and Keats are his main role models.

Now my mother and sister keep asking me about him and what I am going to write about in my notebook. They will never find out; this notebook is mine only and I will note down my big, selfish secrets in it.

§

We, the McMahon family, initially come from Ireland, but moved to Washington a long time ago. My grandmother used to tell me that, out of all the members of our family, I have most of the ardent, Irish blood. Ellen was jealous of me a bit. Granny was right: I was rebellious, demanding, and impetuous ever since childhood, but also reliable and bold. I am no renegade nor a hero; all the McMahons are similar, only I am the most childish of us all – I flash when there is a need for it and when there is none.

§

Robert Underwood Johnson is a son of Nimrod Hog Johnson and Katherine Coyle Underwood. He got his name after his mother's great-grandfather who was born in Tiron County, Ireland. His birthday is on January 12. He has a brother called Henry and a sister called Margaret. My mother says it is important when you meet someone to learn all about that person, because there is no point in regretting it later on.

He has a neat little beard and moustache right above his lips, his eyes are calm, and he wears little spectacles. His starched collar is perfectly clean, his appearance dignified and lordly. He loves the Latin language and finds learning it is not senseless. They are the same – precise and wise.

3

APRIL

Robert Underwood Johnson keeps sending me the magazine he is working for. His handwriting is nice because he uses thin lines to connect words, and writes mature and confident sentences, but a pink message always manages to find its way in all of his letters. He keeps getting more daring and opening up. Finally, I have something that is only mine, someone who devotes his attention to me and only me.

MAY

It seems he likes me. He writes about my reddish-brown hair and smile. My hair is thick, wild, and wavy, just as it should be. I do not need to use metal curlers.

Everything is so sweet and serious. I find it pleasing, although sometimes it seems like a game. In fact, I do want to play. I am more frivolous than him; my letters reflect it. His are more devoted than mine. I sleep restlessly, but I like that, I love it when my whole-body trembles. I love being loved. I enjoyed his looks. I enjoyed him wanting me. He is a person I can trust. For my birthday I was merrier than ever, truly naughty in nature.

JULY

We walk and spend a lot of time together. He is trying to hide his impatience and I am hiding that my thoughts are wandering off – I am with him, but also somewhere far away. My mother tells me I am a coxcomb, and it is high time I should get serious. Poetry, conversations, plans, looking from under our eyebrows, hints of touches. I think I will be able to love him.

He keeps telling me about his editor in chief and friend, Mr. Richard Watson Gilder, and how through him he got to meet many famous people. Mr. Johnson is like a doorstep of a big house – everything starts from him, and he holds everything in his hands. He brings me pastel wildflowers that smell gently. He is a great aficionado of nature.

SEPTEMBER

When we are away from one another, I miss his attention. My mother told me: "Decide whether you want him or not, he has already been yours for a long time now." It is true, I want to live protected and in comfort and to be the first and only to someone, his whole world, I want someone to fulfil all my whimsies and give me everything. What am I waiting for?

NOVEMBER

This is probably the greatest Thanksgiving Day in my life. I am engaged! No, I do not wish to question myself any further.

DECEMBER

While he was going away, I realized he wanted to come back as fast as he could, it is as if he is scared of leaving me alone with my thoughts. Everything is calm now. I have only my little smiles in a silent room where candlelight is shimmering. Soon I will be listening to carriage thumping and the bubbling sound of horseshoes in New York.

His seriousness was interspersed by snowflakes that fell onto his coat, while he was standing in front of the door, tired from the journey, but dignified, and too excited, dazzled by my eyes. He is elegant, I like seeing his rigidity melt like snowflakes, so he looks at me with love, while his sharpness remains. He combines his behavior and clumsiness with his looks, but that is why he is even dearer to me.

The mild touch of his hand, long conversations, promises... I am in awe thinking about the future I wish to run into.

1876

MARCH

Now we have no secrets and I do not even think about them. Sometimes it seems someone pulled me by the hand. Is Robert my soul mate? Nobody ever paid such gentle attention to me like he does, so steadily and persistently, choosing his words. He got to see my character and does not mind when I, for example, write whimsically, when I am demanding, when I get angry. His reaction to everything is always wise and calm. He will be my hiding place, the cornerstone of safety, the man who understands me best. He is going to wish to hold me forever, but the time has also come for me to be held.

AUGUST

I cannot wait for the last day of August to come; it is when our wedding is to be held. Robert spends all his time at our house, helping me with everything. He is also nervous, but his dignity always seems to soften every unusual emotion. I am so impatient I could just jump.

SEPTEMBER

Our wedding was romantic and modest. Robert was modest, the McMahons were merrier and more direct than the Johnsons. I think everybody is convinced I am finally going to find peace of mind and that my capriciousness is now over.

He has not approached me as a man yet. I think he does not wish to startle me. Tomorrow we are traveling to Philadelphia to visit the Centennial Exposition, the first of its kind in the US.

I give him a remarkable look when I am supposedly looking at my reflection in the mirror, when he does not expect it. Do I see shame in his look?

§

Philadelphia is the soul of the US. The Exhibition is fantastic. We got to see the Horticultural Hall with gigantic and tiny plants from the most exotic parts of the planet, the telephone, a small printing press, the Statue of Liberty's right hand holding a torch, that is to be set in New York.

§

It finally happened! We made love! I cannot say I enjoyed it, it did hurt and there was a lot of blood. Robert was caring and worried throughout the whole experience.

DECEMBER

I would like for our passion to become a sanctuary of completely surrendered souls and bodies. I often get dry quickly, but my succulence remains trapped – although I wish to drip and drop out entirely. I cannot, I am not even invited nor encouraged to do so. I wish to give myself so that I no longer know of myself after the act of love. After making love, we are aware of who we are.

Robert says I am soft and rough. I love playing with those words. I sometimes get cheeky in such games. It happens rarely, but it happens. I may wish him to subdue me, to tie my hair in one move, maybe that is why I challenge him. I wish for him to get stronger.

He will never read what I uncover in this notebook; it is my freedom. He often calls me "my dear wifey".

1877

JANUARY

We have arrived in New York a few days after Thanksgiving. It is magnificent, completely different than low-key Washington. New York is the proclamation of all things new. It is diverse, its faces are modern, people are busy. New York grows rapidly, every day, it seeks a lot, and it provides a lot as well. Robert is in love with me, and I am in love with New York.

We frequent at the home of Mr. Gilder and his sophisticated wife, Helena de Kay, in 103 E 15th Street. Gilder had participated in the Civil War on the side of the Southern Army. His eyes are sad, and his moustache is big and thick.

We listen to chamber concerts at their place. I believe I manage very well because I am friendly. Helena is a painter and a model for other painters. She is so fragile and tender that I cannot help my jealousy of her activities and career, even if I wanted to. A dark yellow energy bursts out her paintings. She is active and a founder of painting associations. She is always on the move and all distinguished New Yorkers know her. When she speaks of herself as a model, she becomes incredibly alive, completely different, extroverted. as moist as forest soil. They have a son called Rodman.

The moments we spend with them are marvelous not only because they are kind and entertaining hosts and dear friends of ours, but because we also get to meet the New York elite, all the artists I'd heard so much about, and other interesting people.

The brown bricked house at the brink of Mary Hill area in 327 Lexington Avenue is soon to be ours. I felt good when we viewed the house.

FEBRUARY

Manhattan is a marriage of crowdedness and amplitude – its streets are sometimes overcrowded, and you can even reach the island's edges, where the open sea cuts one's view. The sounds are also different here, somewhat hoarse – one can hear horse huffs stomping, the squeaking of merchants' pushcarts. All merchants yell in the streets – medicine sellers, hat sellers, umbrella repairmen, people who look like sandwiches wearing advertising boards over their clothes, shoe shiners, newspaper boys, boys who do tricks or play the street organ, girls selling matches and flowers....

It feels good. New York speaks all languages and is constantly humming.

The subway is also loud; it takes time to get used to the metal bars above your head and hums coming from the avenues.

I love the Fifth Avenue. And the elegant Delmonico's restaurant at the corner of 26th Street. I love its striped awnings and the Palm Hall.

No other city has a store like the one from Broadway, between Ninth and Tenth Avenues. It is five floors high – it is a shopping mall. It has the biggest assortment of silk, carpets, shawls, dresses, all your heart's desires.

Manhattan is strange, entrenched by water and long lines of wooden docks. Powerful steamboats and ferries reach it. They simply hurdle towards it.

I usually walk the *Ladies Mile*.[1] It is located between Broadway and Union Square and the most extravagant stores can be found in it. Its shop windows are made of thick glass. My walking dress is made after the newest fashion, with a long train. Young men in liveries open doors for the ladies and welcome them in their shopping.

At Tiffany's my senses vanish.

Robert and I stroll in the evenings when beam of light illuminate the streets.

At Central Park, I experience a mystery of winding trails and spiteful waterfalls. It is surrounded by marble castles; those are the Fifth Avenue's richest residents' homes.

MARCH
We have met Joseph Jefferson at the Gilders. He is a comedian actor. His acting is natural and spontaneous, as are his

---

[1] *The Ladies Mile* – a historic district in Manhattan (located from 18th until 24th Streets and from South Park Avenue until Sixth Avenue) where the biggest shopping malls were located until World War I. – *All notes are the editor's.*

conversation and socialization skills. He seems to be a good teacher. We watched him in his legendary Rip Van Winkle role.

§

We have finally moved into our home. I will rearrange this house so as the visitors feel pleasant and warm as soon as they cross our doorstep. It will be our sweet home, the warmest and the most loved place in the city, a hideout for good, creative, and interesting people.

I can wiggle as much as I wish, in Robert's heart.

§

We have a very loud furnace, a golden brown, jute sofa and golden damask draperies. We bought antiquities at an auction – six lira chairs and a Sheffield silver tray with grapes on the edges. We had our photographs framed. Robert insisted to frame a photo of me done at the Paul Tralier's Washington studio, right after we got married. He says I am so cute and melancholic, so romantic and tender in a pelerine, and half-turned towards the world.

He brought me hot gingerbread sold in the streets; I love it a bit more than the big pretzels.

We have hired servants, two reliable Irish women, who are also our relatives. They are called Josie and Nora. We do not ask them to dress us in the morning like rich people do.

MAY

New York has changed me. It helped me open up, it gave me new blood. It aspires to reach the stars. Everyone in Washington noticed I've gotten much louder. Can I reach even higher tones? I can, they are somewhere inside of me, I just need to lure them out.

Robert's mother is a wonderful and caring woman, she played the guitar and sang for us and seems to be starting to like me. Robert's sister Margaret is married to Anthony Johnston, a well-known trader. His brother Henry, however, is even more serious than Robert. Henry is lean, almost skinny, and his eyes are big. His personality is more piercing, whereas Robert is mild and quiet. Henry went to law school and has been an attorney for five years now. He is living in Richmond, but he goes to Washington almost every week. His wife is called Lilian.

My Ellen is about to get married. Her fiancé is called Martin Kaveney. He chose her and she obediently accepted his marriage proposal. Mr. Kaveney is also a trader. Ellen does not have expectations that make her burn, she does not wonder what will happen, nor does she have set expectations of pleasure in advance. I too should be like her.

AUGUST

After lovemaking, we still know who we are, but that might be good for marriage: to be on safe ground.

Robert expresses feelings of joy and lets go rather more in his letters than when we are facing one another with our clothes off. When we look at each other naked, he is often silent and contrite, as if he wants to spare me. I am trying to show him he does not need to.

What can be more important than being safe in every possible sense?

SEPTEMBER

I bought a satin dress and a fan with ostrich's feathers that inspires my passions to come alive.

DECEMBER

Robert's shirts have to be perfectly white, his striped daily pants must not have any freckles. I shall convince him to buy a coat with a karakul collar.

We bought a Steinway piano.

§

I told Robert I am pregnant! He kissed me, he wanted to carry me, he chanted, hugged me, he is distorted out of happiness. I have never seen him so silly.

Pregnancy puts me to bed. I cannot walk or rush around the city that much anymore. It is nice to say "we". Robert now pleases me even more, in all kinds of things.

§

I've acquired another evening dress. It is a cherry-colored muslin. I also have new white formal goatskin gloves.

15

EARTH

1878

FEBRUARY

Everything is open and we know what is to happen. Robert told me I am sometimes erratic, that at one point I think of one thing, on another occasion – of something else, that I get mad and then quickly forget why I was being angry in the first place. There is some truth to it.

AUGUST

I must note down in my notebook that now I am a mother of a small boy we call Owen.

DECEMBER

I kiss my son's forehead, his little fingers, his cheek, I keep watching over him, I am him, and he is me. Robert is now even more serious, he is the head of the family, a father one could only wish for. Owen is as soft as silk, loud as the noon, it is always daytime with him, there are no nights, I never sleep, I do not remember sleeping, though I probably did. But the softness makes up for everything, and it feeds my soul when I feed him.

1879

JULY

I am with child again. The feeling is similar, although I am not stunned, only tired. I am carrying another child under a pale pink dress with tiny wrinkles on the bosom. Robert brought me pink roses, he is teasing me: he says I should give them a chance as well, aside from just the red ones. He is ever more in love with me, as if he is growing, as if he is getting enchanted again, stronger than when we first met. I am stable, although sometimes there is an expectation full of restlessness waiting for me just round the corner. I would never like to see him suffer.

AUGUST

Our entire family was here, as well as Helena and Gilder, and all of our friends – on our son's first birthday. I do not think as I used to about cracks through which I cannot slip my skin and look for bodily sensuality that would make my heart spume. My life is now subordinate to commitments. Robert's predictable stability is welcome in our family life, he now erases my wishes that run out of the circle. All is well.

He keeps writing poems and plans to publish them soon. In his pieces, he is flying far above the clouds, although his face looks strict when he is at his writing desk. He writes thoroughly, steadily, with discipline. He first takes notes on blue-lined sheets of paper, and then when he believes a poem is done, he copies it with care onto a new white sheet of paper.

I would still like to rip his restraints when we are intimate. I tried, although I have not reached far, but I cannot talk about that with him. He is too much of a gentleman to tear my skin, bite my lip, angrily ruffle my hair, and breathe out bite marks on my shoulders. This is why I too step back, and everything remains in the middle, decent and dignified.

1880

FEBRUARY

My second childbirth was more difficult than the first, but I am already forgetting about it. I brought our little girl into the world. Her name is going to be Agnes.

NOVEMBER

We got a dog, a black Labrador pup. We shall call it Lord Hamilton.

1881

JANUARY
Robert wrote a poem about wintertime at the library. He was looking at Gramercy Park and its black fence. He wrote about roses he remembered from his father's rose garden in Indiana. The roses he had never seen again.

He is never melancholic in the real world, only in his poems.

FEBRUARY
Owen was entertaining the guests at Agnes' first birthday. He is talkative and also likes to listen; he was showing his new shoes to everyone and asked them to tell him something interesting.

Ellen and my mother visited us as well. Ellen is pregnant!

JUNE
Ellen gave birth to a healthy girl, thank the Lord. We will soon visit her in Washington. Her name will be Rose.

NOVEMBER
Scribner's Monthly became a newer, prettier, and better magazine; it is now called *The Century Magazine*. It is still at the corner of Fourth Avenue and 26th Street.

Robert is going to be writing about interior decoration and old furniture from the colonial period. There will be more poetry and painting in it, which he is quite excited for. The magazine is going to be a home of the spirit. He is spending all his time in the office with Gilder, who is editor in chief now. Unfortunately, Dr. Holland has died. I am frequenting at Helena's when our husbands are at work.

Although I try to hide it, Robert feels I am longing for something more, so he tries to compensate for it with more worrying, work, words of endearment, and devotion. I am his and he is fighting for my thoughts and body. For a long time now his heart has been sitting in mine.

§

Robert is going to publish his two poems in *The Century*. His words are neat. It is as if he was embroiling, but in a very disciplined way, with lots of ornaments. Scholarly words, put together in harmony, do not drag you full force forward but with their intellect, they are nearly perfection.

A poem about me is very dear and as childish as I am. "The Love Calendar". My birthday is in May, and he wrote a poem about trying one's luck to find love in May. He also tore some attempts and threw them into a bin with disappointment. The poem's rhythm is faster and simpler, as well as the words, just the way I like it. So far, no poem of his is truly seductive, but charming. My birthday had turned it into a love poem, but also into a piece of advice to everyone that this month is the best month to find love in. When parts are cut out and rejoined into one dear flower. Other months are windy, wet, arrogant, cold as pearls. "Love has the seasons, just like the year," Robert says, and is grateful for the month that brought me into life. "May is here and the hearts will do what they wish for."

I sat at the piano and played the keys out of order. The salon was buzzing with sounds. The kids got scared.

1882

JANUARY

Robert is thrilled by inventors, he says inventiveness is a special form of art, both genius and practical at the same time, and for such an art one needs to be courageous and capable. He feels that the inventor's mind can reach the deepest truths and deepest secrets. He received a task to write an article about Thomas Alva Edison for *The Century*, which is now located at a new address (33 E 17th Street). He is going to visit him at his laboratory ranging for two blocks in Menlo Park, New Jersey. Edison's nickname is "the Menlo Park Wizard". I could instantly imagine a dark, secretive lab and my first association was a wet night, the rain has just stopped, and in the backyard there are big trees with heavy branches.

Edison the inventor must be some kind of an eccentric working at nighttime. A crackling sound of short circuit is loud in the dark. He invented the light bulb! It is a round magic lamp with a pointy top that emits the light. Robert says Edison invented the phonograph as well, a device that records sound.

MAY

Sweet children's questions and their discovery of the world make me simply not think of yesterday nor tomorrow. Kids seem to recreate the world they are surrounded by. Ellen will soon bring Rose to us. This time they are going to stay a little longer. I love her, but I do not tell her everything.

JUNE

Today the whole city is talking about Mr. John Pierpont Morgan, a financier and a banker who has only yesterday installed the electric bulbs in his house in the corner of Madison Avenue and 36th street. His whole house is illuminated. It is rumored that the light bulbs produced a lot of sparks last night, but it will all be fixed very soon. We must pass by it and see the light. The lighting was installed by the Edison's Electric Co.'s workers. Gas lamps are soon going to go to oblivion.

People are saying a lot of people are afraid of Morgan because he is very quiet and smokes one cigarette after another, and his nose is unsightly – red, like a schnoz, all bloated due to a dermal disease, terribly ugly. They also say Morgan's look is mesmerizing. I will have to see for myself.

§

We have passed by his house with the Gilders. The Moon was hiding, so the light had no assistance whatsoever. His whole house is illuminated. One could see its magnificent beige pillars and marble. The details are not visible from Madison Avenue, but as a whole – it might appear it is a bright day in the middle of a black night because of all the light coming from that big and mighty house.

AUGUST

We are in Bar Harbor, Maine. Ellen and Rose are visiting us for a while.

We are going to garden parties and horse races. Main Street is always bursting with life, I like the big pillar clock and vivid colors, the yellow and dark brick color. I bought a pink lady's parasol. Bright colors are everywhere, completely different than the gray and green coast.

DECEMBER

It is easy to find a solution of everybody else. But how could one find a solution for oneself? When we kiss, I wish I could feel Robert's breath more and more. His kisses are but shorter now and I kind of feel his diffidence. It is his current maximum point.

What can I do to melt Robert away? Our bodily love is but friction and nothing more. If I could just bite him! But I cannot seem to manage it. It is all getting down to his pleasure every time.

1883

MAY

The Brooklyn Bridge was opened, with fanfare, fireworks, and a cannonade. It is the best birthday present. We have walked on it at the promenade. Its construction reminds me of a spider web. It resembles o-shaped legs. And it has two eyes as well.

JULY

Robert met Tommaso Salvini, a famous Italian actor, who is in the US on tour. He was our guest. He is a vital and bright-spirited man, with smart eyes and big moustache. He set on stage for the first time when he was fourteen. He was telling us about his great success in Alfieri's *Oresto* and his participation in the Italian independence war. Robert says Salvini is the greatest performer he has ever seen.

AUGUST

When I hug both Agnes and Owen and gently press their heads on my chest—and feel their little bodies under my biceps in puffy sleeves—I feel like an antique vase with wide handles on both sides. I am completely calm on such occasions.

We go to the outskirts of great American forests that are getting ready for the fall. Robert thinks nature is the prettiest and the most powerful, the most beautiful of all human creations and buildings.

Mother is not feeling well. She does not complain about anything, but I can see everything is difficult for her, including herself, and the perennial tiredness is starting to show on her face.

§

My mother has died. We buried her yesterday.

NOVEMBER

Robert was telling me about a young enthusiastic member of the city government, Mr. Theodore Roosevelt, who visited Mr. Gilder to discuss a park protection plan. Parks are Robert's greatest love, so he immediately liked Mr. Roosevelt.

DECEMBER

New York is honest all the way, its contours are straight. They can be very sharp if one does not get by; and if you learn to get by the whole world is your oyster.

New York is wanting. When it gets what it was wanting for, then it can offer you everything.

1884

FEBRUARY

New York got new trolleys, powered by electricity.

APRIL

Robert is yearning for nature, he writes down all the stylistic figures he can think of, he says March's hair is freezing, he yearns for velvet air in the fields and plan tassels hanging from the trees.

JUNE

During his holidays in Point Pleasant, near Long Branch, New Jersey, Gilder informed us that General Grant finally accepted to be interviewed by Robert for *The Century*.

SEPTEMBER

The Century started publishing Mark Twain's novel, *The Adventures of Huckleberry Finn* in sequels. I enjoyed his *Tom Sawyer* piece when I read it.

At the beginning of the novel, Huckleberry Finn says that change is all he ever wanted – to go somewhere new.

Mark Twain catches the reader's interest, there is no stopping; I am drawn into his play and do not wish to stop.

NOVEMBER

Mr. Twain visited our family home. That is, Mr. Samuel Langhorne Clemens, because Mark Twain is his literary pseudonym.

When I excitedly received him in the salon, he immediately resolved the question of his name by saying: "Oh, for God's sake, just call me Mark."

Owen and Agnes ran towards him, and he greeted them with a joke. He is very direct, but in fact is the funniest person I have ever met. We were laughing all the time. He is an unusual man: his moustache is big and hair restless, his look is piercing and hidden behind his smile – but not because he is mean. On the contrary, he is a spitting image of witty wisdom assessing what degree his jokes need to be in conversation, depending on what his interlocutors are like.

Anyone would wish for Mark's life so far, because he is adventurous and likes sailing, but I doubt they would manage to lead such a life. Everything he told us, both happy and sad, was told with a dose of humor and in his particular manner. I was thrilled by the way he turns all life situations to his advantage. "Mississippi is always hungry," he said at one point, with a mixture of melancholy and laughter.

There is still a boy in shabby pants crouching from this man, exploring the world around himself. Boys are of a strange kind, carefree and always ready for an adventure.

His voice is cheerful and sparkly, he likes toying with serious stuff. He was telling us about his wonderful wife, Livie, and their daughters, Suzy, Clara, and Gene. Suzy is his favorite. He also told us about his journey to the Rocky Mountains. He tried to stop smoking a thousand times.

He won all of our hearts.

DECEMBER

We have installed light bulbs as well!

1885

NOVEMBER

We are soon setting off to Europe. It is so strange to leave this world and go to another.

Street sellers offer us baked pears that smell delicious.

I am too excited to eat or sleep. Robert's mother came to take the children to Washington. She is a wonderful creature who finds kind words for anyone. Robert once told her she would see only the best even in the devil himself.

The house is so strange when empty. I thought it would be more passionate this night when we are left alone, but Robert is the same. That is why I took over: I love unusual new situations, even if they bring restlessness. That is to say, I love only such occasions, the ones that make my stomach rumble. I tried to give myself to Robert in a different way, more openly and provocatively. It did not bother him, but he took me in the same classical way – the only way he knew. I did not manage to take him with me.

§

Our boat is called "Alaska". Our first stop will be Liverpool.

"Hungry waves," Robert said. It seems that there is a spot in the middle of the Atlantic that separates the two worlds. When you pass by it, you seem to get another life.

DECEMBER

We are headed towards Naples—leaving Liverpool, London, and our time in Paris behind us.

We made a stop in Avignon, because Gilder gave a recommendation to Robert to visit a Provençal poet, Mr. Joseph Romanillo.

It is so nice to visit different cities because you seem to get a pinch of their smiles and forget about yourself in the meantime. That is, you get more alive, and it is as if you are a different kind of you.

1886

JANUARY

Everything is different in Italy – the less fortunate are joyful and careless, perhaps the most careless of all. Time is getting slower here and it is as if we are taking big, heavy steps. The sky is wider and smaller than in the US, but it is more intimate and brighter.

FEBRUARY

Naples made me stop me taking my crazy notes. We were not bothered by the noise nor screaming at all. The sea was grey but full of golden reflections. The city is white, and it smells alike, even though the streets are all but white.

We have visited the Nuovo and Del Uovo castles, ate the most delicious lentil pasta and spaghetti with mussels (here the food for the poor and rich are equally delicious) and we were very idle.

On our way to Pompeii, I was thinking about how the most difficult task is to understand your own heart.

APRIL

Everything tastes like the sea in Sicily.

MAY

Robert says England makes him feel at home, and he is right.

JUNE

It is nice to be Robert Underwood Johnson's wife. We met Robert Browning yesterday. We were at a luncheon at Mrs. Zhen's, who organized artistic and literary gatherings.

§

I keep telling him he should trust the female instinct more and that your feeling is more important than your reason. Our instinct and emotions allow us to evaluate more than in cold thinking.

We are two worlds. Hot and cold blood. Dream and reality. Sensitivity and restraint. I evaluate people based on my feelings and he based on their words. I run and chase and he stop by and returns.

JULY

All I have ever read about Paris was true. Its charm and beauty are indescribable. The Louvre is wonderful. When you enter it and walk the paths of the royals, you are simultaneously a queen and a grain of sand.

I was looking at a painting in the Montmartre for a long time; it was next to a few other paintings, with similarly bright colors, from the same artist. Nevertheless, they portray still life, flowers in vases and this one portrayed the Luxembourg Park. The shapes had dark contours and the peacefulness of natural nuances is broken by two coral-colored ladies' parasols. Their contours are smeared and seemingly unconnected to others, far from each other. This image offers tranquility and light, but tranquility can easily fall apart because the coral color seems to be prying about, as if it was screaming – coral-colored dots can take the visitor way into a completely unforeseen whirlpool.

§

The children will be joining us soon. I am bright as the colors in that painting. I want to take Robert to an unforeseen whirlpool. I want to go mad from passion, to be younger than we are, to love each other wildly and more freely. I sometimes truly do not get him. He is an artist and understands all nuances of feelings. He transmits passion into poems. He is touched by trance. But in physical love he is still uptight, usual, unimaginable, simple. He is ashamed when I kiss him here in a different way than is usual. He pushes my hand aback when I draw him closer to me.

AUGUST

All the wonders that surround us are not as pretty as when you hug your children. I have time to hug them in Paris. Robert is going to Athens via Rome, with Mr. Scott. Agnes will be staying in Paris for a year in a monastic school *Couvent de l 'Assomption.*

1887

JANUARY

Owen and I greeted Robert in Naples. This might have been the adventure of his lifetime. He smiled and told me that living with me is his greatest adventure.

He was telling me about the beauty of the Parthenon temple, that superiorly rules the blinding whiteness of its own position.

MARCH

New York has big eyes: when you return to it, it embraces you. It is confident, tall, a mixture of this and that, proud of being so special.

Gilder introduced us to the famous German pianist, Adela aus der Ohe. He has already written a poem about her. She paid him a visit and promised to organize a music night at our house.

§

I keep reading Agnes' letters with longing. She is exemplary and brave. Sometimes it seems to me I have nothing to offer her anymore, she has taken everything, and improved all. And when it comes to Owen, I could now sit with him and play with marbles.

JUNE

Mrs. Johnson brought Agnes back from Paris. Agnes is apologetic. She comes and goes. She is left alone, brought back, she accepts everything that happens to her, without any rebellion.

She started loving Paris a lot and behaves as if she was still there. She speaks French marvelously, and she is telling me about her girlfriends. When I kneeled before her and hugged her, I felt as if the emptiness inside of me was filled back again. Agnes is a diamond we kept missing.

SEPTEMBER

Robert's brother Henry has become a member of Indiana State Senate. He is a Republican.

§

Another Republican entered our circle of friends, and his name is Mr. Theodore Roosevelt. He lost the mayor elections last year as the third competitor. Robert believes in him in every sense possible, he says he is a very practical person. One can notice this immediately: he has zero tolerance for the pathetic and self-deceit. Everything on him indicates a stable and a truly ambitious personality. He is corpulent, consistent: he loves boxing and the navy and says that plants and animals directly come from God's hand. This is Robert's religion as well.

DECEMBER

A poem of an unusual poet, Walt Whitman, called "The Twilight" was published in *The Century*. He writes about nirvana and oblivion. His verses are completely different than all the poems I have ever read before: they are stunning, on the border of disturbance, and quite free.

1888

JANUARY

Happiness seems to be simple. But it seems to be so difficult to find simplicity and dwell in it forever. I build and shape little towers, I keep putting one onto another, wishing to build absolute pleasure. Every tower should be enough, but I want to make a mosaic, I want to arrange them all. It seems I am wrong. I love each of them with all my heart, when I am alone with myself, but I keep longing for an ideal structure. I sometimes dislike being that way, I sometimes think it is the only charm – to keep striving for the heights incessantly.

MARCH

When I am completely alone, I comb my hair, so it becomes thicker and gruffer. I let it stay the way it wants to: wild and big.

DECEMBER

At the border of 16 Gramercy Park, banker Boot's house was renovated and equipped and now is going to become The Players Club for gentlemen. Even the facade was changed: instead of brown bricks, it is now a reddish Italian style building. Robert is invited to become a member, among other businessmen, attorneys, writers, and journalists, together with Gilder. Mark Twain also joined the club.

1889

MARCH

Robert went to California to research and write about gold diggers. I am left with an article about Madrid in *The Century* while he is looking for John Moore, a natural scientist. He finally met a person in love with the nature more than him. Robert has zero vanity, he admires all successful researchers. Maybe nature indeed has an answer to all questions of the mind and the heart.

John Moore says we all come from one fountain and all souls are expressions of single love.

APRIL

The Century published Robert's poem "Flowers of Glory". I cannot wait for him to find out.

SEPTEMBER

Henry is no longer a congressman. I know he has served this country as honorable as he could, and he could have achieved a lot more if he had the time.

OCTOBER

John Moore is in New York. Robert promised to bring him over right after the agreed walk in Central Park, so he did. I completely understand why Robert is tied to this man. His look is big and clear, his soul is calm, he likes everything around him, accepts everything, he is one with his surroundings, with the ground he walks on, he does not need to speak to say it.

When he speaks, his lips (which are hidden under a very long beard) utter full and ripe tones. He is nature's priest.

1890

JANUARY

A small kiss for New Year's Eve, the one that is implied.

I bought a women's magazine, *Harper's Bazaar*. I like fashion suggestions – a collar with satin roses, velvet dresses, and I must buy cocoa for breakfast.

FEBRUARY

We met Stanford White, a young New York architect, who visited us. This year, the building of Madison Square Garden II is to be finished instead of the old one in the corner of 26th Street and Madison Avenue. The project was financed by this city's numerous powerful people, Morgan being one of them.

White designed the interior of The Players Club. He is an unusual creature. He has a wide, curly, intimidating moustache and an old man's look, and his soul is clearly very disobedient. It is very easy to notice his inborn disdain, which, in his case, does not evoke negative reactions at all. There is no arrogance in him, but elitism that is his by right. He knows what he will be and become. He does not highlight his knowledge in conversations, as it is not really necessary, because it is noticeable he knows a lot. I like him and would like us to become true friends. He is intelligent, decisive, and ready for anything. Robert will hire him to design the magazine cover.

§

44

I must stop by the dressmakers on 210 Fifth Avenue. I need a new cashmere winter dress.

MARCH

Our house is a home for many great people. Thomas Commerford Martin, an electric engineer, visited us today. He used to work with Edison and now is the editor in the *Electric World* Magazine. He still has a fresh British accent, which makes him charming. He seemed to be too shy, but that was just my initial impression; he is but extremely careful. His eyes are expressively round.

§

Robert is writing a poem about Chopin's fantasy. He is calling for silk in his words, thrilled with the exterior. Silk is placed on a pedestal. I want it in my wet hair and between my legs.

APRIL

I hope I am not anything like women who think about the width of their dress' folds. Life is art. We write our names in the earth's body – in stone, clay, or sand.

NOVEMBER

The new Madison Square Garden was opened today. White also made himself a nice apartment within the building.

There is the nude goddess of Diana's gilded statue on top of the tower. The whole city is talking about it. It is scandalous. What else could be expected from White than a sensual provocation? It is Stanford White, or Stany as we now call him, being closest friends.

White's wife Betsy is not fond of White's new apartment. It is rumored that, besides the eccentric nude sculptures and rare books, he also enjoys the crude company of different young girls. He changes them as he pleases, and as the time passes by, he gets more eccentric, demanding, and perverse.

1891

APRIL

An aspiring English poet, William Watson, paid us a visit. He writes traditional, disciplined poetry, similar to Robert's. Robert still loves reading the revolutionary Walt Whitman, although it seems to me I sort of feel him better, even though he still writes blank verse. It seems to me you can say more with free verse, since words are more powerful free than rhymed.

1892

JANUARY

Gilder introduced us to an English writer who is touring the US. His name is Rudyard Kipling. He was born in Bombay and is heart is tied to India. This is his second visit to the US, but now he is traveling with his wife Carrie. They are on their honeymoon. Kipling is on his way to becoming a great writer, his ideas are very exotic. He is a man who is both strong and soft, harsh and emotional, decisive and prone to commitment.

MARCH

We have arrived in Florence and are living in small hotel rooms in the heart of the city. I have a great wish to create a paradise for Robert and myself, our own little heaven. I want us to wait for the dawn together, to get lost in beauty, and for me to pull his hand equally. The Arno bridges are our labyrinths, I laugh and want Robert to laugh more. I want us to wander.

§

Mr. Salvini invited us to a dinner in his villa. He dominated the conversation for the bulk of our time there. We also met his sons, Alessandro and Gustav.

After dinner, our host recited a poem about Columbus, written by a young Venetian poet. These people's leisure smells of soil and sweat. It is juicy and contagious.

APRIL

The rain is pouring chills all over Venice, and the Sun brings gold. We met Twain in front of a restaurant at Saint Mark's Square. He was accompanied by his old lady friends. I love that man very much. His gift to pull you into his funny stories is majestic, it dazzles with joy and ease of living. This time he told us about a prophetic dream he had during the time he was still in Mississippi. Namely, he dreamt of his brother's death on a ship in detail. When he came back home, it turned out his dream was unfortunately true, to the very last detail.

It is possible to see and dream the future. Messages appear in people's dreams. People are connected with dreams. Miracles exist.

Mark Twain is a workshop in which all the stories from this world are gathered. He loves Italy because its soul is warm. It is completely different than France that, as he put it, has no winter nor summer, nor moral.

In the end, when he encompassed all the beauty around us with his look, he told us with a momentous smile to never abandon our illusions because they can prevail even when we are gone, but our life would then be over. I will remember this.

§

We met Twain again. We were walking along an open gallery on the east side of the Uffizi court and noticed a strange man gazing at a painting. When we approached, we realized this man was in fact Twain. He did not notice us for a while because he was astonishingly immersed into an ordinary image in the street. At first we did not want to interrupt him. When he did notice us, he jumped, laughed, and stretched his arms to hug us. Then he was all serious explaining us this is the only painting that drew his attention of all the gallery's masterpieces – whose value is supposedly greater. He added that one cannot enjoy such masterpieces while is so fun and enjoyable to observe this painting. Then he laughingly said he is glad all the great masters of painting are dead. The only thing that bothers him is that they did not die earlier.

§

The change of the weather is noticeable, I am sleepy, but this does not prevent me from enjoying Asolo. We met a famous actress, Eleonora Duse. She knows what she wants and does not hide her feelings like I do. I think there are no variations of happiness and unfulfillment in her, she is probably always equally serious with dignity. She is very intelligent, and her face shows she deeply thinks about everything. Such a woman would reach wherever she pleases. She does not fall down because she cleared her way. She is happy because she is living her dream.

SEPTEMBER

America is sweet, Europe is salty.

Owen is soon going to Lawrenceville School in New Jersey, and his departure is erasing all reconsiderations and reflections. Of course, he is excited and ready. Robert is steady as a rock, and I am doing quite well too, I know my child needs to live his life and learn how to live away from us.

OCTOBER

It is kind of boring in fact.

Robert is happy he found us amusement for this evening. Have we already reached that point to have to find stimuli in the outer world to regale ourselves in the evening? Eleonora Duse is in New York and tonight she is playing her role in the *Lady with the Camellias* for the first time in front of a US audience. We welcomed her in our home. The party was grand. Gilder and Helena were especially jolly, I think the diva set a good vibe for everyone. I felt the excitement was only Eleonora's, and the rest of us got ahold of its parts only, like dew drops, and got stronger from her. I want to be the spring – of warmth or dew, it does not matter, it is only important for me to be the spring, big enough so other people can drink from it.

DECEMBER

Our brown house is an unusual shell, gathering famous people. We met Antonín Dvořák. His face seems to be roughly carved, seemingly petrifying. He brought a different energy, strong, decisive, and tall. He came to New York to become the director of the National Music Conservatory. He played on our Stanway. His fingers are a fighter's, he played explosively, and his music was gentle, Slavic, an incompatible combination, that made us all silent. Artists give their best, completely, at one point, that we, the audience, devour in a moment. It seems that what they give is ridiculous, it vanishes so quickly, but the spark keeps spreading, we spread it, through other people, we enlighten ourselves and approve of it, we get better and caring for other people because a piece of art touched us from within.

Their heart turns into something small in us, and then again into something big that comes out of us.

FIRE

1893

FEBRUARY

Sherry's Hotel became a new mundane place. His restaurant can compete with Delmonico's, they are now rivals. Stany is glowing with joy.

I love the quadrille, I feel solemn when I dance. Robert is getting on well too.

MARCH

New York has the best hotel in the world – the Waldorf Hotel. William Waldorf Astor opened his 13-floor hotel today, built at the corner of Fifth Avenue and 33rd Street, after having his late father's house torn down.

APRIL

Robert is on his way to Chicago to the Columbian Expo. It will be the greatest world fair of wonders. Stany fulfilled all the commentators' wish to remove Diana's statue – it is now at the top of the Expo's building.

MAY

I do not like it when I do not take part in an event, I want to see and hear everything he sees and hears. I am jealous! I am thirsty!

I want a miracle for myself.

I am 37 and I am observing my hand on my chest when I am laying down. It is thin and smooth in dim light. When I stretch my fingers completely and take a better look, the top of my palm wrinkles a bit, as if it gets flaky. I put it back on my chest and feel its distant smoothness. Am I moving forward or backward? I am mature and ready. Or am I a child that already has children who are also grown up? Am I starting my story or just finishing it? What can I start doing?

I can do anything.

JULY

We are all in Maine, Ellen is here too. Self-loving waves talk of unusual things too, their rustling sensuality makes me want to cry. It seems to me I do not know when I am lonelier, when he is around or when he is not, so when I look at my thoughts in a real way, it seems to me I am crazy and ungrateful.

SEPTEMBER

Owen founded a literary magazine called *The Lit* in Lawrenceville and is its editor in chief. He is only fifteen! My enterprising and creative child, he has taken all the best from us.

DECEMBER

A famous Australian diva, the soprano singer Nellie Melba performed in the Metropolitan Opera. She sang Lucia of Lammermoor. She was at a reception at the Guilders and we met her. She has a strong look and an unforgiving character. She behaves like a diva… maybe even too much, but it suits her.

Robert was excited when he came back from the editorial office. He was intrigued by something. He is trying not to show the change on his face, as if everything needs to be perfect all the time. I like the fact that he is curious, wise, and often awake, but I would love for him to present his inspiration: I do not like it when he is silent, when I am waiting for him to write, I would like for him to tell me what he feels immediately. That is why I use the fondling method.

Why is he not more like me? Why is he keeping his exciting thoughts? Why does he not want to tell them to me right away? When will I change him?

I started fondling and cooing without asking immediately what the matter is; I was patient and meek, which was really hard for me to do, and I almost got crazy and bombarded him with different questions. It is hard for me to play games and not be the feisty me, but it was worth it – he finally told me the whole story, and I must admit it is interesting.

Namely, today Commerford described him a wizard who arrived from a strange region in Europe, I cannot remember exactly its name – nevertheless, it is a part of Austria-Hungary. That wizard is, according to Commerford, in fact an aspiring scientist, and he is pleading for him very much since he is enchanted by his personality. Commerford said that scientist sees better and further than us all, and he is even better than Edison.

How intriguing. I noticed Robert was all melting. The description was so attractive that he told Commerford to bring that man for dinner to our place.

Bravo, Robert. What is a home if there are no guests to entertain? That wizard must be the most unusual creature we have ever seen, he must look different, behave strangely, he must wear funny clothes, like some strange being from a fairy tale.

I have never seen a wizard before. Had Robert not highlighted he is a man of our age, I would have expected a grey, old man speaking in codes.

Commerford is going to bring him over to us so he can talk to Robert about an article that scientist could write for *The Century*. Robert is trying to make the magazine modern and progressive, and if it turns our Commerford was right (and I know that is exactly what will happen), both the magazine and the young scientist are going to prosper as well.

He took a nap in my lap, and I cuddled his hair while he was telling me about their encounter. I still need to melt him down: after all these years living together, he still wraps his thoughts into wrapping paper.

Why is he not more like me? If I were him, I would start shouting from our doorstep about that wizard, so everyone could hear and gather before me, I would tweet, without further questions, I would blurb everything in one breath, and....

§

I slowly recall my memories of yesterday, and it seems it all happened much earlier. Is it possible only two days have passed?

I slowly introduce and lure the images that appear one after another, they listen to me and do not meddle at all. I have met the wizard. His name is Nikola Tesla, and he entered our home with Commerford. He is incredibly tall, has royal standing, refined elegance, and is poised and calm. He was taking his white buckskin gloves with two black buttons off so slowly I could not stand it, as well as his perfectly tailored black coat and a fine long tailcoat with a satin passepied. He made me feel so impatient and calm at the same time. His face was long and puzzled, a true gentleman's face, but of a wise elf as well. He is quiet and pale, at first glance, and I would say a bit aloof, but he does not let his first impression to last long, because he breaks it with his grey-blue eyes, bursting unattainably with strangeness, so that impression turns into its opposite.

His walk is silent and abrupt. The wizard is, as it seems, capable of staying in one position for hours, taming bloody fire burning his chest and fingers. The fire in that man, it intrigued me the most, but it is not the same as mine – witty, orange, made of grumpy, short tongues – no, it is snake-like, hungry, coming from the heart of the Earth. It is set in the finest porcelain shell. I have never seen such a man who is so tender and powerful at the same time.

He was so gentle with Agnes and Owen, and they clicked instantly, as if they sang a song they started themselves, completely naturally and easily.

Robert was enchanted as well, his face was glowing with smiles while Nikola Tesla, the wizard, was telling us about Europe. I was expecting a person who would be more foreign, but this man speaks English perfectly, his manners are silky, and his voice manly.

What about me? I was stunned, but nobody hardly noticed anything.

We sat around the table, and it seemed as if he was around forever, as if he was a part of our family, which was quite confusing. But all that confusion was lost when Nikola Tesla started talking to us more directly. Frankly, this was the first thing that confused me: I thought this dignified and unusual man would keep his distance, but he talked openly about his tiredness and exhaustion, and that all his life is subordinated to his experiments. He firmly believes in his own work. Oh, how decisive he is.

We were sitting there, eating dinner, chatting, all so cheerful, our home was so warm, I felt as if a web of golden flakes was falling all over us and remained in our hair. I was lulled and ablaze. Now, when I can see the scene again, I notice we were all looking at him only, listening to him all enchanted, but he did not try to bewitch us, he simply behaved as he usually would, but then again in such as particular manner. His fingers are long and beautiful, his hair neat and smooth, his moustache clearly prompted. decorating his face, and his eyes are penetrating.

It was quite logical and expected, so, without thinking things through, I spontaneously invited him to spend Christmas with us, as if it was a usual thing for me to do. The kids were thrilled with my suggestion and Robert gave me only one mild look to show I was reading his mind.

So we all sat like that, seemingly reddish and alive, besides him, who kept being pale, despite the wine. I can still see that web of golden flakes' patina all over us. And in one hand move, Nikola Tesla rips it and takes it off. He was speaking with much excitement at that moment: he invited us to his laboratory for dessert, as if he was calling us to a mysterious cave full of diamonds. Since both Robert and I said yes immediately, he seemed to have gotten his wings: his eyes had flashed as if he suddenly found a way through a thousand labyrinths, so he jumped up (easily, ably, quickly, flexibly) and invited us to the coach.

And then there was real magic! Warm tears started pouring from my face in the coach, they rolled down from all the unfamiliar excitement, we were silent, taken aback from his strong energy that led us firmly through the city, along Gramercy Park and Washington Square all the way to Fifth Avenue. There were more people in the streets that night than usual, or so it seemed. I wanted for the ride to last longer, but also to get to the wizard's lab as soon as possible. I cannot tell what was more beautiful – to ride with him in sparkly silence, to hold my hand on my belly that hurt from hope and expectation or being in the lab itself. At one point, while we were still sitting in the carriage, it seemed he looked at me differently, with curiosity, although that very moment that look faded away, and I realized I was probably exaggerating, since he was probably only enjoying himself, in advance, for showing us his kingdom.

Although, that moment, that look keeps possessing me.

His laboratory was full of strange devices. Perfectly clean and neat. Heavy and fresh fragrances were mixing in semi-darkness. I am unable to describe it with veracity. You could feel metal and rainy fragrances. Stale and moist, sort of. Long cables and dark devices, one could barely see them, vanished completely when the scientist drew the black curtains. And then one could only hear our breath. Robert and I were as if in another world, and Mr. Tesla was still moving around silently, preparing the spectacle, warming our curiosity and excitement up. Time was speeding up, as well as my heartbeats, to the point I could not bear it anymore.

I felt he was moving, but I could not hear him. Robert took me by the hand one second before innumerable flash lines and shapes flew by our heads. I have never seen such a thing in my life! Rustling, golden, orange, and blue clouds, fast and playful, seemingly without a goal, flew all over the place without colliding, and my eyes seemed to have been filling with some sort of... light, the sun? I do not know.

I was trembling in fear and pleasure. Mr. Tesla stood mute, as if his body had elongated, he seemed to be as tall as a giant, and his hands were even bigger holding a big light bulb shining with warm light. He was happy, it was a right, calm, inner happiness, unconditional, godly. He was safe. A majestic giant, king of light, a beautiful magician, a true wizard, but what is Mr. Tesla?

He finally managed to draw relief, joy, and wondering from us. Then he lifted us up even more by showing us what the world is intrigued by – the motor he invented, with a light flash, above his forehead in a park in Budapest. It is a motor with a lava core.

He stayed in his lab when Robert and I went home. Who knows when he will go to his room in the Gerlach Hotel in W 27th Street? We stayed outside for a few moments, silent, listening to the rustling and buzzing sounds that crept in us.

I was alive in a new way, as if someone woke me up all of a sudden, which is why I was disoriented, but I know I was smiling, and so did Robert, we were looking at each other and our eyes were sparkling.

.   §

I keep thinking about Mr. Tesla. He is transparent. Weak and strong. How can he be both transparent as a ripe petal and impenetrable as granite? He moves without making a sound. He is slipping through the air. He seems dignified. His face often appears to be made of stone. He is often absent, his spirit is not present. His movements are as soft as lace. He has long bony silky fingers and a sinewy palm with plump mounts. His hands can dig canals and emit the light. How can this be?

§

He talks of electromagnetic waves. I do not know what kind of waves I feel, but there are waves between humans too, in any of our interactions. I am overwhelmed by his waves. Those are invisible powerful circles traveling from him towards me. They spread from him, like when you throw a stone in the water and see how wrinkles reverberate on its surface. They meet in me. Like rosebuds.

§

I cannot sleep again. Robert is sleeping like a baby, so I snuck out of the bed, and am now sitting in the salon. I feel hot all the time. It is cold outside, but I feel hot. Everything is tiresome, my every movement, I keep sweating from every little move, my armpits are wet, and that sweat is somewhat heavy, and I am not inclined to it. Is it because of my age? I am already… Am I changing? Am I losing my womanhood? Am I getting heat waves? Am I getting older?

I must be beautiful, more beautiful than ever!

How can I think of such a thing? I can. How can I? And Robert, if only he knew!

I am still young and beautiful! I have just looked at myself in the mirror, my contours are unclear under such weak light, I am all alone in our salon, writing in convulsion, in dim light. A watery and unclear Kate was reflected in the mirror, but she was pretty, her hair was thick, eyes big and her skin young.

I do not know where this heavy sweat is coming from. This is not me. Or, maybe, those are some poisons I got free from, some sort of nausea I threw up? Maybe I am me, and something of mine which was unfamiliar to me got out on the surface? What is going on?

§

Robert found me in the salon early this morning. I fell asleep there. I must admit he was confused and in wonder, although, in fact, my dear Robert was worried as ever. There was no reprimand in his voice, and God knows there should have been.

I dreamt of Mr. Tesla. I have never had such a dream before. It was real! I turned my back away from the mirror and saw him sitting still, but it was as if he enclosed a small space and air around himself, and was its sovereign emperor, and the rest of the salon was trembling, and the colors were overflowing. He crossed his legs and looked at me. He looked the same as he was at dinner, only his eyes were black. It was a great, mirk black color. In fact, his eyes were turning into two pulsating black holes. As if he was calling me: I could not hear anything, he did not say anything, but he somehow managed to communicate with me, and I had to start walking towards him. I was grunting, pausing my breath for longer and longer. I wanted to touch his face, but simultaneously I was afraid. Wanting and fearing. Can the two emotions go alongside one another? "Katherine," he said without moving his lips. His eyes were getting blacker and blacker, and widening.

Then Robert woke me up. He told me I was screaming.

§

I bought damask napkins for our Christmas dinner. I want everything to be perfect. Energy and elegance gushes keep blowing like the wind in the fall. Everything seems to be like it is our first time. Agnes and Owen are excited because Mr. Tesla is going to spend Christmas Eve with us. Robert is excited, too. I am more clumsy than usual, I keep dropping things. I know everything needs to be ideally clean and sterilized for him. Tablecloths, cutlery, *everything*. He washes his hands several times a day, in restaurants he inspects if the dishes are clean enough, and he additionally rubs his cutlery with napkins.

§

Holiday candles were illuminating us differently than usual. Mr. Tesla was sitting modestly and unobtrusively, maybe it was a bit uncomfortable for him. As if he was trying to tell us he is a foreigner after all, that he is not a part of our little world. One could notice he felt uneasy, and it was as if he wanted to say it, but his cheeks finally turned red due to such closeness. His body language was showing something opposite of his thoughts. He liked us.

That man is a lighthouse. He is standing alone on a rocky coast, he can see everything, he illuminates everything. But he is also a cup, a silver cup waiting to be filled with wine, warm blood, kisses, tenderness – even though he does not want to admit it.

He was chatting with the children, telling them of his childhood adventures, how he was petting a tomcat and a field of shimmering sparks appeared above it. Then he asked them if they knew who pets the nature. The children were listening

65

to him attentively. They laughed together. He was joking with the kids in a decent manner. He is not an offensive prankster. That is good. Some people hide their own evil by mocking others. There is zero evil in Mr. Tesla.

"Dinner was splendid, Mrs. Johnson." I knew that, I paid attention to every minute detail. He was telling us about his father and mother, about his sisters, his home, how he snuck out in the night to read even though his father forbade it because he was reading too much. He merely mentioned his older brother, a shadow marked his face. A blink of a lighthouse. Eyes shut.

He is incredible. A boy, a man, a ruler.

He was telling us how he conquered the deep breathing technique. I tried to do it all night long, but I gave up. I cannot do it: I was breathing too fast and clumsily.

Robert went to the library to bring a collection of Whitman's poetry to read. I was observing Mr. Tesla's lips that moved slowly, as if he knew the lyrics by heart. They were juicy, free, fresh, and sensual. Robert was reading, the words flew into the Christmas night, and each and every word was like a vow. Or was this my wishful thinking – that Mr. Tesla would become a part of us?

Can he lift his dreamy eyelids and keep looking at us with devotion? Can he give himself to us completely? Would he ever want that?

We were all enjoying the food. Roast turkey was just right, cranberry sauce was smooth, goose pate never better, peas incredibly green, and the Parisian salad was gone within moments. Punch was perfect.

He stayed until morning. The day was red.

1894

JANUARY

"You have wonderfully started the New Year's Day, my dear," Robert told me and mildly kissed my nape. I was touching the piano races and remembering the basic steps. I wanted to spill music onto the frozen street, so everyone can hear it and bring guests. So it will bring thee guest.

§

Today Mr. Tesla celebrates his Christmas Eve and I have decided to send him flowers. I must do something, I cannot settle in any way. I would rather visit him personally. The flowers will speak on my behalf. I chose the pretties white roses in the flower shop. They were big and innocent.

§

There is no answer. Today he celebrates Christmas.

I cannot even think about what he is doing. I am thinking about what he is doing.

§

We are children. I am a girl watching a small windmill Mr. Tesla sent me in response to my flowers. I love it that he brings about a child in me. Robert is serious, whereas Mr. Tesla is both serious and frivolous at the same time. Sending this windmill was an easy move for him. Robert is neither easy nor spontaneous. He must always think and reconsider things, and even to previously ponder doing something crazy (and carefulness always seems to pervade). Robert is like a stable and necessary fireplace in a home. Nikola Tesla is like the most spiteful flame. The warmth of an empty pipe moves the windmill. The note read: "This is the most beautiful invention!" He sent me the most beautiful invention ever! How unusual this is. What other lady could receive such a gift? I now have the most beautiful and the most original gift in the whole of New York! All the petals that rose this morning in lazy rooms as gifts to wonderful ladies are nothing compared to my sophisticated windmill sweetly turning its wings.

§

Today I was smoothly looking at him straight in the eye, seducing him while he was drinking tea. I wanted to cause at least an uncomfortable vibe between us.

§

We were at his lab again. Robert participated in an experiment and Mr. Tesla has orchestrated everything from the darkness. I observed Robert in disbelief as the strongest power currents, a system of the scientist's high frequencies, went right through him. Robert was, in fact, a conductor that illuminated the lamps in the lab. My excited Robert, I could rarely see him in ecstasy, and now he was glowing from outside. Mr. Tesla's ecstasy was crumbled, his lip smiled only for a moment, and I managed to catch that little movement. He did not stop, this spectacle is just another step to him, his everyday life. He is both modest and guided by great light that burns his forehead's skin when he bravely outplays the nature.

"Mrs. Johnson, how do you like Mr. Johnson in this role?" he asked, turning the unlit side of his face with invisible curious spheres.

§

Oh, what a night! White, golden, lascive! What is going on? I am burning. I could not look Robert in the eye this morning. He went to the editorial office, kissed me as per usual, and I hid my sin deeply under my sleeping gown. It was important only to hide it away from my face, while Robert was quickly leaving the room.

Then Agnes asked me to help her with her hair, and my sin started burning. I endured the pain while chatting with Agnes, touching her wonderful brown hair, her shiny curls. I endured all the while she needed me, and then I withdrew, went to the master bedroom, and unzipped my dress. I did not feel relieved. I was trying to recall my dream, and the freed red stamp, that was hiding under my dress for long, became ever stronger.

I dreamt Mr. Tesla was coming to get me, I was set already, and the coach was waiting for us. I was very young, and Mr. Tesla was the same age as today. His eyes were grey-blue again, and I was not afraid; on the contrary, I was free and light, childish and carefree.

We entered his laboratory, it was not dark, but completely the opposite: everything was white in there, and all of a sudden it was morning, completely unexpectedly, and golden rays of light entered the room through the open windows. Mr. Tesla hugged me and kissed me, and I kissed him back.

The kiss was soft, smelly, mystical, stunning, and warm. He took my breath away and it felt good.

§

Owen is soon going back to school and he and Agnes thought of asking Mr. Tesla to let them ride his coach, which was waiting for him in front of our home. He immediately said yes and added they can do it whenever they want. His outer stiffness immediately melted away.

§

What do I want: to be loved as a friend by Mr. Tesla or for him to fall in love with me? Friendships last longer.

§

Robert came back from the editorial office with a letter in his hand.

"Mr. Tesla," he shouted, "is saying thanks for your flowers!" The letter read he must thank Mrs. Johnson for the wonderful flowers, since he has never received flowers before, and it left an unspoken impression on him.

Oh my God.

We are friends. I want us to be friends forever. He told us about his birthplace: it is a place with gorgeous flowers. He could simply guess what I was thinking.

He took a little step further from his spiral distance, and I got close to him completely, as hot as Venus turning my head towards the Sun. How close is he to me if he is that distant?

§

I do not know how days are passing by; nevertheless, there is nothing lazy about them, everything is quick. Robert is working harder, Agnes is more joyful, Owen writes jokes in his letters, everyone is looking for something and in a rush. At least it seems so. I am there for every one of them, I cheer them up and organize and respond to every question possible.

The end of January arrived so quickly. It seems as if we stepped into a stellar year, and nothing will ever be the same. I did not have time to think of myself – although, it is not an excuse, to be honest. The last words written were of Mr. Tesla: "an unspoken clue." He visited us after that letter, I did not write about that. I did not want to, I was afraid.

I do now.

He visited us at dinner, he was sitting straight, smiling, and recited Goethe's *Faust*. His reciting is dear and serious, not pathetic in any way, fluently and without errors, convincingly. Later I described all the images that went through my mind while he was speaking, all the colors and face expressions. He told me I am imaginative. Who is that perfect man? A scientist, a poet, an angel? A devotee? A secretive being? He sees everything, he hears everything and feels everything. He is so sophisticated, elegant, strong, and wise. I find his laughter the hardest, I get lost for a moment.

Who is that man? Could he ever love me?

We, the Johnsons, ease his loneliness. He has no house nor home.

I am afraid. I feel nice. Never better.

I want him beside me, I want him for myself only. He has strong mechanisms to defend from love. He is not mine. I would like to have his baby. He is not mine. I would like to lie beside him during the night and to talk with him in the darkness. He is not mine. I would love for him to take care of me. I would like to take care of him.

I accept he is not mine, but one part of me is rotting away. I accept he is not mine, but one part of me is shining.

I want to press him with my body against a wall, so he has nowhere to go. I have no dignity longing has no dignity, it does not come with a price tag. A thousand tongues flicker in my mouth.

I want to dance till I drop down and subdue, to listen to music, to feel its round, plump body, to shed manly tears.

§

Antonín Dvořák finished a symphony in the US. Robert wrote to Mr. Tesla about it, and he got tickets. Mr. Tesla and Dvořák did not meet officially before we introduced them to one another, but Mr. Tesla said he has seen the composer in Prague.

Mr. Tesla travelled all over Europe, persistently and diligently, before he had decided to come to us.

§

We were listening to the *New World Symphony*, directed by Dvořák. I am fascinated. In the beginning, he used music to describe childbirth that is not shy at all, and it is immediately proven by a storm. It is a split that separates the old from the new. Then starts the music resembling sea voyage, a decisive expedition.

America is the new world for others, but the first for me. Dvořák masterfully covered his experience in America – he introduced the tones of prairies, the voices of the wilderness and the thundering of the West, that quickly cross the entire country and reach the East. A search, a heart, a step, a home, a house – between them and within them is America's being. Dvořák presented the explorer's common songs, the dark tones of the prairie, the rebellion, a strong will, dances, cities, and the dawn. This too is America. Playful power. The power that is implied.

Later, at Delmonico's, Nikola Tesla showed us one more time he is the best billiard player in the world. Dinner was delicious, as usual. Mr. Tesla was telling us about the importance of chewing food properly. People usually swallow it voraciously. I have never seen such a meticulous man. His meal is a ritual.

Maybe he is exaggerating a bit. Everything he does is beautiful to me.

"Music is love and love is music," the educated Robert from above says. It is the essence, but I would like him to say it with a tone spreading down the street, like when music creeps out of salons and concert halls with haste.

The art changes the world. When a person hears or sees an artwork, his consciousness changes. The layers of impressions come around. Complex thoughts change the world.

§

This evening, the menu in our house was similar to Delmonico's. I have spent a fortune, but I was trying to make an exhibition. We have had fresh mushrooms on a toast, crabs, lamb chops, stuffed eggplant, and peach pie. I drank maraschino. Mr. Tesla said neither the menu nor the atmosphere are behind Delmonico's. He wanted to be polite, but I could feel he had a wonderful time and is being pretty honest. I love pleasing him and being exclusive.

It seems Robert is more fascinated by him than me. He keeps mentioning him and analyzing him aloud – who he is and where he is from. He keeps stressing how his look is clear, his behavior is cultivated and refined, how genius he is and to what detail he knows classical literary works. This is good, because I too can get fascinated, completely free and without causing any doubt. Besides talking about the children, I think all we talk about these days is Mr. Tesla. We read his letters aloud, as well as Owen's, we comment on them and giggle. I have an alibi. I hide craziness under my pillow, and I pull it out in the morning and spread it all over my face. I can talk with my husband, completely freely, moreover – it is desirable – about the man I am fascinated by. Robert and I seem to follow his movements all the time, and he keeps us informed, we get closer, and his letters are getting more frequent. I follow, in my mind, this scientist's big, elegant steps he proudly makes along Fifth Avenue. Do those people turn around after him? His unusual might is clearly visible on his forehead. I want to be able to see it myself alone. There, in the city, he belongs to everyone. He wants to be an inventor for the benefit of the entire world, I know it, but I also know he wants to be only ours. In fact, only mine.

I am happy. It is as if I am traveling to the unknown, in a romantic train cart, and I know only good things await me at the end of my journey: warmth, acceptance, knowledge, and closeness.

I see his spots in all colors, they are blurry, they overlap, kiss each other, those hazy spots, that are simultaneously bright. What is he? He is crushed light. His body is made up of a plethora of light particles in all hues one can think of. They are tangible at first, and if you look twice, those spots play and run away, they penetrate one another, just like the ocean and East River meet.

I play with Robert too. When we mention Mr. Tesla, my heart beats for two reasons – it is happy, and it is hiding. Fascination is beautiful! Life is beautiful!

When Robert kisses me, he is shaking, I am everything to him, he loves me only, I am his whole world, and I sort of defend myself from his kisses: I shake my head away and rest it on his shoulder. Can he tell I am different? I kiss him back because I should.

§

The three of us were at the salon, preparing to go out, tucking our scarves in. I played a game of knowledge and ignorance – Robert does not know it, I know it, and I want Nikola Tesla to know it.

§

Sunday can estrange one person from another just because they are so close, so one can naturally wish to be left alone. I have been taking care of Agnes and Robert since Thursday, they have influenza, they have been lying down, almost voiceless and in delirium. Robert is feeling better today, and Agnes is still on fire. I felt alive again when Robert asked me to write to Mr. Tesla.

"Dear Mr. Tesla," I started my letter, trying not to let my handwriting give away my longing and impatience. The entire letter had to appear certain, and even charming, and I made it. I even ordered him to come right away to visit us, as a favor. I have not even thought of how brave that is, I did it out of impulse. The letter is now on its way to him, and I am starting to feel hot, but not because of high temperature.

§

He came! He listened to my plea – or did he just come because of Robert? I cannot tell. When he arrived, I welcomed him. It was the first time we were alone together. Maybe it was a bit uncomfortable for him, but he was certainly trying to hide it. My hair was classy; it was obedient and mt=y waves thick, smooth, and glossy. I easily ran down the stairs and opened the door widely. He brought cold with him, as well as the city's live fragrance, but his face was still pale and soft, untouched by evening frost, not red at all. He really put walls around himself and does not let anything influence his body and mind. Oh, that moment we had! He knew Robert and Agnes would be confined in their beds, but he did not expect to see me with such a big smile, swaying and nonchalant. I tried to seduce him, I carried out my attack, seemingly harmless, but still mildly – I am not a person who exaggerates, but I am a person who knows what she wants. I think spending energy on daydreaming is romantic, and one can enjoy it, but if I turn my desire into a pearl smile, step up on the scene and give what may, but if nothing happens, I will think of it in a few days. The moment was ideal.

Tesla embraced my smile and returned it.

"How are the patients?" he asked.

"All the same."

He was dear and open at that moment, but when I raised my hand to touch him, it was as if he closed himself and started walking behind me.

I continued playing even besides Robert's and Agnes' beds, but only with my look – I was looking for those bright crystal eyes. There is no arrogance in him and yet he manages to make himself known. He must have been born with that inborn aristocratic behavior that does not need to be explained nor highlighted. Very skillfully he turns his own complexity, I am not sure anyone will ever understand, into a seeming usualness and simplicity, as if it was mundane and usual, while he is simultaneously and devastatingly different than us, as if he was from an unknown world.

I was playing at the border between fear and shame. I was looking at him in the eye when I gave him a cup of tea, imagining myself kissing him on the lip. Right now, while I am writing this, when he must be in his lab and Robert and Agnes are asleep, tired from illness and lying down, I think of repentance. I cannot explain even myself what is going on with me. It is a big wave that lifted me on the surface, and nothing remains the same anymore.

§

I am lying for the first time. Am I lying or not saying things? Robert does not even know there is a reason for me to lie. Does he know it? Can he know it? Can he see it?

If only he knew, his disappointment would shake me from the bottom up. But would I continue longing for the wizard? I would. What kind of a person am I? I am split into two. It is not my fault. Is it not? It is not. I am. Would Robert's words be full of despise? Full of hatred? Would he understand? Would he still love me? Would he only be sorry, so much that love would disappear? Or would he get mad to take away everything he gave me? No, this is my Robert.

What would happen? He might know it. He might see it. He may be silent about it.

§

I cannot believe the conversation I have had with Martin! He is perceptive because I feel lucky and hooked. We were talking about Mr. Tesla. Robert was in his editorial office. Martin was telling me what I already knew so well: that Mr. Tesla is working too much and is exhausted. He is honestly worried about his friend, and we agreed on it. He almost does not sleep, because he is working all day long, without even thinking about the consequences. He is guided by his higher goals and has the enthusiasm and energy, but we are all wondering how long will he make it, where his limits are, and why is he making such effort to reach them?

"What can we do for him?" I asked Martin with a sigh.

"I do not think I can talk him into reason, but I am sure you can," he responded without a blink.

I? I would and I could, but how? I would love him, I would provide him with support, but that is impossible. There are two strong reasons for it.

I looked at Martin curiously, acting innocent.

"I?"

He then decently explained I should keep warning Mr. Tesla of the possible consequence's exhaustion can have on his health. And what is more unusual to me and what I am, I admit, glad about is the fact that, as he looked at me as if he was revealing me, only I can warn him in that way and I of all women – whom he is afraid of – can influence him. This is true! I mean, I hope it is, although he is incredibly stubborn. But what has Martin noticed? How does he know it all? Am I that obvious? What must then Robert think? Has Mr. Tesla told anything about me to Martin? Martin must not know that I, as it seems, have caught a few Tesla's curious looks. I think he does not look other women in that way. It is not my vanity, I am being realistic. But I thought nobody else noticed it. I tried to keep calm as much as I could while he was telling me I should give Mr. Tesla a lecture about taking a rest at least once a week.

By the way, Martin is going to publish a book about Tesla's inventions and writings. He has been gathering his data very diligently.

FEBRUARY

He pronounces words calmly, clearly, and plainly, but nothing gives an impression of him being slow – he is sure and abrupt. He is persevering. Even though his stories are like a fairy tale of the future, when he tells them, they all seem possible and I trust him – not because I am blinded, but because I feel he knows it. Robert says his words are prophetic. Yesterday we talked about Italy and an overseas journey. Tesla's eyes lit. He turned around towards me and spoke to me as if we were alone. Oh, how much I wanted him to hold my hand as he was saying with devotion and excitement that in the future people traveling across the ocean in a steamboat will be able to read the daily papers from around the world and use pocket devices to communicate with their friends in New York who also have it. They will be set up similarly and people will be able to use them to communicate no matter where they are! How could this be? It sounds incredible. It will be a fast world where everyone is carrying those little devices, communicating and reading. What other power shall such devices have? How will the time pass by then?

While he was telling me that, Tesla's look was as if of a wild animal. Or was it a look of a mystic who does not really speak much or has he decided to enlighten me at that moment? In any case, it was piercing.

I can hardly imagine it all. What would that pocket device look like? How can anything reach people in the middle of the ocean? How can I read the news if I am in a steamboat? He understands it all. All those wonders are already in his thoughts, and he has seen them. I do not see anything, I do not understand him, but such fire in his eyes could mean only one thing – he is right, it will all come true.

I felt desire and fear again. When he turned around and got closer to me, as if he was telling me all confidentially, that fire in his eyes burnt wildly.

I am happy, I am rocking in sparkly clouds, I am not thinking of anything, I tremble from the beauty, all of a sudden and uncontrollably, this has never happened before: my whole body starts shaking and then I feel mild calmness.

He is thrilled by how the American way of treating influenza is successful – you drink a mixture of a brandy and 20 grams of quinine and then you go to bed.

§

Martin's article about Nikola was published in *The Century*. The two of them have different characters, but they respect each other, and Martin too is enchanted by him as we are. There are tiny troubles here and there, and they also spark from time to time.

Robert and Tesla, I believe, will never have trouble with one another. Robert is not a man who holds grudges. When he start feeling love for someone, he stops thinking, he just lets himself go. I know it best. He lets people whom he loves to lead. I used this for small victories. I could rule. That is, I rule, but I try not to cross my limits. I live comfortably, with a husband who is tolerant, but it is not a complete freedom mature girl now have and aspire to become independent. I would make it on my own. I would find that unquenched thing that is calling me from within. But then I would not have Owen and Agnes, Robert nor our lovely home!

We met Miss Marguerite Merington. She is five years younger than me, unmarried, and as far as I can notice, has no intention to get married. She is an artist, a playwright. She was born in England but came to America when she was very little. Freedom is what she aspires to with her distance. Simply put, she does not attract anyone, she does not want to, she dresses usually, maybe even a little stiff, and she wants to be her own and alone. She has big pale eyes. I asked her if she was really that stiff and I believe she is, she is not pretending. She seems happy and content, but how can a woman be content with such stiffness? Probably absolute freedom makes up for taking away everything for the benefit of it. She does not want protection, to be admired to, she does not overdress, does not show off her attractiveness, the dazzling side of herself, and she does not want anyone's help. She speaks through her work. But what is happiness for a woman?

§

When I look at myself illuminated with love, it seems I am an unexpected person, a mature Washington chestnut, that has now cracked.

I think Robert would forgive me anything—any sin—so long as I told him. Of course, he would be mad for a long time. But I have power over him. Robert would forgive me....

I read Martin's article. It is true, as Robert said, that Tesla's charisma worked on Martin to write even better. One can feel the admiration he has for him. Martin wrote Nature sometimes highlights the good by creating people who contribute to their nation with their transcendental meaning, but such people, the Americans, were born in exile. What he in fact wanted to say is that people in Eastern Europe are mostly idealists, but sometimes someone appears to make up for their impracticality with one's own ability. And of course, America is the country that accepts those Magnificent people, by offering them working conditions.

This is true. America appreciates work and devotion.

Martin put it so nicely when he wrote that Tesla's inventions and lectures give away the impression his soul is imbued by poetry. I can feel it, too.

Martin then wrote about Tesla's discovery of the reversed magnetic field (I have heard about this, but I do not understand it quite frankly) and how Tesla and Edison terminated their cooperation. Tesla is, in fact, for alternating current, whereas Edison still tightly clings to direct current. It is wonderful how Martin described Mr. Tesla's experiment he performs in his lectures, when he lets the current pass through his body and emit shimmering lumps of light. That is good. And by the end of the article there is a beautiful photo of him looking at the world slantwise, and his image is even milder in it. His lips... are even more sensual. His look... is even clearer.

§

Martin wrote to my husband: "I believe she (that is, I) has certain power over him, as much as a woman could, besides his sisters." Robert knows how much I love Nikola, but he thinks my love is equal to his. At least I think so and hope so. My love is mine only! Martin felt something more than that. He did not tell Robert anything besides what he wrote in that letter and both of them see my love as a form of respect, friendship, and enchantment. I hope it is. They must! After all, I would sense if Robert felt anything.

Again it was hard for me, but I also felt glad about it. Am I the one who has power over Tesla, as much as a woman could have? Those words are grand. If only I had such power, he would be mine. Since he says he will never get married, but is married to science, maybe my influence on him is the furthest point one could ever reach. What does my influence imply? A smile, giving way in small things, stolen looks, frequent letters, thinking. The fact that he even listens to me? He does not like many women, it bothers him when they wear pearls, he does not like plump people, overdressing, tackiness, he is sick of such people, he vomits when he smells camphor, he cannot touch other people's hair... The fact that I am his lady friend? The fact that he might sometimes want me?

Did he ever want me? When I think of that body, I get chills that stop my reason for a moment. It is a wonderful moment, even though it is insane. And it lasts for a short time. I quickly go back to reality, where such thoughts are probably impossible. Inexistent. Did he ever want me? Is that my power?

Martin wanted Robert and I to influence Tesla to accept an honorary doctorate offered by University of Nebraska. Robert thinks Columbia University should do it first, because it would be more appropriate to the achievements of the Nikola Tesla. He said he will write to them and suggest it.

Did he ever want me?

§

Robert made it. Nikola Tesla was awarded an honorary doctorate from Columbia University. Yale did it, too. He is officially a Doctor of Science.

The better Robert is towards me, I get more nervous and start loving the man who is cold and unreachable even more. Robert is infinitely careful. I am cursed.

§

The storm was waiting for long to knock down over the city. For a long time, the white air, so proud, was playing with our senses telling the whole city how powerful it is and that something terrible was soon to happen. That "soon" lasted for hours in such a terrible atmosphere. And then it started snowing in frenzy.

I was nervous from the very possibility of a blizzard. It did not touch Robert in any way. He asked me what was going on. I was upset he is not taking notice of what was going on. Maybe it would be easier for me if he noticed? I was upset by boredom. The boredom of suspense. And the fact he is composed. That is so indifferent! That is so tepid! He does not know me! He does not even suspect it! Why would he not free me by recognizing it?

We were sitting by the fireplace and Robert was following that snow blizzard with his everyday look.

I do not know how he cannot show his rushes. Writing is his rush, but he is an ordinary man when he is not writing. In fact, he was not so ordinary until Mr. Tesla showed up.

I am cruel. He is wonderful, gentle, refined, thorough, and wise. But in comparison to that look that make the winds clash....

Are women cursed because of their longing for mysterious dazzlement and strong unreason leading to an unknown direction, completely opposite than the known, open, everyday?

I decided to write Mr. Tesla a letter and then I briskly got up. Robert was following me with a warm look. I was as perfect as careless wildflowers enjoying their simple splendor. His love has always been mature, tolerant, and protective. It is even harder to aspire to fire when there is calm lake water beside you. My one hand is in that water, enjoying dark blue lake eyes, and I would like to put my other hand into fire burning from those ever-playing eyes. That man emits something that upsets my body. Even when he is sitting upright, when that position resembles Robert's composure, he quivers, grabs, he ardently wants, he shines.

"What are you doing on these stormy days? We... are wondering if anyone is coming in this evening to cheer us up, say about 9, or at 7 for dinner. We are very dull and very, very comfortable before an open fire, but two is too small a number.

For congeniality there must be three, especially when it snows 'in my country'."[2]

Let him come tonight, tomorrow evening, just let him come!

§

He did not arrive neither last nor this evening. He is working.

I dreamt we agreed to meet in the city, in the middle of the night. I went out easily and silently, and the moment I stepped outside in the street, fear crept up. New York was strangely, almost spookily calm and my footsteps echoed down the street. My heart was pounding and, as the beats got faster, I walked faster, surrounded by stagnancy. There was no end to Madison Avenue and my throat was clasping, but now that I remember it, I feel my search was incredibly vivid, undead – because life is but walking with lots of passion, on the brink of fear.

I have power over Robert and Nikola Tesla has power over me.

MARCH

I have noticed Nikola Tesla gave me a few curious looks. There were few, but he was looking at me like a man.

§

---

[2] A letter from Katherine Johnson to Nikola Tesla, in: Margaret Cheney. (1981). *Tesla: Man out of Time*. New York: Touchstone, p. 126.

Mark Twain is in New York! He will stay in the city for two months even though he often half-jokingly says he does not like it here because wherever he wants to cross the street, a carriage gets on his way. Robert wrote to him and said to stop by and visit us if he can.

§

I was not even aware how I missed Mark. When he starts overwhelming us with his jokes, laughter, and good taste, only then do I realize what we were missing all along. Conversation with him is always easy and witty, unburdened, and full of silly traps. He came hopping and brought us the spring, singing, fidgeting in his chair, and then he played the Stanway. I wanted to hear more about his daughters, they have grown into two beautiful women, with a mind of their own, thank the Lord, as he said with a smile on his face. He wrote down something on the napkins, mumbling as usual. He is used to writing down a word or two, as if he was hiding, and then he gives us a clear, innocent look, in a normal way.

Mark is going to visit Tesla tomorrow, in his lab. Another fantasy is coming up, another miracle.

§

Robert told me Mr. Tesla photographed him and Mark in a new way, using some king of cold light (Tesla's invention). He was talking with excitement, and I was happy and jealous. Robert loves Mr. Tesla as if he was his brother Henry or his sister Margaret. We are the same, we love the same person, in the same way – we worry about him, we protect him, we keep thinking about him. In fact, it is not in the same way, it only crossed my mind. There is a big difference.

Speaking of which, Tesla and Twain immediately recognized one another. Those are two glorious spirits, each in their own way. Tesla told Twain his books gave him a reason to live when he was young, when he was on the brink of death. Mark started crying. I cannot imagine neither Twain crying nor Tesla being weak.

§

My husband loves the man I am longing for as if they were brothers. I am longing for my husband's friend. I am longing for my friend. I am worried about the man I am longing for as if we were kin. He became a part of us.

They are going to The Players Club tonight, with Mark. He said he will beat Tesla in a billiards game. I do not know what I am going to do this evening, everything will be boring for me.

§

Tesla is wearing gloves only for a week. He then throws them away and buys a new pair. He also wears only white silk shirts. He sleeps two hours only. He knows everything, he counts everything, he does not let anything swing by.

§

Robert started calling him "Nick". In my thoughts I call him that too. Sometimes I mutter it out loud and he does not complain, nor does he give me funny looks. He accepted it.

Robert and I were sitting with Twain in the Gramercy Park when Twain said, completely nonchalantly and in fact looking us deep in the eye, that when we get old we will regret about everything we did not do, instead of everything we did do. He is completely right.

§

"My dearest wifey," Robert frequently uses these words of endearment. He is writing about me. He published a poem called "Her Smile" in *The Century*.

My dearest wifey,

your smile is the prettiest in the world,

as if a rose would be happy

for having a human image.

APRIL

We spent a quiet evening with Nick. We were sitting in the salon and without any fuss we enjoyed each other's company with just a few words. We were all quiet and gloomy. As soon as he arrived, Nick, however, was talking enthusiastically how happy he is with the new photos, especially the one with Joseph Jefferson. I did not see them yet, Martin has them. Then the conversation died out and we all enjoyed it as if we were half-awake.

I want him to take me with him and take me with no preparations, with no introduction, with no tenderness!

§

This evening we discussed wine. Nick enjoys it, he says quality always tops quantity. He would prefer drinking good wine less frequently than having it in abundance. He says the only thing he is missing in the US is good wine. Unfortunately, he did not get a package of it that he had ordered from his uncle. The bottles have probably been broken during transportation. We will try another time.

I am intoxicated even when I am not drinking wine. He is not even a little when he is drinking. Self-control is what he aspires to, he does not cross the line. He told us how he overdid it when he was young. He was mysterious about the details. I would love to see him loose and intoxicated! He is a man who had been longing, who experienced everything, tested his boundaries, and now is absolutely dedicated to his one goal. He enjoys things with moderation, and his grand delights' lechery reveals in his sharp, grey look. I want to reach that boundary. True peace comes only after having explored the boundaries, after we live through great and risky experience. Without them, peace is fake.

It was not noticeable I was imagining going through his hair with my fingers, how our naked backs touch, how I was looking at him and eating his rocky shoulders with my look. Or maybe he did see it? I would like him to have seen it.

§

I like the fact that Nick has an urge for luxury. His appearance and behavior are already of the classiest gentleman, his attitude in combination with his wizardry builds an incredibly interesting person.

Today he was all ears when Robert described the Waldorf Hotel's glamor. They are similar – our dear scientist and the prettiest hotel in the world: they are the first, unique, luxurious, eccentric, born glamorous. It was noticeable he was longing for that sparkly perfection, that nonchalant spillage of valuables in banquets, that smoothness and sophistication. The jewels in napkins in banquets. That hotel is missing only the most famous diamond – mister inventor.

§

We were at his lab again. Owen came home and we went there as a family. Agnes often says his hotel room is truly a mystery and we will never get to see it. She was thrilled she was to enter his other quarters. The air is different, electrified, the lamps are magical, the coils are endless. That laboratory is his home. He sleeps only two to three hours a day and after lunch he goes straight to south Manhattan. It was an early, soft, spring evening. Mist-shaped blue lightnings were spouting from the laboratory windows. We saw him letting lightnings into his body, drinking them. We all shone, and he drank them. He was pleased when they entered his body, he allowed them everything, they were caressing him. He loves them….

MAY

The new age has begun. We now know we, the Johnsons, are definitely and officially in Nikola Tesla's heart. It is not just me, but this feeling is beautiful, nevertheless. We are special. He gave Robert a nickname – Luka Filipov, and I am Mrs. Filipov. Those are our new names – Nick calls us that way. For the person who has the hardest glass wall behind his openness and closeness, these names are pet names. We are special! Robert and I. Me and Robert? Robert has a name too and I have only a last name. I am jealous.

One day, I will be only Katherine to Tesla!

For now, I am Mrs. Filipov.

He came to us last night with a poem, as he said, written by currently the most significant Serbian poet. He told us his name, but those words did not ring any bells for us, though I recall the poet's nickname – he is called the Dragon (Zmaj in Serbian).

Robert got interested in Serbian poetry and he wants to publish it in *The Century*. The evening was warm and fresh.

Tesla spoke with deep appreciation about that poet, as if he was bowing him. Poetry runs through our friend's veins, it is in his sighs. Poetry is his respect, his dedication, his work. Robert is a wise poet who creates when he is alone, bringing about the feelings he does not usually show. He is serious and thorough. Nikola's look is pure poetry, especially when he turns around towards me and looks at me that way, sometimes he disarms me. I must not give in.

He said it will be hard for him to translate Zmaj's poem because his works are tightly connected to the Serbian culture and identity. That made him nervous, because he wanted to interpret the verses as best as he could.

He stood in front of us as if he was on a stage, holding the paper in his hands, and started interpreting the words, pronouncing them loud and clear, mimicking them with his hand.

Luka Filipov is a Serbian falcon who captured a Turkish pasha (it is some sort of a military title) in the middle of a battle, he recited the poem. His name is in the ending of each stanza, and Nikola would take a deep breath when he pronounced it. Luka! Luka! The stanzas ran one after another. It is a heroic poem, invoking sense of pride.

It seems that such is the Serbian people, dramatic and proud. He was silent for a while after his recital, as if he was again showing respect. Then he woke up and cheerfully said Robert is his Luka Filipov. Robert was overjoyed. "Mrs. Johnson is my madame Filipov."

It was as if we were knighted. Everything was so solemn and new to us. My Nick.

§

Every time he visits us, it is as if a new fragrance conquers me and refreshes my senses. It would be impossible to get used to the aroma, as if it was a perfume you stop feeling after a while, because he is always differently magical.

It hurts me and I enjoy it. Parts of my body are starting to hurt when I think of Nick or when I am beside him – my hands, my shoulders, my stomach. But the pain is not strong and piercing, rather blunt and persistent. I enjoy my sweet imagination, as if I am a young girl again, so I dream and idealize, and the image

96

of my beloved one is always on my mind. The only difference is that, in fact, I cannot idealize him: Nick is much greater than I can imagine him with my ordinary mind. I enjoy the sweet uncertainty: he may be unattainable, he might be attainable, and the pleasure lies in hope. Then the pain and pleasure mix, so I have no idea how I really feel.

I love sweet possibilities, when the end pleasure is postponed, maybe forever, and maybe not.

§

I wrote a letter to Nick, asking him to join us in our trip to the Hamptons. It would be perfect! When I think of not going with him, I no longer wish to go there at all. I should have used my persuasion methods to make him even consider it. It is hard to invite a person when you know he would not even want to hear about it. That is, he will listen, but he will not obey. My words will be of a passer-by, words that exist for but a moment. Nevertheless, my hopes remain.... If only I could see him relaxed, not uttering a word, not thinking about his inventions, just sitting beside me, observing the ocean, sitting together with me beneath the Sun. If only I could see him rest.... If only I could provide him with all the warmth and closeness I have in me, the innocence that appears when we are on holidays.... If only I could feel the time stops when I am with him, when days are longer. If only I could see him through the window sleeping on the porch in peace, intoxicated with idleness. If only we could talk about the ocean. If only I could feel the sweetness of his fingers.

He responded he will feel sad when we leave, but it is impossible for him to join us.

He is an elusive being.

§

He finally accepted our dinner invitation. I have been begging him for months.

"I had formed the firm resolve not to accept any invitations, however tempting; but in this moment I remember that the pleasure of your company will soon be denied to me (as I am unable to follow you to East Hampton where you intend camping out this summer) – an irresistible desire takes hold of me to become a participant of that dinner, a desire which no amount of reasoning and consciousness of impending peril can overcome."[3]

Do you know that I get overwhelmed by the desire to go on a holiday, not to go away from you, to observe summer storms in New York, to feel the warmth of summer showers, to follow you, to take care of you, to listen to you?

I want to let go and give in. I do not want to live a life following rule. The summer is near – everyone is moving out of New York. Only one person is staying to procreate. I want to disobey.

---

[3] Nikola Tesla's letter to Katharine Johnson, in: Margaret Cheney, *Tesla: Man out of Time*, p. 127.

He visited us last night. We were laughing and joking. This morning, the city is wide, it expands my lungs and eyes. Maybe something will happen.

JUNE
He forgot about us... he is not even thinking about us....

He can do anything if he wanted to. He is laughing, he comes to us, and goes away.

JULY
Nick was puzzling at Delmonico's during his 38th birthday celebration. He quickly switched topics and it was hard to determine whether he was uncomfortable for being the birthday boy, or if he was, as usual, thrilled to be the focal point of the evening. He sharply told us he was born at midnight and has no birthday. He was telling us about his sisters, childhood, and how he was born in the middle of a stormy night. What other time could this real-unreal being be born at than at an undetermined, timeless, mad time? You cannot reach him, do not even think you can subdue him, and you cannot ever fully understand him. A restless night's fluid is running through his veins, and it ripped the Earth's crust with its golden arrows to help him be born from it.

§

I am happy, dressed in silk and satin; he was looking at me, he likes me, at least a little, he would have to think, at least a little, maybe he will think about it, he was happy, he was pleased. Happiness is when I am present, when I do not ask myself what has happened and what will happen, but attentively enjoy all the things that surround me, when the reflections of looks, streets, pillars, and lights reach me. I am full of his energy, desire, and smile, and now I can walk around the city and share my smile, without worrying about them going away, my chest is full of pleasure.

§

Nick was interviewed by Arthur Brisbane. They had a conversation at Delmonico's. The text was published today, and it reads Nick is the greatest electrical engineer of today. The cover page shows a picture of his with light shining from his body. It is a light shell.

§

Last night I was sitting alone in our porch, waiting for midnight. All of my dearest souls have already fallen asleep and made the summer house warmer with their dreams. I have uncovered my shoulders. Exactly at midnight, behind the scattered, seemingly harmless rough wool clouds, a sound broke off in the distance. This was a greeting made up of thin lightnings that ripped the sky like a combination of numerous swords. I was not afraid at all, I enjoyed their alternating calls. I have uncovered my shoulders even more and let the freshness into myself. They knew who I was, they reckoned me sitting on the porch, nude and ready, and they continued shooting and going wild. I shook from cold touches, as if I am already wet from rain, but it has not started yet. As the wave passed and shook me from head to toe, I opened up. It was as if you opened a shrine, and you felt the old smell coming from it. The wind blew it away sharply and quickly and immediately replaced it with the smell of burnt air. I wanted the lightnings to keep going wild, to brand my naked shoulders. I approached them. They were gone.

They left me with rain that spurred all over my skin in droplets, like male seed.

§

Kind of incidentally, Robert left the "Irish Love Poem" on the table for me to read it again. It was a poem about me. Its rhythm is fast and jolly, faster than his usual poems. It is a cute description of the moment we met, how likeable and sightly I was, so juicy and vivid. The sweetness of my eye is incomparable, it cannot be found anywhere else, he says in the poem. It is true. I have a fairy's nose. My cheeks are red as cherries. He wrote loving me is passion. You have not opened my passion yet! Katherine is hiding beneath naughty Kate's mask, Robert says. It is true. But, Robert, Kate is the real Katherine, that naughty, passionate girl, that is the real me, Katherine is a mask. Katherine is, as you say, dear, serious, patient, and poised. I am Kate. You are asking yourself, Robert, in the poem, whether you should attribute sunshine to Kate. You know her, and yet you do not frequently summon her. Kate entertains you, Kate is childish, and Katherine is your spouse and support.

Oh, Robert, I want to be Kate only.

§

The sunlight is reflecting on the pale grey sand, thus erasing my sight. No, it is not the light coming before Nick the scientist's eyes when he has visions of his inventions; mine is ordinary, coming from the beach.

AUGUST

I wrote a reprimanding letter to him. I told him his telegrams are much too cold and meager. I told him he is being cruel, which is the opposite of any American's behavior and of anyone I know. We all bond with each other. He can live without anyone.

SEPTEMBER

We are back to life. It is even more exciting because everyone is now talking about our friend; he is popular and wanted. Famous salons and stylish madams are making up tactics to steal him away from us. New York currently has no intriguing a person than this new, young and successful man. Tesla the scientist is interesting to them in numerous ways. Nobody is as elegant as him, nobody is as tall, as wonderful and unspoken.... The more the newspapers write about him and praise him, the more people recognize him. He is elusive as much. He enjoys being interviewed, he looks at his future audience seductively while he is being photographed, he becomes everybody's word and breath, but is untouchable, we cannot find or hear him, he is flying around Fifth Avenue, he finds time for everything, he gives himself to everybody, and he is nobody's. It is an art. He is still working like he used to, whenever he finds the time.

I observed his picture in *New York Times* and read the text. He is simultaneously revealing and validating himself. A star is being born. Our Nick. My Nick. He is going to visit us tomorrow.

§

When I saw him, it all came back to me and filled me up, I am now breathing more easily, and only now, when burden is alleviated from my chest again do I see how big it was.

He is still pale as always, especially in comparison to us, who are fresh and rejuvenated. But he is shining even more. His wings are even greater. He is aware he has climbed a few steps up.

He is not haughty. Nor does he brag about to us. He does not feel the need to highlight anything. He is now just more aware of the fact the whole world will know it too, and he has dressed a suit with more stars on it. He was telling us about the Niagara Falls and that he has signed a contract with Westinghouse. Robert remembered Chicago World Expo, Westinghouse's stand and a metal egg spinning on a table covered with a soft material, it was only one of our friend's magic spells. This means that they had met back then!

Nick will conquer the Niagara Falls with his inventions, he will remotely transmit electricity and the entire New York will shine. No, the whole of the United States! The whole world! That will help him finally show he will have heroically beat Thomas Edison. I could live off his energy – I could only look at him and listen to him all day long, I would not need to any food.

§

"You must always smile, Mrs. Filipov," he tells me, "that makes you even prettier."

§

He described something that is impossible but, as he says, is going to happen. I love his certitude and his persevering faith. He said in the future energy is not going to be transmitted neither through wires nor wirelessly!

Where does he come through? Where do his visions come from? How can he see a machine in the middle of a room started by its medium's energy circling around it? How can he see the non-existent? What are those ghost images in front of his eyes? I love his eyes furrowed with shooting stars' golden tails.

OCTOBER
We have introduced Nick to White, we both like to connect the people we know. The two gentlemen immediately recognized one another.

Agnes and Owen, who have argued they are no longer little for a long time, enjoy when Nick is telling them bedtime stories. It all started yesterday, on Saturday, and it went on today as well. We have made an agreement with him. I cannot believe it: he was at our quarters on the second floor of our home, so close to our bedroom, and my dreams, he flew by it and entered the kids' rooms, that smelled like milk, powder, and babies again. His voice was cotton-like. It seemed the night was deeper than it was as I stood, stealthily, by Agnes' room's door. I was trembling from the gentleness his voice was emitting, now quiet and fairytale-like.

NOVEMBER

It is snowing for the first time this winter, the air is sharp. It started snowing violently this morning. My eyes become paler when it is cold outside. Robert always laughs when I say it, and he convinces me I am looking at myself in the mirror too much.

We were sitting by the fireplace, chatting as usual, and it was very pleasant by the fire. Robert kept noting down something in his little black notebook. At first, all seemed like it used to, but then I felt something was missing. The two of us are a bit boring of a company to one another. Robert would never say such a thing. I was bored, me, the ungrateful woman. And here I am, writing a letter to Tesla to visit us because it takes at least three for a company. That is a nice diplomatic bait. "Two is too few." Those are common phrases I can skillfully and politely hide behind. It is snowing, we are expecting him because it takes three for a company.

§

I dreamt the night has come and the snowy blizzard has just passed. I was riding with Nick in an open carriage. He was silent, looking in front of himself, and I did not have the urge to speak, I was looking at the sky interspersed with whitish fog's fingers that slowly scattered around and dispersed. Blue lightnings were holding aback and went further. The night was wet, the sky washed, we were riding around the city, by the newly constructed rumbling railway. The whole city was swelling despite the indigo night's silence that tried to calm his pulse. I have never felt more peaceful.

§

Twain came to celebrate his birthday at Delmonico's. He ordered a terrapin just for fun, and to see people's faces, and, thank the Lord, a salmon with tartar sauce. He loves November just because it is his month of his birth. Robert, Nick, Mark, Livie, and I were all sitting at the restaurant, completely unaware of the freezing rain that occupied the city. Mark made us laugh again and again. He told us he is very old now and can remember only the things that did not happen, and when he was young, he also remembered the things that happened. We are all getting older, we must all go through it, Mark claimed half-jokingly. I tried to tell something similar to Nick with my look – we are getting older, it is true, but why would we not use the time we have?

Why are you devoted to science only? When will you realize my thoughts? The time is passing by. It is time.

DECEMBER
We are preparing for Christmas differently this year. The secrecy is in me, the sweet, pale red as a warm cinder in a pile of black, rocky, cold coal. Nick is coming. I enjoy monitoring food preparations, everything is already ideally crispy in my mind. The cookies' glaze will shine, and Christmas Eve will be

warmer and more solemn to me. He is a part of us. Christmas Eves are always tucked in, despite the cruel coldness that makes the windows freeze.

Christmas will be our little, important tradition. We are a part of his world. He will come all serious and official, and we will cheer him up, make him blush and warm. He will bring the smell of the street and winter to our dinner table. That day, our home will be his home. We are going to eat roasted walnuts, apple sauce, chicken croquets, English plum pudding, and roasted hickory.[4]

§

He told us how after his mother had died, he got a gray hair strand on the right side of his head, and the color was back after a few months have passed.

He still loves his mother. Such connection is so unusual, with deepest respect. When he talks of her, he expresses his most human, moon side. Usually, he is the sun, two light beams are piercing from his eyes. He gives us sunlight. When he talks about his mother, those beams remain, but his face is silvery, his shoulders move differently, I feel the shadows' coldness, I see the moonlight. He feels he owes something to his mother, as if he has not given her enough love, because she had deserved more. It is as if he is aware it will be impossible to ever pay his debt to her, he was not able to do it because she

---

[4] American walnut.

gave him more. That love is gloomy, frustration that makes feel cold. He wants to be connected to her even now.

His love, so it seems, can make the dead ghosts alive.

Who is he? Where does such strength of his come from? How strong are my loves? Will I ever be able to feel his lips?

1895

JANUARY

Last night he came late, Robert and I were ready for bed, it was a few minutes after midnight. He stormed in like the wind. I quickly dressed my peignoir, my hair was down, and I ran down the stairs after Robert. I felt my thin sleeping gown underneath it, as if I was dressed in it only; in fact, it seemed to me I was nude, as if my body was rejecting everything from itself. I found myself between discomfort and flourishing, between shame and ember. His lips were pale, blood free. The children heard our rattle and woke up, thrilled by the fact the wizard came out of nowhere in the night. The carriage was waiting for him for hours. He left very late, just before dawn.

§

We escorted Owen. I have been laying all day in my night gown doing nothing, I do not want to listen to anyone, I want to be all by myself. I want to enjoy the silk touch.

FEBRUARY

I was walking down *the lady's mile*, window shopping. I did not think about anything. At such moments true signs appear, when we are seemingly not ready, when we let everything come to us without having first prepared.

A girl was selling postcards. At first I did not want to take a look, turning my head to the shop window, and she followed my look and waved with an image of the Niagara Falls. I bought it instantly. It is Nick. His work is being spread and celebrated, and soon it will happen, and I can catch a glimpse of the future over the signs, and look at it in the eye. I managed to enter a part of his electric field, and I keep getting messages. I cannot imagine how he might be feeling – he can hear everything, he can enter all known and unknown fields. His ears rustle and crackle, and the past and the present combat right before his eyes. He takes the images he needs, has a glimpse of them, sorts them out – only the platinum are worth it. I gather every sign of his, as precious as a four-leaf clover. If only I could engrave them into my skin.

§

What do I want him to be for me? A friend, a brother, a lover? Do I want to be with him? Do I want to be tied to him too? Probably. Is that even possible? Do I want to lean on his arm in the morning, right after I wake up? Is that possible?

What would I taint? He is my being. I do not know where he actually came from. I do not know whose he is. Is he mine? Could he be mine? Could he be mine for a moment? What do I take him away from?

A brother? Love? A friend? Something is pushing me towards him. I want to worry, to touch him, listen to him, love him. What is that?

I am an adulteress. I am cheating on him in my thoughts, but that does not justify me, at all. I am cheating on Robert.

He erased all of my past thanks. No, I have erased them!

"I love apples," Mr. Tesla says with a dull voice.

Would it be easier for me if I did not see him? Would my pain lessen? No, I cannot stand not seeing him. I want him near me all the time, no matter the pain. I feel happy when he is around, even though the feeling is barbed happiness.

When he is close, I too know why I am here. When he talks about food, hotels, shoes, scarves, the city, hand cleanliness, his plans, when he talks about anything, he starts pleasant waves that move into my dress, and then into my body. Then I want to push my waves back at him and let them enter his jacket, cuffs, and his hair section. It seems as if they cannot protrude him. They remain inside of me like needles, pricking me. But the agitation causes such happiness!

I feel happy when I observe his royal, slightly gruff, behavior at dinner in Waldorf. Last night he returned wine and sauce, he said their quality is poor and undignified for his dinner table. At first, he was rough. I like his gruffness. In fact, that means he is consistent and a perfectionist. Then he drank chocolate liqueur with me, we were looking at each other, trying to catch each other's looks, through small glasses' thick ground glass. His eyes were female and mild, sparkling like the crystal glasses on the table. The whole world's tenderness, female sensibility in his eyes and his pale lips, he was a person undiscovered again.

Everybody was looking at him, there were a lot of people there, as usual, especially the ladies, who all came to Waldorf only because of him. He was looking at me only.

MARCH

Happiness is spreading warmly through my body as Nick slowly reads stories to my big Agnes. At dinner, the two of them laughed, hiding what it was all about. After that she drove in his carriage.

I am a girl and a woman at the same time, ready for everything.

§

It is nighttime but I cannot calm myself. Almost 24 hours have passed, and it is already the 14th. The moment lasts... And he said 13 was his lucky number! If I am finding it so difficult, I wonder how he must be feeling. Robert is not sleeping either, he is in the salon, he did not go to the editorial office today, he was with Nick all day long. There was a great misfortune! I did not anticipate anything, I have fallen asleep as usual. And then Martin called us.

Oh, dear God, Nick's laboratory in Fifth South Avenue has burned down. It is gone. Burned to the ground! His magical place where he used to spend his nights and days is now gone in a moment! He was, luckily, at the Gerlach's. All of his devices and equipment are destroyed, his notes, papers, ideas, exhibition items, all of Nick's hard work. How is he feeling now? Today he was distraught. No, that is not the right word. Stopped? Cut down? Colorless? Dead? I am unable to describe it. When we arrived, still all muzzy, angry, and agitated in disbelief, we had to believe it. We saw him wearing a tailcoat over his almost nude body. The morning was slowly entering the city, revealing the toothless face of the burned down floor and the screaming grey horror on our friend's face. It was so horrible looking at shaky walls' dead parts and the devastated voiceless hole where black slimy liquid was floating, a mixture of demonic water and oil. Nick was standing in front of us like a desperate person at a funeral, at moments like a passer-by ready to accept his fate, and in fact a devastated being from whom this obvious death ripped out the power of reasoning.

He will find the strength to move on, he has it in him. If only this night would pass. I cannot calm down. My heart is beating like never before, I wish I could vomit. I cannot change my clothes, I do not even want to try to go to sleep. I cried today, Robert held my head in his lap. I cannot even shed a tear now. Why did this happen? It is not fair. It is not possible.

If only the dawn would come, Nick will regenerate when the new day comes. I know he is not sleeping now. Why would I sleep then?

If I could pet his hair now, drink his tears, put my hand on his forehead, as I do with my children. He will go through this, I know it, but... I would....

§

It was so creepy, even now, the day after, as if it was all happening again: the memories are settling, causing an even greater tempest in me.

After having received the call, Robert and I immediately went out into the city, wandering around New York in order to stop Nick from wandering. We knew he was distraught. I wanted for us to find him so badly. So we could provide him with at least some warmth and compassion. We did not manage to find him though, as much as we searched. We fought for him night and day when we ran around the empty city. On a dead night, New York has a grey breath. Life is smoldering, in the balconies though, on the other side of the windows, but the two of us were entering places where people do not go during the night, into the emptiness, we knew he was looking to find brutal loneliness.

I cannot transform my words into silent fear, there is a cramp that blocks everything; for a moment, we did not know where we were, we got lost in our city looking for the person who was hiding his broken heart. I cannot describe the chills that emptied my heart, the dark secrets of the city that were grinning, revealing, adding fear. How can I express how much we would like to help him, now more than ever? If I could, would it mean anything to him? It would not. Our tears and compassion cannot change anything, we are helpless. I wrote a worthless letter calling him to visit us. Even if it were possible to send tears by mail, it would be in vain all the same. Could compassion help in such moments? Even if it could, he does not wish to receive it. Why would he not want to come to us? We would help him at least by providing him with our understanding.

Nothing was insured in his lab.

§

He is in a bad condition, he does not wish to see anybody, and does to wish to be seen. He is crushed. I pray for him, and I wish he could get up and move on as fast as he could. "Mother," Agnes said quietly, "he is a star."

APRIL

Martin published the sad story about the fire in the *Engineer's Magazine*. He was not sentimental, but even his realistic portrayal was enough to shock and evoke compassion. While reading it, I remembered the horror and the blackness. I felt as if the black dead remains of the instruments are in my stomach. If something I made ever burned in such a cruel way, I would never manage to recover from it.

But our Nick is different. Difficult moments inspire him to keep fighting. And he memorized all his notes by heart!

Nevertheless, only now have his cloudy eyebrows started to clear up. The struggle will be difficult. His spirit must fight a real loss. He is a giant. A phoenix. The most painful thing is, as Martin wrote, the fact that Nick is going to have to make room for new research again.

§

How can one alleviate the pain of a loved person? It cannot be done. We all bear our own pain on our shoulders. How can nice words help? Words in general? Maybe poetry can, it is the music of words. Robert probably thinks that since he wrote a poem "In Tesla's Laboratory."

It is hard to describe the phenomena in it: the fast-approaching lightnings, the hissing darkness, unusual objects, the metal smell, the silence of windows behind heavy curtains and a perfect order in everything. Monster-objects were spinning around themselves in that magical place, they were twirling wildly, the balls were shining in unusual colors, the fire was biting, the air was burning, the whole room was breathing deeply and exhaling freshness, and the wizard let electricity go through his own body and lit the light bulbs with his hand. How could one describe such tiny sparks that were blinking passionately, as the first stars in a summer pale-ink colored sky? How could one describe us, the untaught persons, who voraciously swallowed such sparks and the hissing freshness?

Robert described the lab's apparitions. They are not phantoms from the past, weeping ghosts, wraiths dressed in a cloud, but blessed spirits waiting to be born, and thoughts that will unlock the shackles of us all.

"Their smile is like a happy interruption of sorrow."

I like it. The smile of apparitions, sparks, stars, white balls, colorful balls, they all burst out of laughter so madly, and wiped all the thoughts coming from the visitor's hear, but first the sad ones. After the bangs, freshness remained in our thoughts and bodies, letting go and letting in, reconciliation, fresh emptiness.

"Listen! that murmur is of angels' wings," Robert finished his poem.

He is right. That sentence says it all.

Another Martin's article about Nick was published. A year has already passed since Robert, Martin, and Nick agreed to publish the photos that brought such joy to the scientist. Martin had been keeping them locked up for a long time. The negotiations on publishing them did not go smoothly.

As expected, Martin praised Nick in the text. He used powerful words, and he is also very practical. Nikola Tesla, the architect of the new era that has just begun. This is true. In fact, Nikola Tesla is so new and different – and that is frightening at the same time. Then he described Nick's oscillator, and finally the photos have been published. They have been made under phosphorescent light. They are so wonderful, unclearly clear. Globe-shaped light seems to permeate people's bellies, and the darkness that covers them says it all, only if the spectator gives in to it.

Mark is portrayed in the first one, standing behind a light, awake and wise. Then comes Joseph Jefferson, who seems to be shining with light, as if he was bathed by it. Then there is Marion Crawford. And another photo of Mark, and in the back stands Nick. At a first glance, he is unnoticeable, in the darkness, consumed by it. And when you look closer, you can see he is young, fresh, and lean. He looks indifferent, but he is the maker of everything, and he is observing his work with love. Another photo portrays gigantic light, sharp tongues coming from a dark cone.

New York will be thrilled!

§

The relationship between Nikola Tesla and Thomas Edison can only be described as war. The journalists call it "the war of the currents". In that battleground, Nick is a person who does not wish to intentionally attack or take away anything, but a person who found a new, better war, and wants to present it for the greater good. The great Edison takes it all personally. But the two of them know each other perfectly. Nick told us about Edison's persistence, but also of his cold vanity.

I am afraid Edison is capable of all kinds of combat. Nick is hovering over a war field completely innocent. He is persistent because he is confident the better system must win, and not because of his personal glory. Everyone enjoys fame, and so does Nick, but his work is not hierarchically under it. I am not saying Edison became a scientist in order to become famous. I am only afraid: Edison is now like an endangered animal, the rivalry wounded him, and he feels he is going to be defeated. Our Nick is looking for a location for his new laboratory. He is making gigantic steps again. His life is an enraptured struggle and eternal presenting. He is not understood by many because he is so advanced when compared to the rest. He must suffer because he is the best. It is hard to be at the top.

In comparison to Tesla, the great Edison can also be small, but he will not be able to accept that easily. A wounded beast always tries to defend by any means possible.

We are reading the headlines these days. "Who Is the King, Edison or Tesla?" *Troy Press* writes. They also quoted the actor Joseph Jefferson: "Edison is overthrown, and Tesla is the newly crowned ruler."

I believe the old king is grinding his teeth while Nick, the king to be, is hovering over the hate directed towards him. And I am not referring only to Thomas Edison. The giants always have numerous enemies. It is sheer luck the gigantic step is so big to skip ahead them. I hope it is.

MAY

He escorted me to Central Park today and was telling me about oscillations. Everything is oscillating, he explained, both the sun and our hearts. I trust him when he is telling me about the sun, although I cannot feel it, and I know many things about hearts: mine was beating wildly beside him, its rhythm definitely changed. It is as if he did not notice it, so he went on – he said peace can be attained when man is balancing his trembling. This means I will never find peace! He looked at me as if he knew, he knows everything. His heart is calm.

§

Robert said those are just rumors. They are retold, voluptuously and with enjoyment. Suspicious things happen there, so this does not come as a surprise. They say there was an unusual dinner in Bris' Photo studio in 5 West 16th Street last night, hosted by Stany for Nick and Augustus Saint-Gaudens, a famous sculptor. How do I describe the things I have heard? "Unusual," to be as mild as possible. Scandalous, erotic, debauched, impossible, exciting, sinful, lascivious… Nick was observing how a big foamy cake is being introduced before the guests, and a young girl got out of it, and who knows what she was wearing – the word is she did not barely have any clothes. Darkness in the studio, probably, and those dim lights, with Nick in that crowd, among other red-eyed girls quickly eating pieces of that foamy cake! Those young guests were all poorly dressed. They were looking at Nick and approached him. Has Nick changed his dignified standing for at least a moment? Studio full of ebullient looks, unbridled Stany, giggling half-nude women, smeared cake.

§

I dreamt I was wrapped in layers of thin and sticky ivory silk. I felt hampered in it for a moment, as a larva in its transparent cocoon, and for another it became sensual, it slid down my naked body, its weight thrilled and caressed me. I was wrapped inside of it, it felt good feeling its touch from my neck all the way to my hips. I was laying down on a thin and hard bed made of dark wood in a room filled with darkness. I was waiting, and the smoothness and darkness in me caused both chills and fire at the same time. Creepy fire in velvet darkness. My naked breasts under a heavy satin silk got swollen. At the same time, I was sweating and shuddering in a dark crater, knowing that I am waiting for a good blue ball-shaped light to impregnate me.

§

Stany is going to make New York prettier again. He told us to get ready for it because soon a new gate is going to be opened at the beginning of Fifth Avenue. We will be there with Nick; I hope he will truly return. This Stany's news is the only thing we got since Nick went to Philadelphia, to an expo, to present his electricity transmission experiment. He is going to meet Edison there.

§

When he is not around, I lose my will. Nothing is nice enough for me. It is true I always maintain a relationship with my children, but that is a given. I am like a big tree whose trunk is feeding its leaves – my children, and it will be so forever. I give them my arms – the branches they live on, where they can receive birds to build their nests on, they can do anything. My love for them is stable and eternal. But the tree also needs breeze to caress its treetop, it needs sunlight to feed from.

§

He is back. Everyone can notice his look is special and unusual, but only I can see the flame. I dream of him. I understand him. I feel him. I love him the most!

I cannot tell him that. Does that mean I could admit if we stayed alone together? Am I ready for everything? I am. I am crazy. I will burn. Does that mean I am ready to lose everything? Even him? I would lose him as well if... Maybe he would reject me...

The fire is so strong, it is overwhelming me. I cannot stand it anymore, it burns. Do I love the man who can never be mine? Do I love the man who does not want to be mine ever? I do love him, I, Mrs. Katharine Johnson, a married wife of his friend, mother of two grown children.

He was sitting beside me at the table, and I was melting both from pain and happiness.

§

There is only pain today.

He said: "I do not know how to love."

"Why is that?" I asked.

"Because I can only love the future. Not people."

§

Agnes told me I changed. At one point, I looked for signs of suspicion in her eyes, and she got scared. Kids often know everything.

New York got a new gate on Washington Square. The most beautiful river in the world springs above it – Fifth Avenue. Greenwich Village is beneath it, a true beehive. I was standing next to Agnes, Robert, and Nick, and we were all looking at Stany, who was proud, and rightfully. That man is an architectural genius. There is a tone in me that is outstanding, it always plays differently, and never agrees with the initial melody. It makes it irresistible and attractive, that strong off-key. It is, in fact, a disobedient, free tone. A balanced imbalance. And now he went even further and above: he created an old building too. White-painted wood made a magnificent white marble gate.

At the end of the ceremony, Robert recited his new poem in honor of the former wooden gate. The mayor invited him to do it again before President Harrison.

§

That was a moment I did not think of anyone. I was walking along Gramercy Park as slowly as I could. Gramercy is a strange park, surrounded by fence and exclusive: not everybody can enter. Suddenly, a colorful carousel appeared in front of my eyes. A boy with a round blue cap was showing me a paper windmill. He ran towards me, and the windmill was spinning joyfully. He stopped and it stopped as well. In its handle, right above the boy's tiny fingers, two letters read N and T, probably added, written, carved, I do not know... He kept running, I did not see where to.

I would touch his hair and warm wind would flow over my palm. He never touches other people's hair, even of his dearest – it is appalling to him.

JUNE

Owen got home for the summer break. He has grown so much! He has his own circle of friends now, he is not only ours. I cannot sustain myself from hugging him when I do not see him for a while, I squeeze him so much he starts complaining jokingly I am suffocating him. He has the most curious eyes in the world, a look of a thrush that flew from somewhere all of a sudden and learned how to manage right away.

Nick wrote how a great Serbian poet is trying to present him, as best as he could, a beautiful girl from Serbia, who is enchanted by our friend. She does not stand a chance. He is again in his dreamland where he reveals his secrets best. He quickly starts reading other people's words and gets back to his dreams.

JULY

Not doing anything is not enjoyable.

AUGUST

Twain sent us a letter from Australia. He is giving lectures on his world tour, and is going to visit New Zealand, Ceylon, India, and South Africa. Livie and Clara are with him.

Adelaide, new Morgan's lover, even got to the papers. Morgan can have anything he wants. He buys beauty and stores fortune in his library.

SEPTEMBER

Kipling sent his poem "If" to Robert. I fail every question. Kipling says you are a human if you can stand the loss of what you have been waiting for without a sigh or protest for a great period. I sigh and protest because I do not have what I want, and I can only imagine what I would be like if I would lose at least one wish that would come true. Kipling says you are a human when you are in love but not mad from love. I am so mad from love I am screaming from the inside.

OCTOBER

We got back from the coast and brought a plethora of colors similar to the Italian ones – orange, red, and brick color, heavy grey, cheeky dark blue, and bright turquoise, but Nick topped us again. He needed to run away from the city, the experiences reached him, coming from India in particular. We were still unpacking when a package arrived for Robert, with a letter. There was a book by Swami Vivekananda. The explanation was short and clear – Nick was visiting his lectures while we were away, Buddhism thrilled him, and now he sent Robert that book. He wrote Christianity and Buddhism are religions of the future. Nick's enthusiastic stages are truly the ocean's waves that take everything with them. Robert is interested, but it seems to me that book will influence me more. White foam from Nick's waves is whispering and crackling again in my ears and hair. Everybody else is showing him respect, love, and appreciation, but I am a person who feels him. I am the only person who permanently receives his radiation. Others go to his lab and get excited about his experiments, but I dream of him, I anticipate, only I am connected with him, I embrace his waves. He is the man I was waiting for. I want to dream of him tonight. He is going to visit us tomorrow.

Maybe it is luck.

§

The color of his eyes is water-like. He came and looked at us a bit in wonder, as if he was discovering us for the first time. "I am glad you are at your beautiful home," he said with sensuality. Then he got serious and added that unfortunately

125

he still cannot move into his new lab because it needs to be equipped. He perfectly goes from short sensuality into intangibility. Others do not even feel all of his nuances, only I can discern his toying with speech.

NOVEMBER

Thanksgiving Day has passed. Ellen and her family are visiting us, they met Nick. Ellen and I are now even more distanced, she cannot read my mind. We love each other, but we are not close, not the same. She did not notice a single change in me, not one glowing look, not one possible remorse, no fears. I did not want to talk. Nick was telling us about unusual things.

§

Last night I dreamt I was alone with him – I could see in his eyes how much he wants me, but I cried and cried, and suddenly I turned my back on him. Then I stopped. When I woke up, I cried because I have made a bad move in my sleep.

§

When we see each other, he surprises me almost always, even when I know for days in advance I am going to meet him. My whole-body shakes; he moves my mind, as if he removes all things from the table in one hand gesture, and most of them break. Then our waves swirl around one another, so close, we are so close, I could almost press my cheek against his, or even hope our necks will caress. I want to serve him, pour his drinks, be close to him. Sometimes I feel a painful trace on my neck, as if tiger's claws would have marked my skin and tendons. Then we spin around, at anything is possible and impossible at the same time. We do not touch each other in this reality, but it is still possible in another one, I know it. What is impossible – becomes possible, what is not happening – starts happening, possibilities tickle me, imagined images cross my street, and I try to keep the conversation go as per usual. I put my silk scarf onto an open wound from the claws.

The new laboratory is similar to the old one, so mystical and dark. Everyone can see the experiment only once. Nick got to have wire roller charges again, similar to a necklace, metal stands, cone shapes, inexplicable things.

DECEMBER
Streetlights arrived in 42nd Street. Roosevelt became the President of the New York City Board of Police Commissioners. We introduced him to Nick.

Christmas is coming in a few days, and Nick is going to spend it with us. We will bake beef; he likes eating thick, top quality pieces. I saw him only twice this December. Far from eye, far from heart – that proverb is true! Or is it the opposite? Maybe the heart distances from the people we see every day? How can my heart distance from the wizard who is to illuminate the world? His fierce look is a brand on my shoulders. He is a heavy black wind, fruitful rain, omniscient light, he has all shapes, and is almighty.

Robert sent him a Christmas dinner invitation. The reply arrived quickly. Maybe it is the most beautiful word we Johnsons ever received from Nikola Tesla: he wrote he is going to come to his 327 Lexington Avenue home. Robert hugged Agnes and me with glee. When Owen and Nick will have arrived, we will be a complete Johnson's family. Come what may, wherever the orange hot lava, that runs from my heart every day, goes, if it returns to the Earth's heart, and if it ever cools down, no matter what, I will love Nick as my family's dearest. Robert said jokingly we are very honored – Nick is coming for Christmas, and he started communicating with the richest people in New York – with the millionaire John Jacob Astor, for example.

The whole of the United States knows who the Astors are. Their Fifth Avenue house is only a part of their wealth. His wife Ava is a spiked lady ruling the Fifth Avenue and all mundane places in the city.

§

I do not regret it. On the contrary, I am shaking from excitement, as if the strongest current is just passing right through me, and I live. I feel no fear as I am wondering what is to happen. This questioning destroys me and reassembles my broken parts at the same time. I am dying and regenerating myself in quick short cycles. This is very similar to giving birth, when a woman's body is ripped, and a new life appears from it. I am torn, and my life energy is being regenerated, and again, and again, and again. But anything is possible when you tremble because of Nikola Tesla!

It started as usual. Our dear Owen arrived on Christmas Eve. Our eternal boy. just what he should be like. Agnes is a cultivated girl with golden eyes. Sometimes it seems to me she is Ellen's daughter, because their character is very similar. Agnes is a true lady too, as if she has blue blood. I am glad she is not one of those girls who spill their smiles very early. Robert is the pillar of our home. Then Nick arrived, the elf from a faraway country, the newest member of our family. The youngest one. A child and a father. A wise guy. He memorized the whole of *Faustus* by heart, and he recited it to us, quietly.

Agnes and I set up the table with the servants, while Robert, Owen, and Nick chatted. Whenever I interrupt their man conversations, the energy seems to change.

But that is when I add fire! I do not know how to speak about science, politics, and the society as they do, but I feel those topics better. Love is God's gift we mortals are wrapped in, and then we can do anything.

I felt I was tender and soft: all of my dearest were gathered around the Christmas dinner. I have never been happier, more fulfilled, braver. Everything was in perfect harmony. I bathed in a thick beam of light that blinded me.

I have not tried the wine, I barely touched the food. I was enjoying my family's enjoyment. This is luck.

By the end of our dinner, Nick and I stayed alone – it gave me additional courage. Then I gave in to desire, I stood up, and put my warm fingers on Nick's. He did not expect it at all! He snapped out of it. My heart was pounding (and it is still beating hard). I, Mrs. Johnson, in my own house, as if there was nobody else in the building but us, have laid my hand onto his.

"Katharine," he snapped as if he got burnt. "I do not know."

He quickly pulled his hand aback and likewise his skin's smoothness was gone.

Still, he did not look surprised. He was only surprised I did anything.

My passion was not unfamiliar to him. Therefore, he knows it.

"I cannot take it anymore," I said with a dose of risk. Somebody could have entered the room all of a sudden.

"I cannot do what you think you can do," his reaction was mild. He could have done it differently.

He gave me a glance and then he looked aside and got up. His look was snow-white. It was as if his corneas disappeared in a moment.

§

Robert wrote about illusions. He says the ships shine in night's foam. The entire heavens are spinning. Our eyes deceive us. Many lights we see are but a reflection of phosphorus on the journey of life.

Are some lights illusions, Robert?

1896

JANUARY

What is a dream, and what is reality? I now look clearly through the window and see the city, the roofs, and balconies. For example, I do not see the ocean's blue. Or could I see it if I decided so? What we see in a dream, is it reality, only from a different dimension? If it is not, why do we then have such a harsh feeling of reality in a dream? What is true, reality or dreams? What is clearer? What has more worth?

I still cannot completely return to my tangible self. I am sitting by the window, looking at the city, but I am still half asleep, while it lives, it managed to survive the morning.

I am alone, everybody is in some other place, everybody is doing something, everybody has a vocation. Is reviving dreams just another dream? When images in an inner eye go quickly, are they alive or dead?

I dreamt of love. I was already nude, and my hair was down, and beside me Nikola Tesla was lying, completely dressed and, as usual, all starched from head to toe. He spread his arms on the bed and was carefully watching me. I wanted to take his gloves off, frightened at first of whether he would allow me to do it or not, but when I revealed his wonderful hands, he also smiled and everything else was easier. His tailcoat, shirt, pants – I started undressing him slowly, but he did not complain about me getting so close to his bare skin. He still did not touch me, but I could tell he wanted to, he was waiting while I felt his body's scent, his red scent, penetrating and so strangely dry. When he lit up naked on the bed, I felt pain in my left shoulder, as if a poisonous arrow stinged me. He touched me there first, knowingly. I felt the strongest heat I have ever felt, his branded touch was engraved on my body. Then the most distant signal fire woke up in my body; I have never been more aware. Nor more awake. That is why I am wondering: Are dreams only a different wakefulness? As he was moving his hand down from my shoulders onto my breasts, I have reached the border of sanity. I was looking at blackness that waved on the last point of existence. When he touched my genitalia, I spread my arms, that were pulling me backwards until then, and felt dark satin on them first, not gradually. It was a soft touch of being welcome.

Strangely, he kissed me only after he touched my intimate parts. White fuzzy heart was born from the first connection in a thick black mass. It was like the head of a ripe dandelion. Nikola's lips were juicy, completely opposite to his scent, deep and tasty. They were taking away my conscious, this insolence feels good. I got down, kissing his naked chest, his big hands, going back and forth to the same places several times again, wanting to kiss and moisturize every part of his skin. We were rolling around on the bed, intentionally, unintentionally, he was wild and sure of himself above me, with his strong arms above my head. He firmly clasped his hands around my waist, almost like a bully, holding my skin as if his hands are metal pliers. I grinded my teeth, I yelled from happiness I felt in pain. I disappeared and reappeared.

When he penetrated me, the white sun started dripping. In fact, its feathers started falling apart, just like dandelion's seed, and were floating around, scribbling around the black mass around us. When he penetrated me, I was reborn. His skin was also white.

Floating lazily and slowly, the white sun's feathers gradually turned into spots of light. I took as much as I could as our love lasted, I grabbed his curls and back, I grabbed and scratched, crazy from love and happiness.

When I reached the climax, I was looking at his eyes that turned dark grey. We then relaxed at the same time. We were shaking, with our wants emptied and completely satiated, under the tiny bright spots. He was looking in front of himself, not at me. I was looking at him. We were silent together.

And now, when this dream reappears in daylight, I am living my ordinary day, waiting for Robert. What am I waiting for? Am I playing a game, am I toying with him or myself? Who am I lying to and why? Am I alive?

Where is that man with whom I was both a snowflake and the mountain, with whom I have experienced the pleasures that were unknown to me so far? Where is he, why does he not come and take me? Why things I want cannot happen?

There is no shame in me, lust is getting stronger.

My body is Robert's; my thoughts, Nick's. I am ashamed, I regret it, but it is true. And Robert loves Nick! How could this be: the man I give myself to with little heart loves the man my heart loves.

I frequently compliment him. They simply burst from my mouth, and I let them go. I always notice his fine clothes and a taste to be well-dressed. I get excited by his black coat, when he puts his bowler hat indeed he looks like a magician. I twitch from lust when he takes out his clean white silk handkerchief. His perfectly brittle shirts rustle, I can hear it, I know only I can hear it, I love how his meticulousness is given away by his austerity, I love how his collar is firm and has straight, sharp lines. When I say good words about him, it immediately seems it was unusually brave of me to do it. But who could stay indifferent to the whiteness of his shirt protruding sensuously, just a little, but enough for one to go crazy? His flexible body is fresh.

§

Green lianas grew all over the pillars of the Brooklyn Bridge. Steam from the boats is going through its construction like spider web.

§

How can I hurt Robert's pure love and pure tears that would run if he only knew? I can. I regret it. I do not regret it. Robert did not hurt me, he just loved me, pleased my whimsies, ran towards me, calmed me down. Robert is with me. His pure love hurts. I spoil everything. I make it dirty. I can. Robert is a creature of nature who unconditionally accepts me. Who is that other man? Robert is a silent creature, apological, and gentle. Nick breaks my body apart. When I desire him, I do not think of Robert, I do not want to think, I only rush into it, without

134

even thinking about the consequences. I cut Robert's goodness, I hurt his kind heart. What kind of a person am I? I betray him, he does not know it, but I do, and that is enough. Could I really trample on his kindness because of this passion?

He would suffer if he knew it. His suffering would slowly kill me. It is easier for me to suffer alone. His wound would never heal.

I love them both. I will go crazy because of him. Robert is an obligation, Robert is a connection, a part of me, my hand, my stomach. Nikola is my eye, my heart, my motion. I want to hug Robert and lean on him, to talk to him about the past. and I want to burn with Nick, to die and be born again, I want to breathe his expirations in and live from that.

If only I could have both of them!

I have respected one of them for a long time now, and I am in love with another. They are friends. To one of them I gave my vow, the other one is forever young, and can have the world under his feet, he is at the beginning of his journey. One of them is safe and durable, the other elusive and always in motion, as if he was everyone's. The risk of it is so sweet.

Everybody says mature, married love is stronger than all incantations. It seems to me you lose when you do not listen to your heart.

How can I hurt the goodness? I cannot go against myself. You cannot choose whom to love.

I am jealous of the time Robert spends with Nick. I would gladly kidnap him, at any moment. I am ashamed. I think he wants Nick all for himself.

§

Robert suffers from ulcers. He is gloomy and vulnerable. I am taking care of him the best I can. Nick is sending him funny letters. He is teasing him that he is overreacting, that he is a coward. The city is tired. I am full of elan. I run around, wander, dream, sing, burn, fly.

§

He too must be asleep, dreaming of me! His devotion and restraint would have never allowed him to admit it, but I think it had happened before. We are two connected creatures in the same wavelength. I will ask him about it. In order for that conversation to happen, I must plan for us to stay alone, and not to wait for the opportunity to happen by chance. I am very interested in what he will tell me, how he explains my voices, my signs, dreams, and premonitions.

You love me, Nick.

§

Nick took John Jacob Astor and his wife Ava to his laboratory. In fact, Ava was only visiting for dinner, but did not want to see the lab. Even better if you ask me. I want for Nick's laboratory to become famous and visited, but with as little women as possible. John Jacob Astor IV's wife is the mistress of her own salon, perceived in New York as her court. Her endless house's front door is made of gilded bronze. She wears a diamond tiara she paid a few million dollars for and, besides, everything else she has is made of diamonds. Terrapins are served in her balls, duck croquettes and goose pate, and at her parties, she arranges apple flowers in wide golden bowls. Her ceilings are also gilded, and furniture was bought in European castles and palaces. Her home is illuminated by majestic chandeliers, onyx, and brocade.

Nick is overjoyed. He is after big shots and one of the biggest ones dined with him last night and visited his magical place. He has no time to think of Mrs. Astor's snobbishness. Stany too attended that dinner party and the tour.

Robert's pain subsided now. I have not. I would not call it restlessness, for I am in a different state now, which is much worse than restlessness and distraction. I feel weak, tired, and desperate. At one point, it seems to me I have been alive for a hundred years, and on another – like time flew by. Lots of things have happened, and in fact, nothing ever happened. I am no diamond, I am but a regular beach pebble, one in a myriad. I cannot fight my own irrelevance. Robert usually says it is important how much love we gave to other people, that love persists even when we are gone, our verve and efforts and our thoughts remain and sway above all the rocks, and someone in the future is to catch and receive them.

That gives me no comfort. I am laying without any will, feeling blunt pain on the back of my head.

Oh, how inessential am I to the wizard who wants to master time, to give us rain when we need it and let sunshine into our hearts when we long for it? His mind already sees all those machines that control the weather, in his thoughts bright rainbow colors always keep flowing, he drinks from them, so bright, sticky, and burned, he swallows them feeling no pain, he drinks the light. He is happy with his projects and his burning desires and with communication with other worlds. I have a wish that can never be granted, no matter how many times I sent it to God. I want that self-satisfied creature, and my desire is doomed to fail well in advance.

How does he feel as a person whom many women dream of? They run after him. What kind of a feeling is that? He must know. Does it matter to him that he is the only fantasy of a woman?

§

And? Then what? Would my soul be able to feel or see anything? Does it matter all my love will keep swaying above the rocks and rivers? Where is the real me, me who wants everything now? I want to be rewarded in this life. I want to live.

It is so strange I wrote this. At the same time, I do and do not want to live. I could arouse my enraged desire, but I have no urges because frustrations have kept it locked deep inside, so I cannot move myself.

§

"...if you have not forgotten me entirely or forgotten to be fond of me – *I have forgotten to forget*... Be human, be kind and come. You know it is Robert's party. Perhaps you will come for him."[5]

I am prepared to say please and get down on my knees, only for Nick to come. Only he can alleviate my tiredness and desperation. How strange it is that he thwarts my desires, but makes it go aflame, he brings me death and life.

He came to Robert's party. When he visits us, he gives me strength. He was more casual than usual, he was laughing, looking at me with a smile, teasing me. I am still filled with joy when I think of it.

§

He probably never even thinks about me, he has successfully returned to his cocoon. Come what may, I do not regret it, I wanted it to happen.

He visited us this morning and found me alone, I had a longer breakfast than usual. "Today you are beautiful, Mrs. Johnson," he said to me, "and as fresh as the spring." I did not sleep enough that night.

"Thank you, Mr. Tesla," I responded wittily.

I stepped out of the dining room into the kitchen to tidy up the dishes, and in such situations he would sit still and wait for

---

[5] A letter from Katherine Johnson to Nikola Tesla, in: Margaret Cheney, *Tesla: Man out of Time*, p. 149.

someone to reappear. However, this morning he went after me. I put the plates very slowly, I could feel him observing me. I turned my face towards his. He was looking at me as he usually does. But the location we were standing in was unusual, hidden, never before has he walked in in there. I approached him without thinking, I put my hands onto his tucker and pushed him with my chest onto the wall. He was in shock, but at that rough moment I was completely calm. I nearly screamed when my face was close to his: "I no longer have shame!"

At that moment he was mine, caught up, he could not move, he did not know what to do. I felt his body was getting warmer, he did want it after all, but it lasted for a few seconds, and then he got together, cooled down, and forcedly moved aright.

"I was wrong. You are not," he said.

He was not rough, he did not break away, he did not want to humiliate me, he just stepped aside.

Blood was rushing through my cheeks. As I was thinking what to do next, he already calmed down, without even looking aside, and said: "I have another dinner at Waldorf."

I thought he would leave immediately. Courage and humiliation fought inside of me. There was no regret. This too shall pass, it has passed for him. I am laughing and crying.

At that moment, when his body was getting warmer, his eyes glistened. He cannot deny it.

Everything was hard again, just like when you get stuck in beach sand. Your face is near living waves, you feel the water's freshness, but you cannot even move, nor enter it.

I do not regret it!

§

He is toying with me. That is both wonderful and cruel. He sent me an invitation to a celebration at Waldorf and he changed his handwriting and my last name on purpose. "To Mrs. Johnson, the beauty of the ball." His teasing is wonderful because it excites me. It is heavy, because it makes me sad, I wish it were true. For him I swallow sugar and salt at the same time. I am both the sun and rain he wants to control and send them back to the Earth when needed. I am under his influence, time in me turns as he pleases.

What is he doing with my desire? He puts it into a drawer, turns it into light breath that cracks above a dead lightning, he holds it in his hat, in his gloves, and undresses it and dresses it back, he throws it through the window. What is he doing with my open offer I threw in front of him? Nothing.

§

A famous French actress Sarah Bernhardt arrived in New York. I do not like her photos. Her look is dreamy. Her mother was a courtesan. Nick told us he met her in Paris. He was strange when he was describing her.

§

141

He went to dinner with Sarah Bernhardt. On the morning after that, he came to tell us about her. Robert was all ears, which made me even more upset. I could feel the story's tone and that woman's aggressiveness, who shamelessly puts her desires onto men's collars, so of course all her endeavors will succeed. Nick was even stranger. Sarah means something to him.

§

"I have had a wonderful time with you at the ball, Kate." Nick did not say it in reality, his voice woke me up from a dream. Thoughts he turned down reach me, they are mine.

§

Robert wrote a short poem "Premonitions".

There's a shadow on the grass

that was never there before.

§

If he wanted me, I would give myself to him without thinking. Wives cheat on their husbands all the time. I could bear the mockery, the contempt and Robert's disappointment. Only if the other party wanted it, I would risk everything for him.

§

Harper's Bazaar started publishing postcards from Paris, from Miss. Katharine de Forest. Good for her. She lives as she pleases, she enjoys being in Paris, she gets invitations to all the salons and art galleries, and she can write about everything after that, and even gets paid for it.

FEBRUARY

I must immediately talk to Nick. I will rewrite my letter to him:

"I have had such a wonderful experience the past three years. So much of it is already gone that I sometimes fear it will all pass away with me and you of all persons ought to know something of it for you could not fail to have a scientific interest in it. I call it thought transference for want of a better word. Perhaps it is not at all that. I have often wished and meant to speak to you of this, but when I am with you I never say the things I had intended to say. I seem to be only capable of one thing. Do come tomorrow."[6]

§

Was the morning terrible just because of Nick's response or is it because this nasty weather would never clear up? Even Robert, who is long accustomed to my changes of mood, was looking at me in wonder. He lets people bang their worries, his inner peace and dignified standing allow him to patiently wait for people around him to find the middle ground, and then he continues or starts to converse. It would be very unlikely for him to comment or criticize something about another person.

---

[6] A letter from Katherine Johnson to Nikola Tesla, in: Marc Seifer, *Wizard*: The Life and Times of Nikola Tesla. Biography of a Genius. Citadel Press, 1998. p. 106.

That is called being truly distanced. Sometimes I would prefer he told me what he really thinks, to even get into an argument with me. He thinks he speaks enough with his waiting and restraint. That is so faceless. I do not like silence. He even teases me I love being dramatic, I would be good for the theater because all the emotions are exaggerated there and new layers of anger, desperation, and hysteria are being added. Now that enrages me even more.

It is not Robert's fault at all. It is not right for me to transfer my bitterness to him. Nick replied to my yesterday's letter. Not only can he not talk to me personally, but he is going to dedicate all his time to Sarah Bernhardt. I curse the day he met her. She is a weasel. He is taking her to dinner again. I know I will be chasing my tail all night long, like a dog. He is watching her perform in *Isiehl*, and she will be taking him somewhere after that, to a special place. She is so forceful, so flirtatious. She buys people. How does not Nick see through her? Why is everybody enchanted in her presence? How do they not see how sneaky she is? She pretends to be fragile, and she is not at all, she is a cold pile, moreover sly. She likes using people. She has a poker face, and yet she manages to make men run after her to protect her.

I do not know how to do that. You can see what I think and want right from my face. I cannot play two games. Or can I?

§

I wrote a reply to Nick. I told him it seems lovely friends have him captured.

Robert says jealousy is mostly a sin towards oneself. One wastes time thinking of others; you could have lived your life and enjoyed its fruit, but you annoy yourself.

§

He says dinner was more than interesting. Sarah was with him and Swami Vivekananda. Nick is thrilled and intrigued, I notice when someone's presence moves him. It rarely happens, and it is exactly why it is important when it does.

Swami is doing yoga and he reestablished Hinduism in India. He says all religions are real and true. He came to the US to give lectures on famous universities. Nick is especially fascinated by Swami's insistence on self-control. Can Swami achieve more self-control than you, Nick?

I dream awake, I look at my reflection in my own writing, I dream and imagine. Could Robert see and hear through walls? I am scared and excited. He is here now, he will open the door, but he does not know he should suspect something. I will kiss him on the cheek when he gets in, I must.

MARCH

I saw Swami's photo in the papers. He is wearing a turban and his lips are like a river delta. He appears like a calm statue.

Even novelties cannot lighten my mood. Earlier I managed to find joy in the little things, now it all seems so pointless. Little things cannot fill up your life if you long for something grand. In the earlier days, I would rejoice about new fashion, such as bicycle shoes – knee-high, with laces. Katharine de Forest wrote the prettiest dresses in Paris are made of white serge. I am not interested in that either.

§

Robert published his "Ode to Greece" in the Independent. He wrote it a long time ago, when he visited Athens, on Parthenon's stairs.

§

He cannot fool me. I send him my thoughts and words. He must be getting them in one form or another! Maybe he does not see or hear them because there is a wall around him. When he is working (and he is always busy), he is in his light cloud that does not let anything reach him.

Nothing is certain. He can reject all of my colorful arrows. He can see them and bluntly ignore them. Nothing is as important to him as science. The Niagara calls him. I can imagine and form words as much as I want. Who could be strong enough to compare to him, to get near him, conquer him?

I remember a travel article about the Niagara, written by Mrs. Van Rensselaer for *The Century* (I envy her – she is a traveler, writer, publisher, she turned her adventurous spirit and freedom into words). She is the first woman who is an architectural critic. She wrote the waterfalls are so mighty, only the brightest light can show all of their beauty, the nights there are blinking, one must walk around the whole area for more than a week in order to notice all the details, as beautiful as a structure of a cathedral. The nature surrounding the Niagara, she writes, is most seductive in May, when all the trees get leaves and blossom. May is mine!

The Niagara is a spitting image of what Nikola Tesla imagined before he came to America.

And what about the love? Could love find its way through the light clouds?

What kind of love is it when it breaks your body? How can I send it to him if I am so weak? It is a paradox. I love him so much, my love is stronger than the power of Niagara's water falling down from the cliffs. But it is not enough. Even such love cannot stagger a person like Nikola Tesla. I send it away, it returns, it completely breaks me, and then I cannot bare to send it any longer.

§

I barely saw him this month. I did get his letters, though he usually wrote about Swami – he is thrilled with what he was saying. Every man has a potential deity, and the divine in ourselves we can wake with our work and prayers.

He has got his science and his goal, pleasure does not depend upon other people for him at all. What should I do? Sometimes it seems I miss only one grain of star dust for pleasure. He does not find anything hard, he is tied to no one. Does he have a heart? Has he ever fallen in love? Who is that man?

He is the master of self-control. He is a senseless being, aware of being born to reach the top in science, to make the planet behave differently, to open eyes for us all… That is great, but do not forget it is also senseless. He works for all of us, and we are all equal to him? He is a machine.

He has not visited us for so long, but he wrote to Robert he has the time, but he will not come unless our guests are famous.

"Look at his signature, Kate – Tesla, the Great Inventor!" Robert's smile is round and standard.

Nikola Tesla is a cruel machine. Paradoxically, that machine dedicated its life to the humanity. But for us, individuals who long for him, he has no time, he cannot give us even a piece of his heart.

§

It is not Nick's fault my pleasure relies on him. It is not Nick's fault I want something more, and I already have enough.

Swami says to choose an idea and put it on our life's pedestal, to think all the time, to imagine all the time, to live that idea. That is the road to success, that is how you build a spiritual giant.

§

Confusion dug out the evil from my soul, that little prickly evil that has to make everything uglier in order to feel better. That evil must hurt everybody around itself in order to feel fulfilled. Oh, that fulfillment is so miserable! It lasts for such a short time. Then regret comes. Maybe I am that great evil? Why do I flatter myself?

"Knock, and it shall be opened unto you." No, not all doors open! Some stay closed forever. Should I abandon all my hope? Maybe it truly is high time I threw everything down the drain and break its neck.

What gives me the right to consider Nikola Tesla's door legitimate at all? How could I even think I was right, I, a woman who wants for the adulteress' door to open for her? And I even quote Jesus! I should repent. I should admit everything to Robert and cleanse my heart. Both moves seem so easy when I write them down.

APRIL

We were walking down Fifth Avenue. Robert was waiting for us in Central Park. There were boys with two-colored hats playing on the lake's shore. The girls were wearing white and red plaid dresses. The pretzel seller shouted. Nick was walking faster and faster and responded in short sentences, but he was neither rough nor unpleasant. He is hiding his tenderness towards me deep inside. He is a pink and fragile tenderness, as soft as a kiss. It is truly trapped, deep inside of him.

Nick's cramped tenderness and I, a woman who has to but does not want to, hiding my own tenderness. He is walking beside me, so close, under the brave sun, and I cannot even touch him, my hands and shoulders hurt and there is only one touch that could cure them. I must endure the pain and feel the happiness. I wanted for us to stop, to stop everything, to melt myself in the sun. What might I be to him? A shadow-friend.

149

A woman who prays for him. That is also nice. That, too, is a lot.

That is little… I do not know. I am happy to have met him, that he illuminated my life. But having his hands beside his body burns me, undivided warmth runs through them. If only I could put my warm hand onto his chest… The fire you must swallow burns the hardest. And even when you swallow it forcefully, your woes do not go away because a new fire emerges since he is there.

"Am I walking too fast?" he asked when the sun got down onto his look.

"We could be walking a bit slower," I replied. "So we can spend as much time together as we could."

"If the lady wishes so," he accepted half-wittily.

"Is everything wasted?"

"Nothing is ever wasted, everything has its energy, and it lives forever," he responded as if he gave me solace and almost as if he could not wait for the moment to be like that.

Who am I? A spectator of a great being. He told me matter is a manifestation of energy. He can create everything. What could I ever offer to him? Friendship? Will it last forever?

It is hard to pretend being a friend when you love your friend.

§

He sometimes writes something full of life and cheers us up. Now we all take part, and it is dear Kipling's fault. He are

150

voraciously reading his new work – *The Jungle Book* – Robert, Nick, and I. Agnes cannot even steal it from us, the elderly. I wrote to Owen about this siege.

Reading washes sorrow away. I penetrate the stories, they are the reality of us all. Kipling took us all to the Indian jungle.

§

"Now this is the law of the jungle..."[7] Those Kipling's words sound so peaceful and imminent. The law of the jungle is ruthless and perfectly ordained. When I get back to that sentence, I feel a cruel atmosphere, as if in a fairy-tale. The laws of the jungle are better than all human laws because they are clear, and the animals respect them.

All day long I have been talking to Robert and Agnes about Mowgli. Today I read the monkeys kidnapped him. Robert read less than us. We were imagining how the ruined city where monkeys live might have looked like.

The artists are there to offer us an escape route. When do we really live? When do we reside in our everyday life or when do we enjoy the art?

§

Nick wrote about *The Jungle Book* again. He says stories are magic and he loves Riki Tiki Tawi the most.

---

[7] Quoted from: Rudyard Kipling, *The Jungle Book*. Macmillan. London: 1894.

We are carefree creatures lost in the Indian jungle. We must thank Kipling for giving us this joy.

It would be best if we could keep children's spontaneity all life long. Who could do that? Who would dare?

§

Baloo told Mowgli: "The law is like a gigantic liana because it falls on everyone's back and no one can avoid it." This is true. And how can we deal with ourselves when inevitability falls on our back?

§

Mowgli became the master of the jungle! His conversation with Kaa (I get chills even when I think of such a big snake) is rather interesting. Kaa asked him: "So the jungle has given you everything you even wanted, little brother?" And Mowgli responded: "What more could I wish for? I have the jungle and its benevolence. Is there anything else between the sunrise and sunset?" I have been thinking about this for a very long time. Words are true and inspiring, but it is hard to please oneself with one's own existence and sunshine. We all have damned wishes, that distract us from that beauty. Would we feel less alive if there had not been for the wild wishes that devour us? I do not know. Kipling is right when he speaks through Mowgli, but really, who could do that? Mowgli? Swami? Nick?

§

I love our salon when it is full of laughter and wonderful conversations. I love the haste, the murmur, meeting the artists. How unusual our guests can be. When I please them, I simply glow from happiness. We are planning to organize a dinner party for Kipling.

§

Nikola Tesla met Ignacy Jan Paderewski. Our circle of light is expanding. They arrived almost at the same time, we went out to greet Nick when Gilder and Paderewski showed up at the gate. This was not a coincidence, and they later discovered they were connected to each other. It seems both of them were in Strasbourg at the same time. Nick was retelling his experience while working at Edison's factory on promoting electrical equipment and Paderewski recalled his own student days. At one point, Robert and I have not been involved, we were but silent observers, but it did not bother us. I was imagining them as fledglings in Strasbourg. They must have walked down the same streets, but never could have even guessed they would meet in New York, in our house. Life is wonderful. The whole time I have been having a motherly impulse, the purest of happiness. Paderewski played the piano for us. He first played his own composition, a minuet. At the very beginning, a game of sounds and the music remind me of Mozart, and then the tracing of the sound gets lost, but it continues its steps and then blossoms. And then he played Chopin for us, to prove his mastery. One could hear the water flowing, not the piano playing.

Paderewski has a dry look and the feistiest brown hair I have ever seen, so messy and willful; his fingers speak: they kissed our Stanway piano's chords, not softly, but a little rough, but those unusual tones have captured our breath.

I am going to tuck in now and cover myself with happiness and nothing is going to disturb me, I will enjoy falling asleep.

§

Paderewski presented us with his wife, Antonina, and his parrot, without whom he does not go anywhere.

§

Not a minute planned for science cannot be sacrificed. Despite having had Kipling with us for dinner, Nick could not make it. His dull tone of rejection remained unchanged, it is implied he is calm and poised. "I am sorry I cannot make it, but I will be there as soon as I could."

Can you not at least once cross the borders, ruin your own plans, give yourself wildly? Can you not enjoy at least a moment of laziness?

I know, Nick, then you would not be what you are, then you would not achieve your aspirations, you would not be such a wizard. I know it all, and I know nothing.

Again we moved to the jungle. Mowgli, Baloo, Bagheera, and Kaa joined us. I could feel the scent of moist lush greenery and hear the unknown sounds. Everyone was there, besides Nick.

§

Robert's poem called "A Chopin Fantasy" is gorgeous and powerful. I am also in it. He suggests we leave this world, for just a moment, full of rules and customs and visit the warm places, where free time is a duty. Robert speaks in that way in his poetry but in the real world all he does is work, he has no time to relax. This is both good and bad. He works for all of us. I wish I could do something, too, not only to live off his hard work. He would never let me struggle. But that would mean leaving a mark, working hard!

After that suggestion to me, one could hear Chopin's music in that poem of Robert's without fail. A strong melancholy reverberates. In it, the ships tremble in breeze like white doves. Robert then goes back to talking to me. "Something is bothering you." Something is bothering you, my dear. He says I should be happy, not to think too much, to enjoy planning to be happy more. A dream of happiness is happiness, he often says that. Working on achieving happiness is also happiness.

§

Can Nick feel the spring's breath? Does he blossom and melt? Does he ever change? No, he is stable, always running in the same frequency, dedicated and calm, the outer world cannot shake him up, not even the power of changing the seasons! He would put his open hand in front of him and stop every attempt of meltdown. Then he would continue working.

I wrote a letter to him, asking him to come and improve my mood. I said the spring used to bring me joy, but now it just makes me sad. I also wrote:

"I wish that I, like you, could go on forever and forever in the same routine, without break, living my own life, as you say you do. I do not know whose life I live, it has not seemed my own."[8]

I personally have no goals. My children have them. Robert has them, he was born with a mission and a plan. I was fluttering around, playing, but what have I actually been doing? Everything happened so spontaneously.

We are all alone with ourselves. And what am I doing so alone? What am I doing? Nick enjoys his solitude, he had chosen that path. The world is his goal.

Oh, let him come. A piece of music, fun, and laughter with him would cure me for a while, his look would be my elixir, I will not torment myself with these big questions anymore.

He can hear the sky breathing before a storm, he understands what the lightnings are saying, they come because of him and wound New York's peaks. They caress his hair. I am jealous of them.

If he can hear the messages coming from the whirring sky and the loud call of distraught hissers, can he not hear my soul's message? Can he show no mercy?

§

Even if I followed my lifeline (I do not know if I ever searched for it or have I been dragged to some other line), I am definitely

---

[8] A letter from Katherine Johnson to Nikola Tesla, in: Margaret Cheney, *Tesla: Man out of Time*, p. 142.

not doing that right now. I follow another person's life, I live another person's dream.

MAY
Sarah Bernhardt's fashion opinion was published in *Harper's Bazaar*. Her shoulders are wide, her profile kind of thick—almost plump—I do not know what men see in her.

JUNE
We are getting ready to travel to Maine. We are going to visit Bar Harbor once more.

Again with the lemon-colored houses, the rhapsody, and fireworks of blue, roses growing around tents, meat-colored rocks, the afternoons that never seem to pass.

If only I could look at him, so calm and relaxed at the beach, almost unreal, to hear the waves create foam, and him just standing there, so monumental and quiet! I wish he could be strong as he always is, so ordinary, so usual. I wish I could look at him in the morning, doing nothing, just watching me and that all the world's times would stop at that moment.

JULY
Owen came. Agnes and Robert are impatient to leave the city as soon as possible. Sometimes I think the city alone is my best friend, that only its soul, hidden underneath all this avenues and streets, can exactly feel my own, ever so thirsty.

JULY

When everyone goes away, I usually sit on the porch and watch the passers-by. I have no desire to take a stroll. Owen is accompanying me very often, sitting aback in his rocking chair, nibbling a blade of grass, and telling me about school ending. He often repeats one and the same anecdote a few times, and I can always listen to him because he always tells them differently. He is soon going to go to Yale. My boy has grown and changed so much, his face is now longer, life has made a toll on him, but it is noticeable he turned everything into a positive experience, both his youth sufferings and mischiefs. My son takes everything easier than anyone I know, he is open to new things and does not question them.

It might be a little odd that Owen shares more than Agnes with me. She does not keep many things secret, she is just not that comfortable talking, but Owen speaks his mind all the way. He does it both consciously and unconsciously. Agnes is calm, stable and serious, and Owen is an adventurer. He will be able to grasp what I could not, to bite the bullet, and he will be able to do what others do not, which will give him a chance to fight.

§

"Imagine," Robert said, "how hot it must be now in New York." And then Agnes relieved too, thinking it was a blessing we are here in Maine, and Owen smiled gawkily. His life is full of fun time, wherever he is.

§

I wrote he is making a fatal mistake because he thinks he does not need to rest. I added he must be so tired he does not know what he needs.

In response, he sent me flowers.

§

Isolated and torn off of him, at least physically, I can hear my own laughter before his arrival. It feels good going back to one's own life. For how long will it last?

AUGUST

I am worried. Nick returned from the Niagara, and he is back in town, alone and tired. I beset Robert to send him a letter. He says I am being dramatic. I am restless in this rustling peace between butterflies.

I must write to him and invite him to come. I can write as much as I want, but I cannot influence that person sitting in his lab. I can no longer stay here. The time stopped, and he must admit it, to obey, he would stop being in such a hurry for a while.

§

There is no answer. I made Robert write to him as well. He will melt away in his lab!

§

There is no answer. I know he is on a brink of illness. Who am I to appropriate him? Fire drips from my fingertips, and peace, dream surround me.

Twain's favorite daughter Susy has died. She suffered from meningitis. In his letter full of stoicism one could still see endless despair.

SEPTEMBER

He is able to perfectly cut off the outer world from himself and from us and he does not find it merciless at all. We are in New York, but we have not seen him yet, nor do we know when he will wish to meet us. He only wrote he is exhausted, and he is not communicating with anyone. Even a short notification is a privilege for us. The little we get from him should mean a lot to us, but it is still too little.

He is worried about humankind, we are worried about him; everyone suffers for one's own reasons.

I now do not like staying alone at home and that happens so often. I look myself in the mirror and I still cry. I look at my red eyes and strangely, in the midst of the known and the unknown pain I look pretty to myself, my eyes are beautiful, although red. I may slowly be losing my mind.

§

Tomaso Salvini's son Alessandro has died. He had only just started to conquer the US.

§

Sarah Bernhardt is in *Harper's* again. In her report from Paris, she now mentioned Katharine de Forest and she praises her influence on the fashionable hats industry, because she was the first one to decorate them with big flowers.

Sarah Bernhardt was a courtesan like her mother! There is something fake in her. Alexander Dumas agrees with me, too.

OCTOBER

Owen is getting ready for Yale. Yale should get ready too. It will get cheekiness, devotion, and work, and another famous student to be, I guarantee it.

NOVEMBER

We have read in the papers that Nick visited Buffalo, where he successfully performed his experiment. Robert sent him a cheeky letter. Robert can joke with the fact that Nick is silent, and we are now like strangers. I pretend to be a part of the joke too. I know this is not true and we are not really strangers, but he is not here… and that is the truth. Two different truths.

I call upon him. I no longer write letters to him personally and Robert wrote this one after a while. I call upon him in my thoughts. He can hear me!

§

His greatest success! The first electricity transmission was carried out from the Niagara Falls hydro-power plant to Buffalo. He verified his knowledge and dreams, proved everyone he was right. His is a wide path, a path of a being that descended from another world and shed light upon us. Electricity from Niagara Falls is going to be flowing towards us.

I sent him a letter to come and visit us for at least a moment, that I have not seen him for centuries, although I am always on his path.

§

Harper's is now criticizing Sarah Bernhardt for insisting on having Renaissance costumes in the *Lady with the Camelias*. She does not know everything after all, even though she is imagining the opposite.

DECEMBER

He came by last night for a moment, out of the blue, even though he had sent an announcement. We knew he would come, but he still surprised us with a banging entry. I was happy, but mad too. However, happiness overrules – it was his fault I did not see him, he took away my heart and took it away with him to the lab. He did not want to bring it back to me until now. He is a thief!

He had informed us he is coming to our Christmas dinner, and then he vanished faster than when he initially appeared! I saw only his coat's end fluttering down the street. Could it be he left so quickly because I was rough on him? I was truly distraught.

§

He came for Christmas, and everything was as back when we first met, we just continued being friends and laughing as we used to.

How could I have even thought of judging his compassion? He feels the Earth, the sky, the sun and the moon, he is shivering just like the wind speaks, he speaks as simple as snowflakes fall onto the city. I am glad he is lively again, full of strength. The roses he brought last night are daringly bright, their leaves thick. I opened a window and put them onto the frozen sims, they did not even move, they are the same, so strong in their daring bright colors! The frost encouraged them even more, they now enjoy their own beauty with more love! Everything is so unusual with him.

I regret it. I shall write this to him.

§

"I must always when I write to you make several attempts, a system of repression because I can never express what I would say. I did not mean to be severe the other evening. I was only wrapped up in disappointment. I miss you very much and wonder if it is always to go on this way and if I can ever become accustomed to not seeing you."[9]

§

I do not like snowflakes in my hair, they make me look older.

---

[9] A letter from Katherine Johnson to Nikola Tesla, in: Margaret Cheney, *Tesla: Man out of Time*, p. 143.

1897

JANUARY

My hands are dry, whatever I try to do to make them better, it does not work, no treatment works. I am getting older. It is not fair. My thoughts are not older, I do not feel tired or slow, I do not give up, but my hands give my age away. My own skin hurts and ties, as if I was bothered or tingled by it. Robert told me I am exaggerating again (as per usual). He was on his knees by the bed and kissed my hands. Nothing could please me, nothing that could beat this disgusting feeling of tightness. I am desperate. It is too early to be old, I have only started living my life.

§

How does one, who always wanted more, feel when one sees the goal is not achieved? How does one, whose invention is going to be used by the whole world, feel? What kind of a high tide that comes to the final recognition is it? For years, he used to work without stopping, the bad guys wanted to make him trip, he has been waiting for years. He told us a long time ago how he had gotten his idea back when he was in Budapest. How does it feel when you need to stand with a heavy burden on your shoulders, a burden of waiting to be recognized? It must be terribly difficult to take the truth with you, so no one knows it, or distort it, while others brag and prosper while you wait patiently, and you passionately love your idea.

It is a painful truth that wants to go out in the open. I doubt I would be that patient, I would go crazy.

Our friend, Nikola Tesla the scientist is at the stepping stone of his greatest glory. The Johnson family got only a grain from his success's vine. That little grain inebriates as the strongest wine there is.

§

He managed to surprise us once again. He does not sway that easily, he does not enjoy it for even a second. When he had visited Buffalo, he said the Niagara project is already past and he will manage to transmit electricity without wires!

I believe you will make it, I do not know how, perhaps a light will swell under the Earth's crust and travel towards us on invisible tracks. I do not know science, Nick. You said it more than once that humans are born to work, to endure, and to fight, and you personally do not need help and you show your best when you are fighting. But believe me, my dear friend, I can feel your misery and struggles, they hurt me, just like you say you can feel other people's injuries. We are similar in that, Nick! I cannot get near you in many other areas, but I can with my heart. Take me.

§

That being sitting for nights in his Houston Street laboratory, who knows what his eyes are then like (black, dark blue, white, yellow, invisible, fiery, good, evil, nonearthly?). He sits in the darkness intersected with firing lightnings. He observes them.

165

During the day, however, he creates earthquakes and gives statements that he could split the Earth. By the way, he believes the Earth is vibrating all the time.

The Earth breathes, feels, speaks? Is he trying to tell us that? Is the Earth a living creature?

I love it when he tells us his secrets. But he really loves giving bombastic statements to the press. He brags in the most usual way. He simply asserts himself both in his words and glory. And his words are getting more and more incredible.

I love it when he tells me personally I speak as if I were spoilt, and I elongate vowels. I love it when he tells me my hair color is unusual.

I do not like it when he says we are all machines responding to outer influence, I feel uncomfortable. It is more pleasant when he says we are all like waves that move around in space. It is better when I imagine I am a wave than a machine.

We are all waves, as are our thoughts and feelings. I feel calm when I imagine it. The waves are always alive, they never stop reaching the shores.

§

I was observing him. I could see in his face he had reached a point and was just moving to a different sky. Nikola Tesla's steps – what will they reach? He is already sitting with us in a seemingly normal way – but it is as if he was watching us from that other sky. He is still physically the same, but I can see the coral metamorphosis in him, while he strictly holds his back, head and arms tightly upright.

I asked him again, "Are we waves?"

"Yes," he replied, "but when our waves go down, they no longer exist."

"Do they really?"

That question felt so silly. He was silent.

"Some things exist forever," I opposed.

He tilted his head. He wanted to smile, but he gave up. I might have something to say from my experience.

"What is it, Kate?"

"A look, even though the eye no longer exists."

A look that cuts your soul, so it is never the same.

§

John Jacob Astor IV, William Waldorf Astor's cousin, built a hotel next to "Waldorf" and named it "Astoria". He had convinced his mother to move uptown.

A remarkable thing happened today. Nick looked at me as if he was searching for something, he quickly turned his head towards me like a wild animal. It was as if he scarred my cheek with fire. It was just what I had told him to do.

FEBRUARY

New York Times published a story that last night "the most significant night of the New York society" – the Cornelia

Bradley-Martin's ball was organized in "Waldorf-Astoria". There were 800 high society members at the costume ball. For three weeks everybody was talking about the preparations for the ball and now it has finally reached its climax. John Jacob Astor was Henry IV and Ava was Mary Antoinette. Stany had a black velvet and white satin costume. I cannot wait for him to tell us how it went. Everybody wore chimerical jewelry that is being kept in safes, the city's ground felt heavier steps. The hotel was decorated as Versailles from the inside. Mrs. Bradley-Martin had a Mary Stuart costume.

MARCH
Sarah Bernhardt got a bad review for her new play in Paris called *Spiritualism*. Robert has been giving me a funny look while I giggle.

APRIL
Agnes not only agreed with our plan but is thrilled we are going to take her to her Paris school.

§

We met Richmond Pearson Hobson, a young naval officer born in Alabama.

JULY
Our Agnes is wise and patient. I am proud of her, and I give her all the support I could find in my heart. She, of course, accepts it, but I feel she already knows everything, she only adds it. No, she does not ask for more than she already has.

AUGUST

As a ship cuts the ocean's body, I remember four young women with two children on a boat in Bois de Vincennes. All of those new faces were full of life, but not loud and visible at first glance: they calmly and wisely enjoyed the magic of now. That is a trance that does not brag on its own. There is no need for it. You pay it respect the most if you join with no questions asked, without thinking.

Agnes is an obedient, meek, and moderate girl. She already clearly set goals, she wants to have a family, children, she already thinks in that direction and is serious about everything. She has no silly illusions, nor is anything like me in that period of my life. I am proud how my child is so different than me. The most important thing is she is happy about her going back to *Couvent de l'Assomption*.

NOVEMBER

Robert's collection of poems is soon to be published; it contains the best poems he wrote lately. Poetry is an exclusive phenomenon, and my Robert is worthy of that exclusiveness. He is dignified and devoted, just what a true poet should be like. The poem about me and the one about Nick's lab are going to be in the collection. It is curious that translations of the Serbian poet Zmaj's fourteen poems are also going to be published in it.

After the promotion, we are all having dinner at "Waldorf-Astoria", where Nick has a table in the Palm Salon. He demands to always have 18 clean cotton napkins set on the table, arranged as a large, starched pyramid he then uses to clean the silverware – that is already so polished I can use it as a mirror. He weighs one after another, not caring about anyone. He eats slowly and chews more than anyone else. Before he starts eating, he always calculates the food's volume in his plate. Everything must be divisible by three. Even the precious oysters.

§

Robert is proud and happy. He enjoys his success differently than Nick does. He does not go into flames, nor does he glow, but with cold restraint he tells he had deserved an applause. Why would an artist be modest? If he is good, if he faithfully expressed excitement, if his work's rhythm reverberates in people's hearts, why would he be modest? Let him enjoy the attention.

Glamor and applause naturally followed. He was signing his collection of poems, *Songs of Liberty and Other Poems*. There is also the "Irish Love Poem". And I will go into eternity. "A fairy's nose", "cherry-like cheek", "her smile is but like Kate" are all ways I have been mentioned. Someone, when we are all gone, is going to read that poem and wonder who Kate might have been. They are going to pronounce my name – Katherine, Kate, and I will come alive. I will be standing, like I am now, with warm fur covering my cleavage, my hair is going to be silvery and gold as it is now, I will provide support, that is why I am here.

Maybe these lyrics are the most beautiful ones he ever wrote about me:

God, be human,

spare the girl in this woman.

If only I would be the leading star... I should not spoil Robert's day with these words.

We barely got to see Nick in the crowd. Owen was also in the crowd; talkative, as he is, he drew the attention and was socializing with everybody. He is carelessly joyful, hungry with adventures, examining the borders, a true gentleman who enjoys his youth, so spontaneous. He is my upper, improved tone, my voice lives through him.

DECEMBER

Time passes by so quickly. Everything I start doing goes to waste, nothing works for me these days. My hair is crackling. I want him to touch it, to calm it down. He calms the lightnings' urge with one move of his hand, the crackling in my hair would be gone if he would pat it.

I want to lie down like a fetus and have him behind me in the same position, all crumbled and loosing myself in his body.

I wrote a letter to him to come and hypnotize me with his presence. That was a half-joke. A bait. We both know he could take me to another world with his look and I would be different there.

We both know he is not going to come. He must surely know it and I am learning to accept it. I threw a third of my hope down the stairs. My recent girly capability to seduce, I now barely even remember, is silent before his silence.

1898

JANUARY

Nick is in the newspapers again. This time he photographed his hand, and this was published on a whole page in *Electric Review*. In his photos, he draws the attention, giving himself away. He emits himself. I was staring at its every detail, you can see each and every line in it. His hands are both smooth and rough, big and grand, if only he would touch my earring or even my skin.... His striking, wide, milk-white nails, long and decisive fingers, the power of that hand, which he elegantly tucks into his gentle gloves.... If I would let my hair down in front of him....

I went too far. He is not going to touch even the air beneath my earring, not to mention my hair. I let it down in my imagination and these photos break me, I cannot stand it. That man has something rocky and strong in him and such are his hands too: dark, zealous, rough, bony. They move harmoniously, slowly, caringly, gentlemanly. You can see a part of his jacket and underneath it you can see a white starched shirt. The little knoll beneath his thumb is illuminated.

I keep forgetting he is in the room, and I enter unprepared, so my body shakes. That image becomes the only one I see, and when I close my eyes, its light yellowish form is still in my thoughts, like that hand's spirit, insufficiently clear, but untamable and beautiful. However, there are also shadows in the original photo. Nick must take another photo of his hand, so it becomes noticeable how big and free it is. I must suggest that to him.

§

I wrote to him about the photo and that he must come to Robert's birthday party. I am soon going to leave for Washington, so when will I see him?

Robert decided to have the Serbian songs sung in his party, which is going to be a real hit.

I put the magazine photo into my drawer. It is of no use. It keeps shining in my thoughts even when it is there.

My little silver earrings, shaped like three connected leaves, are lying on the table. I do not wear the pearl ones because of Nick, he cannot stand them. They make him sick.

§

Is Martin trying to avenge himself? I cannot believe it. He has been angry with Nick for a long time due to his impracticality and for not cooperating with him regarding the oscillators and the book about him. Martin has a reason to get angry, but still, to let his magazine publish a sarcastic text about Nick – that is too much. How can he attack him that way and leave him? Robert is so angry with Martin. I hope everything will settle. Robert says I am wrong – those who are happy to attack Nick about his wireless transmission ideas are now going to regain strength.

§

Why does the most hardworking person must be alone? Why is the majority either silent or criticizing without a reason? Why is the best person always a thorn in the eye? Why cannot they be happy he is among us? They cannot admit there is a better person than them. They brag amongst themselves and flatter one another, those average people, they sway with their mediocre praise, that comes again and again, almost in cycles, so when a giant enters their space and they realize he is greater than them, they are going to be waiting in silence and attack like evil wasps as soon as they get a chance. Martin's text initiated a series of sarcastic and heavy critiques of Tesla's thoughts in other magazines. Once again, Nick knows something the others do not and is being attacked for it once more. They do not like it when someone sees further. It is difficult for those who are at the top. How easy it is to use words to defeat a better person, to build one's own false value by saying the greater one is not good enough. But those liars will not make it against time.

§

Nick entered seemingly relieved and cheerful. Robert was nuts about the attacks, but he did not want to immediately show how nervous he was. We had dinner. I was quiet. But the nervous energy could not remain hidden under the table for a long time, it was eating at Robert's palate, and Nick cracked too. They started talking about the press belligerence, so I let them exchange their thoughts alone, and I listened to them carefully.

Nick was really outraged. He said he could direct his pronged lightnings towards those ironic critics. All the time Robert was looking for a way to help Nick, wishing him to reciprocate those critics. Nick said he can only reciprocate with his despise.

My being cannot believe evil people exist. He knows it, he can recognize them well, but he is always surprised by it. He cannot believe how some people invest their energy into hatred and lump characterization of others, instead of devoting it to themselves. He cannot believe someone can take a piece of something and turn it into the main story, to judge based on that miserable part, and attack without a solid ground.

"Take care," I said when they both went silent.

He protracted his tight lips as if he wanted to say: "Thank you for caring for me."

FEBRUARY

Washington is the capital city, but it is much calmer and more tight knit than New York. People are walking slowly there, and everything is so wide apart. I love New York's run over and trampled streets, the fact it is getting tighter and remains open, the fact that it is colorful, and loud. Washington has a calmer flow, and it seems the time passes slower in it. My dear Ellen does everything to make me comfortable.

I was thinking about my mom and her last days. Getting old is painful. However you try to be dignified, the painfulness breaks out. Being bright in your old age is rare. I am not young anymore. Robert always tells me I am exaggerating, that my face, look, and smile are youthful, that you can see I am young beneath all those irrelevant features, such as wrinkles, dark circles under my eyes and my rough skin.

I stood still in Washington, as the time, I was not trapped but stopped. White Washington, the city of trees. Its fresh blooded maples, poplars, and lindens feel good. Its power is hidden and mysterious, while New York brags with its power, New York boasts with it but is so unsure that, no matter how much it spends it, its power keeps renewing over and over again.

No matter how much I loved someone, and he wishes to oppose my love, I must set him free. I must stop hoping, imagining, determining him, to limit him with my love. I cannot do it. I want him for myself. And that is never going to happen. He has his own freedom and destiny, that I may make darker with my waiting. I must let him go. Maybe I have a bad influence on his light path.

How am I going to do that? Can I do it? I could try.

I got it. I am going to have him married with another person. Could I stand it? I must. I will find an ideal wife for him.

It is a good idea to have and suffocate at the same time.

"Another crazy idea of yours," Robert said, it seems he only sees my colorful shell. Or is it that? What does he see, what does he know?

This February is so grey. The wind is blowing incessantly, the winter is not giving up, we are all exhausted. I will find a life companion for him. He can no longer say he is married to science. I am going to control my thoughts. I will order myself not to dream of him anymore. I am going to pray before bedtime not to dream of him again. Outside, the wind is moaning like an old man.

§

I invited Miss Hale for dinner, that Nick is also going to come to, and I highlighted that in my letter to him as an important fact. She is, I must admit it, very charming. I will try not to overshadow her. It will be hard to give up on him, especially when he comes and lights us all up with his brightness. I must retreat and glow inside myself. I will hide away my smile. I will observe how Miss Hale looks at him and if she is flirtatious. I will take note of whether he will be looking back at her. I am strong and wonderful as long as the porcelain image breaks in front of me. Could I make it?

§

The dinner was not that bad. My soul was silent during the entire evening. I can cry now, when I take my earrings off and comb my hair, the moment is perfect. I have killed my hope, its whole shimmering body is finally wasted. It is dead.

MARCH

Now my tears are in one of my heart's drawers. That drawer has spiked handles, that stop me from opening it frequently. I think of it and then shake it off. I do not step into happiness, but into a voiceless and waveless space, all tight, but neutral. It seems I am floating in it. There are no thoughts in it.

Thoughts have their own energy, and we can use them to attract what we want, or even what we do not. Thoughts have their own power. But in a voiceless and waveless space, I have no thoughts. It is a different kind of me. I do not know for how long that image is going to live on.

The city is bestirred by the wind. It is forced to twist around the buildings as if through a labyrinth. When it is blowing like that, it is best to relax and lie beside a warm person in your bed. Or at least have that warm person come for lunch. Based on the first impression, one could not say Nick is a warm person. At least the majority could not. He hides his warmth inside, but such warmth is the greatest. He is just seemingly distanced and kind, polished, perfectly clean, which gives away a metal-cold impression.

I invited him out for lunch, to come and give his friends some solace, but he did not send a reply. I invited him again, highlighting that Miss Hale is going to visit us too. She has a mixture of meekness and elan in her, the two colliding features are well balanced. I think she is the right woman for him.

He did not come but thought of us going to "Waldorf-Astoria" for dinner first. He promised to train his appetite by then. The hotel enwraps us with its satin furniture. I love the salad that Oscar, the *maître d'hôtel*, had invented. It is mild and sophisticated – a mixture of apples, celery, and mayo. Sometimes they add nuts too, which makes it even better. The hotel has everything but a dignified walk of the greatest scientist who is planning to move there. Then it will truly have everything.

I imitated our friend's refinement at dinner. It is entertaining. I slowly ate my salad, just like he does. Spicy meat in a cut melon, with blueberries on top and avocado as a side dish. Such an enjoyment, both exotic and mild.

Thank God there were no ladies with pearls at the restaurant, otherwise Nick would not be able to eat.

APRIL

Robert showed me his notes, his poems to be. He wrote April is a lover to all of us. That is impossible. The air's tenderness alone could not satisfy me.

There is an ugly hat in a Fifth Avenue shop window, even though it is from Paris, and it reminds me of bat wings.

The Century published Elizabeth Robins Pennell's travelogue. She was roaming the Alps on her bike. She had felt the wind of freedom.

MAY

We spent a formal day at the Electrical Exhibition at Madison Square Garden. Robert and I walked there. He was holding me by the hand. He was proud and in a good mood. What would I do without him, all alone? Would I ever come to New York? What would my world be like? Robert is my safety. How many steps would I make on my own? I shall never find out.

Nick and Stany wanted to have the Exhibition in a bright, rainbow-colored room, and to have Nick's light bulbs lit up at the entrance. We entered the hall all gleeful. Nick's friend Choncey Depew announced the exhibition of the teleautomaton. The audience is directed toward a pool where the wizard was standing, ready to demonstrate. Love shone from his whole body. A small boat was sailing through the pool. Nick held a small device in his hand, that was moving it in the desired direction, then he stopped and moved it again. We could hear many people around us gasp. A magician without false magic, a real illusionist, a true sorcerer – such is Nikola Tesla. There is nothing to reveal and deny in his experiments, he explains and demonstrates everything loud and clear. When he was done controlling the boat, he spread his arms and held them in the air for quite some time. The audience kept being silent all along, we were all standing in awe. When he finally put them down, the applause broke off. Was that even possible, to control devices from afar? We were all stunned.

JUNE

Katherine de Forest is honest and fun, she is well versed in fashion and art. The quality of her Paris reports is still good. She is full of excitement and adventures, inebriated and joyous. She is writing that red is trendy. New skirts with no rear folds are also starting to appear.

OCTOBER

Nikola Tesla the inventor moved into the most elegant hotel in the world. "Waldorf-Astoria" has it all now. If it pleases him, he can destroy the Brooklyn Bridge with his quakes. He can split the Earth. That is what he said.

NOVEMBER

We are going to throw a grand party soon. I am drawing up our guest list. I invited many young girls. Nick already wrote he is counting on my choice, but it would please him the most to see Miss Merington. She is good, kind, full of qualities. She does not wear jewelry and that excites him the most, she speaks wisely and wonderfully plays the piano. I still have not decided whether she is focused on Nick or is she just enjoying his company, without having the slightest idea about the possibility of connecting with him. I try to withhold thinking about her qualities, but I cannot stand the attention Nick gives her. That is the real truth.

§

He asked me personally whether I would like to go to his dinner. Why would he even ask? For how long are we going to be slaves to formality? I did not dare to cross another line. I must respect the form, otherwise I would lose him forever.

There is a "Waldorf-Astoria" marking on the letter. The letter starts with, "My dear Kate". *My. Dear. Kate.* It is all that I want! To be Kate, not Mrs. Filipov, not Mrs. Johnson, not his friend, but Kate, lovely Kate, his Kate, that presses her cheek against his.

Let all the giggling and charming ladies aside, he called me My, Dear, Kate. He wrote he is happy I accepted his dinner invitation in "Waldorf-Astoria". We are going to rush a bit to be there at eight o'clock sharp, he will greet us all set, with a smile, and we are going to sit like always, elegantly, when we are in his company.

§

Robert was beside me and in that short period of pure fervor, I was like a princess crossing a bridge towards a castle where her Prince Nick is waiting for her. The enchanted prince? Or is the princess enchanted?

§

I am one of the best party organizers in New York. They may not be the most expensive nor extravagant gatherings, but they are certainly the most elegant. Stany, the Gilders, Mure, Nikola Tesla, Robert Underwood Johnson, the intelligence and elegance, subtlety, I who tie them all and take care of everything – it was wonderful. Nick danced with Miss Merington only. There are more things that can happen. Owen also made friends with her, but I can see they can only stay friends, which is good.

Who am I lying to? It is not wonderful. My luxurious necklace was wonderful, covering my neck and cleavage, and its glow was dripping on my chest. My breasts were wonderful, I nurtured them in a special way for the party, you could not see the tiny lines in the skin, my smile was glowing, Robert's support was honest, he was proud how I was glowing, Owen and Agnes were cheerful, our home was the center of the world. But Nick danced with Miss Merington the entire evening. She seemed modest in her moderate light beige dress, strangely attractive. He was greater than the skies. I wished to crunch up into a fetus position. I wanted him naked behind me and hugging me entirely, to crush me with his body, so we can hug like that after we have made love—during the course of which we would have lost our breath and consciousness from time to time.

DECEMBER

He is interested in Amalia Küssner, a famous miniature portrait painter; *Harper's Bazaar* wrote an article about her. She is successful in hiding her years and plays on a girl-painter card. One cannot deny her talent. She has a luxurious studio in the Windsor hotel. She lives the life of an artist, she portrayed the European kings and the Russian emperor. Marriage did not bring her to New York – but art. Nick is writing to me about her – he wants her to visit him in his Houston Street lab. He is now writing about other women to me. Am I his confidant? Am I his best friend? What are we? He wanted to see me like that in his laboratory. He was looking at me differently as well! Or is it just my imagination? I forgot about my mission. I must have him married. Amalia Küssner is a good match. I will be the person to introduce him to that world, to let him see those girls who are dying to socialize with him. I will monitor it. I will help him find a soft spot for other women. There is a place in my heart for that. I can. I must.

He is not mine. He does not belong to me. I must get used to it. I must protect myself. Those are the facts. I will overcome my vanity, I will suppress it to the bottom of my stomach, I wish him well, he must live his life, I have already tied the knot, I am being taken care of, he must find love, he must feel bodily love, he must be with other people, I will take care of it. I have my own life, he must live his.

§

The now famous Hobson arrived in the city just this week. He became a hero after his Cuban captivity. The newspapers are full of descriptions of his bravery. There will soon be another party. Nick wrote he is certain I am going to shine and be perfectly dressed.

§

Hobson was showing off and was at the center of attention. I was glowing even though my chestnut dress had no cleavage; I know Nick does not like undressed women. I cannot be modest and subdued like Marguerite Merington, simply my spirit is not such, I am ardent, but I was furtively seductive, and I am satisfied. Ever since I met Nick, I changed my posture and stance. Back then I would slouch, but now I am like a butterfly spreading its wings. The position of your shoulders shows your elegance. I am happy to even have met him and the fact we were both glowing this evening. Could it be enough?

§

He wrote to Robert saying Ava was sweet. He was at her house. Does Ava realize who he is? Has she even seen through him? Did she see how he is special and made of porcelain, did she feel his unintrusive light, did she notice his fingers are wonderful?

He is impressed, he likes her loveliness.

§

He is taking flowers whenever he goes to the Astors for dinner, and they go to Delmonico's.

§

However, he asked for us to prepare young chicken stuffed with nuts, he is going to spend Christmas with us. He gives his most intimate moments, however reluctant he may be, to us only!

§

Theodore Roosevelt became New York's governor. Robert is proud and also he often jokes with him about it. He really earned it, he became a hero, a leader, he is the best of us all. He still insists we address him only as the "colonel".

1899

JANUARY

Nikola made it, he is in heaven. Astor insisted that the money he is going to invest – being $100,000 – is to be directed firstly to the fluorescent lamps. The whirligig started spinning around Nikola and it spins, and he is all in bliss, lost in the vortex he has been waiting for. But if it were possible in any way, now he is even classier, more certain, now he is the king, the ruler, his feet do not touch the ground. Star dust from the rich and golden hotel fell on his hat, and now is dancing his own part.

Kipling has been traveling around the US for quite some time now, but before we managed to see each other in joyous circumstances, he wrote his daughter Josephine was sick. We must go and see them instantly.

§

I saw the forthcoming death in Josephine's eyes. That poor child, overwhelmed with pneumonia, is hovering between two worlds. Everyone around her is in agony. I changed her head cloths and helped in changing her clothes. Life is leaving her body.

FEBRUARY

Robert is going to publish Mrs. Van Rensselaer's travelogues again in *The Century*. Her writing style is very interesting, with lots of details. I read a description of Le Pouilles Cathedral in

France. I could imagine the gigantic staircase leading to the crypt in that dignified place and Mrs. Van Rensselaer who is carrying a notebook to write down her impressions.

MARCH

"Dear Mrs. Johnson," is how he started his letter. He is interested in her. He said he wants to see Miss Merington at the dinner party I am organizing for my dear Agnes. That is a good enough signal. I will admit, it is not good. He added she was an incredibly intelligent and wise woman. It is true. I agree. But is she the one? Is she going to steal him away from me? From me? He is not mine. I forgot my higher cause once again. I am the audience that is observing how a giant is searching for a companion from afar. All I now see are his intertwined initials on a white piece of paper, but I will manage to distract my view.

§

Dinner was surprisingly quiet. Nick and Margaret were restrained, you could feel the sparks between them, but they did not join completely. Maybe they are only at the beginning? They are both ashamed. It was too hard for me, but I played the perfect hostess role once again.

§

Who is going to learn what things he keeps in his mind? Who is going to foresee his plans? He is not thinking of women at all, any of them. He is completely right to fight for his work and is clinging tightly to opportunities, jumping onto them like a giant wild cat that retracts its claws into soft bodies and rocks, deeply penetrating the victim's body. He is like a secretive spirit of this city, with long metal necks, weaving his transparent web around these tall buildings, as if his face appears in all of its windows, during some of his night visits. It seems as if he is looking at us with his enlarged eye, that spreads and outgrows the very windows, it dissipates and then reappears on another building.

He is planning to go somewhere. But we do not know where to.

§

Martin told us Nick made a deal with *Electric Review*'s editor in chief, now he wants to cooperate with him. That is more Martin could take. Their confrontation has reached its climax. What is Nick up to? Has it got anything to do with the announced departure? I cannot even say the word in my thoughts. Why would I not confront it? His thoughts are long there where he is planning to leave.

The exquisite article in *Electric Review* is followed by Nick's unearthly and seductive photos.

The main impression they give away is their force. A beautified Nick, his veil of light is above his left arm. His look is in love, seductive, knowingly. That is not him. And it is him.

§

I saw an effective evening dress made of purple muslin in a shop. I want it.

Poor Josephine has died. We got a letter from Kipling this morning. Now he has only one child left, John. What should we do, what should we say?

MAY

People of the spring are around me. Nick is packing his bags. He no longer speaks about it, but I know it. He is in love with another place, and he is already there in his thoughts.

The sky is purple. Nick told us some of our thoughts are connected with electrified particles in one layer of the sky, but the majority is not aware of that.

§

I would like to bite myself. I am angry with Robert without a reason, everything bothers me. Everything is upside down. My hair and fingers keep cracking, I am full of electricity, the negative one, the bad-tempered.

Nick is gone, by train to Colorado Springs—the Rocky Mountains' very foothill. He is alone in his carriage, he does not rest his arms on velvet seats, he looks at the stained glass, he is restless. Tre train's chuff is becoming one with the sounds of the night, with the magical speech of Pennsylvania's forests. Then he goes straight to the center. He is wiggling through Indiana, I can see the landscape move away, it seems to me the train is speeding up more and more, the chuff is sharp, the nights are creepy, exciting for him, he is sitting perfectly upright in his compartment, occupied, bought, and guided.

The wizard from another world is passing through my great country's heart.

My America has an open palm, people search for happiness in its hills. My plentiful America combined its wilderness and the world's varieties into an unstoppable whole. In my great America, God showed how much he loves this world by giving it forests and prairies. The more people reach its heart, searching for themselves, for treasure and hope, the stronger it is; the more they use it, the more powerful it gets. Its heart is good.

When will he get back? Will he ever return? His expectations are great, plans already thought out. Who am I to want him to be here? Robert is happy. He knows Nick's departure is for his own and the greater good. I should be happy too. His enthusiasm should inspire me and fill my heart. His work is the most important thing.

§

I have had the strangest fever for a week. It was as if I was pregnant again, as if something wanted to leave my body, as if it was grinning inside of me. So dull and sneaky. Sour and toothy. And then it stopped, vanished. I knew he had arrived in Colorado Springs.

JUNE
I wrote him a letter saying he could probably barely see us, his old friends the Johnsons, from that high position he managed to climb to, and the only thing we would like now is for him to

send us a wireless message. It is a lie. That is the only thing Robert wants.

JULY

Everything is standing still and is sticky at our place. Colorado Springs is famous for its frequent storms. He is standing outside, looking at the silver sky, talking to lightning. His eyes are almost transparent, he channels them and collects them to his fingers. He wrote he can hear it coming way before it even arrives. The strikes come from the mountain range, they split mountain tops and get down to the foothill, into the city. They are luminous hissing snakes, they have a tactics, they draw him near, they want to outplay him in nights that become white from the rain. They devour the clouds and those more daring reach the rooftops. He accepts them and receives them.

§

Everything is seemingly the same, streets will be streets, buildings will be buildings, but then only one tone and one step remind me of him, and his image penetrates me and stretches its branches in my head. The other part of the US is only but another point in which he again draws on the surface of the Earth. What will he find if he cuts the planet's rough skin? What will he hear?

The Earth speaks to him. Deeply under our footsteps its waves are in motion. What did they tell him? I would shout at it so he can hear me when he is walking, and the sparks erupt between the ground and his shoes.

A letter arrived. Centuries have passed since the last one. Robert took it and wants to read it alone. He will pay for this. When it reaches my hands, he can forget about it.

§

The runaway wizard wrote to my husband about the planet's pulsing. The Earth has geomagnetic vibrations. The Earth is pulsing. I believe it.

I believe the signals I receive – in the night, a few moments before I fall asleep, I feel someone's breath, as if it is trying to adjust to something – are not fake. Now I know that puzzle's solution – Nick wants to breathe as the planet is breathing, and I feel it, his breath moved in with me when I was half-asleep.

He is in the midst of the great American silence. The nature speaks there, the time is swaying, it does not run evenly, the sun is spilling from the mountains and flooding the entire city. He is alone there, all elegant. He is taking notes, regularly jotting down his observations. He is like a wolf. He can smell the nature's flicker, the air waves. He does not sleep. He does not breathe. You can feel the silence there and the bang must be primordial. Heavy air collapses onto the ground like an avalanche and the forests are wise, restrained, wild, and dangerous. He is alone there, and happy.

§

I dreamt I put my arm into some dark rift. I was in a forest. A pink fat lightning stroke from the rift. I know I wanted to take something that was not mine, but I could not remember what it was. The lightning burned my palm, and I could clearly see the living, skinless meat. The pain was wretched and salty, I was screaming, but I could not hear myself.

My mouth was open when I woke up. Robert did not feel me getting up.

He knows who he is, and his dreams are not strange. Sometimes I feel so jealous of him. My irregular shaped cracks often connect badly, they mix up, and then I do not know what to do. I have a house, children, a husband, a home, a city, friends, parties. I have everything. And I would like to bite, to break something.

§

I can see how Nick is ordering the lightnings, directing them, calling upon them, stopping them with his hand, and then creating and multiplying them. Colorado Springs is asleep underneath his feet, and he quizzically smiles and thinks of naming the lightnings, he is dancing with them. They merged into a big ruby-colored snake body, listening to their master. He is holding that big explosive body's head with one finger.

Nick is like a spirit over a city on the other side of the US, only no one knows whether he is good or bad, anything is still possible. He lives in his laboratory that looks like a large barn, on top of which there is a ball-shaped antenna. He is the master of the sky above Colorado. He works the most during wolf nights, when little sparks sneak around black forests. I can see them float, tiny lights that move like a dandelion's seeds, floating without a clear goal.

I could not fall asleep again. There is something going on. The light around Nick is neither strong nor red. It is neither crackling nor sparkling. He is dressed in a pale yellow layer of light, pulsing relentlessly and enwrapping him entirely. Even his face is getting lost. The last thing I could see was his smile. In fact, he stays. A smile of pleasure, good and bad at the same time. A smile of a final cognition.

His flickering reaches me. What is going on? I feel a strange smell, as if the sky was burning, when great rains are coming.

AUGUST
Robert sent his poem "Dewey in Manilla" to Nick. Maybe poetry reminds him of us? We are waiting for his response.

He did not come. It would be impossible to see him here in the middle of the night, all fresh, silky, and starched.

§

He immediately replied, only the letters traveled for a long time.

He says the glaciers of Colorado Springs are floating in the sky. He sends us cordial greetings. There is no Kate. There is his ardor for Robert's poetry and noble efforts. He says Robert is going to be reading his lovely poems to the great poets of the past.

There is no Kate.

I can imagine how he is, when he is to be writing to Luka, send a message to the French. Those are the lips that converse with star dust and that are not bothered by rainy air's sharpness that lifts the Earth's first heavy layer. His mind is always in a state of enthusiasm and fascination.

SEPTEMBER

New Yorkers do not realize how boring they are. There are no letters.

Helen asked me what the rarest thing in America is. "Conversation," I said.

I am being too sensitive. But even that is better than being too rough.

My words and my actions do not mean a thing to him. I write "Faithfully yours," at the end of every letter I send him. We write it out of habit. I write the truth.

I never sign as "Mrs. Johnson", I always write "Katherine Johnson". Who is Katherine? In the world of married women of New York, my signature is completely daring and free. In his world, it is the same as any other woman's.

He is married to it, the science.

§

He sent us his photos from Colorado Springs. He is sitting absolutely uninterested and there is a cloud of tiny dangerous lightnings above him, eating, growling at each other, going down, reproducing. They hiss, call him, threaten him. He is sitting, reading, thinking, absolutely carefree. That man is one with the lightnings, they are coming out of his forehead, he creates them. They compress and expand at the same time.

The photos are glorious. One could die from such sights.

§

I saw him this morning. I was not dreaming. I got up at dawn and wandered around our house in a night gown. I could see his voice and hear the light surrounding him through the milky morning mist. The mists are wavy. Bodies are wavy. Everything is wavy.

§

I can see the lightning strikes again, they arrive sneakily, with a sound of the cracking Earth. Contrary to the sound that follows them, their flashes are silent. There are flashes that do not have good intentions, but the scientist tames them, redirects them, and changes their intent. His palms are scorched by blue. I dream and then my dream continues in daylight, I never managed to do it before even though I tried so hard.

OCTOBER

How many times did he manage to provide me with happiness and pain at the same time? He is long gone, and the pain is now dull, but I am also happy because he is happy. For the first time, commitments towards other people are not getting in his way. Today Robert received a letter that read as follows: "I have had wonderful experiences here, among other things, tamed a wild cat and am nothing but a mass of bleeding scratches. But in the scratches, Luka, there lies a mind. MIND."[10]

Luka and Mrs. Filipov, how long gone the time Robert and I got our new names now seems. You are the strongest in combat, Nick, I know it. I wanted to kiss a star for you, I believe it would send you a kiss.

§

He wrote how he created spherical lightnings in his open sky laboratory. He also said he saw a green light.

NOVEMBER
He wrote about incredible things to Robert again. He says in the future he will be able to talk to Archimedes about science. I believe he already does, and he will find a way to bring the past right before our eyes. Will just about anything be possible then? Does that what might have been already exist? If one can talk with the dead, then one could talk to him as well, who is half-asleep. Maybe behind a dark purple curtain standing on the visible reality's tail the two of us could have a completely open conversation. He hears all the words I send him, he reads everything I write here.

§

[10] A letter from Nikola Tesla addressed to Robert Underwood Johnson, in: Marc Seifer, *Wizard*, p. 243.

He wrote to us again with excitement that he found reason in electromagnetic waves.

He is studying the Earth's electricity. It seems that the Earth is a generator of large quantities of electricity, it has a power of its own. We were born from it. When people walk barefooted, the energy directly enters their bodies.

He is setting up light bulbs in the ground and they are lighting up.

You can barely walk barefooted in New York and touch the soil. It is covered by the city.

§

The newspapers are writing that Sarah Bernhardt is playing Hamlet. She is good at anything. Whatever she does is noticeable, the whole planet learns about it. Everybody loves her. Mrs. John Jacob Astor is on the headline of *Bazaar*, as one of the leaders in New York's social life. There is something antique and Venetian in her face. We are surrounded by famous women.

DECEMBER

I may have given up. I would love for Nick to come and visit us for Christmas more than anything in the world. The madness has evolved, it is now toying with me, not hysterically, but peacefully.

Nick wrote he would love to come and visit us. That does not mean he is going to come for sure.

It is two days before Christmas Eve. He did not come. He did not even send us a letter. If I could only see him, for a brief moment, I would regenerate. He is moving the energy inside of me. My hands are cold. It is not because of the winter. I am tired. I would send him a letter today, begging him to come. I am not quite sure whether I want him to know I am desperate or not. Would that even matter to him? Why would he care? Can he read between the lines? Does he even remember? My lines are big and stretched. Silly, childish Kate, he must be thinking that as he discards my letter, probably trembling on a pile of papers; it made him happy for a moment, but he no longer has time, and left his light cocoon undamaged.

1900

JANUARY

He is coming! He wrote he is going to set off from Colorado Springs on the Orthodox Christmas Day.

I used to think that the first impression I would write when 1900 arrives will be only in connection to the number itself. I always counted how many years I would have then, what the arrival of that year would be like, what the new morning would glow like... And now it does not matter! What is important is that Nick is coming. Big old Nick, as Robert called him. I laid onto the frozen, thin ice.

§

Everything is interesting again. I am studying suggestions of opera dresses in a magazine. I cannot wait for him to come again so we can stroll the city together. I am going to buy rose and petunia wreaths and we are going to go and listen to opera at the Met. Night lights on the Brooklyn Bridge look like fattened wiggling stars.

I cannot sleep. Why would I? God sent me insomnia to extend my enjoyment in the sweet goosebumps I get.

§

You could see he feels an impatient void created by his departure, he noticed and put it onto his lips while he was taking his coat off. I stood by Robert and kissed those omniscient lips in my mind. The void was going away, its

201

powers started melting. He liked the fact that I was poised, maybe he expected some kind of emotional outbursts. He knows Kate keeps her whirlwinds in her chest, she learned. I was just watching him watch me. He approached respectfully.

§

I was lying down with my eyes open. A little white ball of light was born in my belly. It spread around my body, growing and growing, all the way to my head, fingers, and feet. The light was quiet, mild, and wise. I have never been calmer in my life. There was no past nor the future in me, not one thought. And then the light perished. I had no questions, no fears, no hope, no plans, no desires. I was bathed.

FEBRUARY

Paderewski is on the front cover of *Bazaar*. I like his photo. It is unclear on purpose, but incredibly strong.

§

Nick is ready and in a state of positive euphoria. He got back even stronger, as if he flew among us from the west. He speaks vigorously. He is not unpleasant, although he expresses impatience. Robert asked him to write for *The Century* again.

He says planet Earth is an electrified body full of electric oscillations. It keeps its voltage with the help of some kind of a mechanism.

I think the Earth is a lot like a woman. She is preparing herself in a boudoir; he arranges her hair, puts on the last drop of her perfume. In her bed, covered with satin sheets, her lover is already waiting for her. All day long she had been thinking what a wonderful night they are going to have, all day long her expectation of longing was cutting down her waist. She is enjoying herself.

MARCH

Nick had another fire. This time not in his lab, on East Houston Street, but very near—one floor below his. Robert received two letters from him, detailing the events. The Jews one floor below his died in the fire. It is a terrible thing. He was scared to death. I was not there, I could not help him. He says he was lucky and very near the end.

My friend and the ending? That cannot happen. I cannot even imagine how we used to live before we met him. That period of my life is too far, as if it had happened to another person. Is that normal?

§

Robert was walking in circles all day long. He only said it was something about Nick and would not say anything else. I do not like it when he withdraws into himself.

I managed to find out what it was all about. Robert wants Nick to write a practical article for *The Century*, both effective and popular, while Nick intends to write a small philosophical work. We are living in a time when newspapers must publish popular texts to be able to sell. But how can he say that to Nick? He is going to describe the world's soul to Robert and Robert wants the reader to step down onto the first golden stair and

203

then not move any further. The scientist is offering the road to the clouds. They are both now having a hard time. They are two friends whose wishes oppose each other. They are both being suffocated by their desires. I cannot help them. I am silent, I do not comment on anything, which is quite an achievement for me.

APRIL

Henry has moved to Richmond with his family. We have a new maid, she is young and beautiful. Her name is Mary, and she is French. She is a careless creature.

§

Robert got back from the editorial office all gloomy. Nick was with him and, based on an ad they saw, they both suspected a certain Marconi is stealing his ideas. I remember that last name, Nick already mentioned him some time ago.

I am going to invite him for an afternoon tea in "Waldorf-Astoria".

§

We are rarely all alone. Those are precious moments. He told me I was beautiful and elegant. He told me he was angry. We were commenting on the ladies passing down Fifth Avenue. I wanted to make him laugh. I did just that.

MAY

I never saw Nick like this. This is the first time I hear about that Ana. When he talks about her, he is fighting himself to gasp.

Her son arrived in New York. It turns out Ana is a girl from his homeland, a girl from his youth. I can see it is an old pain. Nick and a pain for a woman – this is new. That young man is a reminder; she is asking Nick to help him, he wants to become a boxer. Ana sent him here. What does Nick's homeland look like? He told us how he was catching frogs when he was a boy. Forests are so thick over there and winters are very long and cold. A wet winter wind is blowing from the north. Snows are gigantic, you cannot walk on them.

§

Only a crazy person can be jealous of her significant other's family.

But they assume him to be their property, they draw him and call upon him, What was I thinking of? He is not even mine to be jealous of. And that Ana! What could have happened between the two of them? That is a secret not even the stones know. The secret is only his, there is no point in trying to find out. And why would I even care? Of course I care. Why am I interested in ashes? What does that Ana look like? I am jealous of everybody. The past, the present, any twitch of Nick's heart. Whom have I been lying to this whole time? Only to myself. I love him and want the best for him, but I am also terribly jealous at the same time. That period when I was looking for a wife for him was not fake. I was really trying. I was selfless. But I cannot! I cannot fight that shadow woman, that Ana, too. Who is asking me to fight? I am jealous if he ever loved her passionately. I am jealous of everybody! And that tenderness he feels for that young man, it is for Ana's sake. That anger bursts out, now warm and spilled out, it is spreading my skin as an infectious disease. Like pus.

§

Whom am I lying I was not lying?

§

New York is abuzz with electrical streetcars. The number of carriages is getting smaller. Katherine de Forest wrote a book about Paris, her publication is being marketed in *Bazaar*. I read a review as well.

§

Is Stany exaggerating? I love him because he can wipe away borders with his foot, because he does not care, and takes whatever he needs. All of his nights are perverse. On the other hand, he is making his family miserable. If you want to bite life by the bullet and as you please, lewdly, angrily, and voluptuously, your family is going to suffer.

JUNE
I think it is possible, I just need to focus better—more clearly. I am going to send him a message with my thoughts, he is not even going to be aware of it – he is just going to hear the words in his head all of a sudden. I must try until I make it.

§

I was lying alone in the house, I could smell the silence, the sounds of the city were slowly melting away, I put my hands onto my stomach, one on top of the other. I felt my thick, heavy hair on the pillow. My shoulders have been slowly relaxing, while my legs and arms were almost invisible, as if I did not have them.

I imagined Nick's face, that he is beside me, telling me: "I am thinking of you." I imagined him benevolently moving his lips and taking my message. I hope I made it.

§

There is no use, I am a blabber mouth. I could not stand it, I did try to contain myself, but it did not work. I went back and forth, ripping the papers, doing lots of other things, but there was no use, I had to write to him that I sent him a message with my mind. Why am I being so impatient? Why must I blab everything? What am I rushing into, why am I bleeding, why must I know everything immediately, why do I give myself away? I am playing the long game now, Nick does not want to believe there is a possibility to transmit your thoughts.

§

Having fun with my telepathy ideas. He responded he did not feel any telepathic influence and had not thought of me even for a moment. "Dear Mrs. Johnson."

His address was sneering, I know his moustache laughed a bit while he found the time for this brief letter, it lasted for a moment, but the smile was there.

"Dear Mrs. Johnson," he wrote jokingly. I will not give up, he can joke as much as he wants, transferring thoughts is possible!

Mid-July is illuminated by an article published in *The Century*, written by Nikola Tesla himself. His words dispelled all the whispers and calmed them like a big insatiable wave. For a moment, lifeless lull ruled the city. Robert's and Gilder's headlines introduce the reader to the philosophy and the spectacular photos from Colorado easily rule the entire magazine. What power! And what silence!

Out of the eternal different phenomena the nature offers to our senses, there is no other that fills our thoughts with more wonder as such incomprehensible complex movement that we, as a whole, call the human life,"[11] he started. I remembered his assumptions on beings on Mars and claims the human progress is going to be speeding up.

He put it so nicely when he said life is "an incomprehensible complex movement". Who are we? Why are we here? Where are we headed to? What am I headed to? What am I doing? Will I ever realize it?

How will the humanity progress? When will that machine emerge to help me communicate with others while I am on the go? What will come after it? How will people live?

Do you know, my dear king with a light crown on your head?

§

---

[11] Nikola Tesla. (1990). *Problem povećanja ljudske energije (The Problem of Increasing Human Energy)*, Belgrade: Nikola Tesla Museum, p. 11.

They stopped breathing under the grey wave, and then the enemies advanced, those who cannot stand it when someone is glowing so much and is advanced so much more than them. Those who wait for the donor of truth and good intentions armed with envy, who do not know how to receive goodness, reject it, and then throw it away—considering it forced. Nick offers them solutions and his thoughts, but they consider him an arrogant enthusiast. What kind of people are they if they do not know how to receive the goodness delivered to their address?

They keep attacking him from every side, they yell from *Evening Post* and *Popular Science Monthly*. The greater the genius in a human community, the bigger the shouting at him is. They say Nikola Tesla is a lie. Edison... an old rival.

Our Nick does not care about the attacks, they make him stronger. Good for him. I would cry if I were him, I would get angry, I would fall down. I would not be able to stand if someone said I was a liar and I know it is not true.

Robert, however, said a true thing: Nick returned from Colorado without any practical inventions. But, Robert, he is guided by visions, he follows them, he talks to the silver spine of the night, he illuminates the ground. I know you know it and I know you speak with best intentions.

JULY
Robert cannot wait until we set off to Maine. I am silent. I am a good actress. I am happy, packing and planning. If I could just stay!

Ana's son died from severe injuries caused by a boxing match. Desire burned his heart, he overestimated himself, he wanted a difficult opponent. Nick is grieving for him as if he were his son. He is not leaving the hotel, not even sending us letters.

§

I am reading an article in *Bazaar* about women who have employment. I am not one of them. I am also reading about women who play tennis. Paderewski is also portrayed there, as well as the photos of his Geneva Lake house.

AUGUST

The water in front of us in Maine is heavy and greyish. In the morning, blue nuances blend in that opacity, as if in aquarelle. The ocean is dangerous and merciless. It simply does not ask any questions, it only takes away from you. I am sitting on the porch, not moving.

I do not accept defeat, I do not welcome it. I want to fight.

§

I was sitting on the slope, watching the water across the meadow. Then I imagined having his eyes instead of mine. I felt tingling. I was thinking of him every moment, imagining how he sees everything instead of me.

I must write all of this to him! I must call him up!

§

Finally, I received a short reply. He is not coming. How could I even have hopes?

Are the images I am communicating to him even reaching their destination? Are they visible?

§

I cannot determine whether dreams make me happy or sad. At first I saw a huge black grated tower with a golden half-round dome on top. The tower was as slender as a pyramid. There was nothing around it. It drew me near, so I entered it. I climbed up the rough stairs up to the middle of the tower and there was a chamber with lattice door. The shapes behind that lattice heard me and approached me. Those were athletic, good-looking men, their faces appeared one after another, and they were all wearing masks. However, I could see their fiery looks, they wanted me to set them free. I knew Nick was among them, I was looking for his glance underneath all those masks and was confused at first: it seemed all of them were the same. I knew I had the opportunity to set only one man free and the error would be fatal. All of their glances drew me near, some of them were even angry. Soon my confusion disappeared when I recognized him. I chose a glance under a regular green mask that covered a man's whole face. In a sea of trembling, captivating, sinful and seductive, at second glance, his indifferent mask revealed something captivating and seductive from the inside.

When we left the tower and put our feet onto the barren ground, he did not want to take his mask off, and I did not want him to either. It felt good to simultaneously know and not know who he was, to feel him with my body, scent, and thoughts, and not to be able to see him entirely. His mask was like second skin, it was perfectly clinging onto his face, it was thin.

He immediately wanted to take me, I was ripping my clothes, crazy in desire for him to penetrate me as soon as possible. He kissed me only once, I felt the double skin of his face around his lips, and then he plunged his teeth into my chin. His moves were sweet, and then were getting stronger, his whole mouth was sweet, the sweetness was going out from me, moisturizing the soil. I made it easy for him, helped him penetrate even deeper. During his last twitch, when the mask made a pleasure induced jerk, I screamed, and opened my mouth so much that it hurt.

§

If only I could be like Agnes, who does not question herself tirelessly, but does everything she needs to in holy peace. Or like Owen, who solves many great questions when he messes his hair up, goes for a drink and shares with other people. It would be better to be like Robert, who is unsettled by philosophical questions, but he usually deals with them by loving the nature and people, and also by accepting his own duties with dignity and peace. Questions then leave him at peace.

I cannot chase them away. Is it because of boredom? Maybe the reason is really so ordinary. One thing is clear: I could never be like Nick, who has the answers to every question, even those to be asked in one hundred years' time. I cannot even try to compare myself to him.

How strange. My neck still has no wrinkles. I have tiny wrinkles around my eyes that make me look ugly. All the old people must notice changes gradually, like me. When do they accept them, when do they become a constituent part of them, when do they get used to their face? When do they realize they are old?

§

Clouds look like claws.

§

Women act out, write, travel, dance, do something useful. What about me? *Bazaar* published Marguerite Merington's "Poem of a Boat". They all managed somehow in life. I am neither here nor there.

SEPTEMBER

It is not classy to stay in the city during the summer. We were escorted by a thin, dull rain when we were leaving Maine. It stubbornly prickled the water and smeared the horizon. Maine was a golden jail, a paradise island where I feel sad.

The city accumulated the heat and is filled with the summer more than the beach; Italian yellow and warm curtains have spread around the buildings. New S-shaped corsets are trendy, there are no more hourglass figures – the swan figure is popular now.

§

He is now showing a good opinion of himself; he feels good when New Yorkers find him the best dressed gentleman walking along Fifth Avenue. When I was running out of the house, I saw him step out of the carriage. He was wearing polished shoes, he had a glowing glance, he was walking bashfully. I stopped for a moment, refrained myself from screaming, and running into his arms. He brought little suns on his hat and a walking stick, on his shoe tips, an even more quizzical glance, he came so full of himself. He has more sun in his body than us.

When he spoke—we felt he never changes his behavior towards us—he is still the same sincere, trustworthy Nick we all knew, he could never become a snob, forget his old friends, but I can see there were no changes and his letters are flourishing, he is bragging, now he is a part of the high society, the big Michigan Lake whose surface is polished, flat as a mirror, and he is that big dark green lake who knows it all and to which everyone goes to.

§

Morgan announced his daughter Louisa's wedding with Mr. Herbert Sutherly. It is a great opportunity to gather all the people that mean something to him in this city, to measure their strength. Nick got their wedding invitation. He is so happy about it.

§

He came to tell us what the wedding was like. Her wedding dress was, of course, bought in the Woth's; I read it in the papers. President McKinley was at the wedding too.

OCTOBER
Mark Twain is finally back in the States. He was greeted by many people and journalists when he was landing. He is going to come and visit us with his family as soon as they find a suitable house to rent.

§

As always, Twain was writing his thoughts on the napkins, fidgeting in a chair. We talked endlessly. He derogatorily talked about Shelley, he cannot stand him. Livie is as tender as a ballerina. Twain says we are all crazy, and the sooner we realize it, all of our life questions will become clear.

NOVEMBER
They say Morgan's daughter Anne, a girl whose youth is already eaten by seriousness, is stubborn and persistent. When she reaches a certain age, she will wear a permanent stamp of sharpness and seriousness on her face. They say she is giving Morgan such trouble, but he has a soft spot for her, because one loves the most what one cannot attain. Oh, how I know this is true.

I saw her in the city, I got the impression she is calm, that her spirit is older than her body, it seems she has a man's will. And at the same time one could notice a Renaissance veil on her face, a Renaissance layer that is yet to show itself. A Renaissance, antique, strong veil.

She is already around thirty, she is not that young and innocent, but she is still a rich favorite living in a house in Madison Avenue. She is very interested in Nick. He was telling us about the first conversation they have had. He was visiting Morgan for dinner the day after Thanksgiving. He is somehow interested in her! I did not notice any enchantment full of elan, but they have made a special connection.

He showed them colorful light bulbs in which lightnings struck the flying spider web. When he brought them to our house on one occasion, my hair got up from that conundrum of colorful flashes.

He gave Anne his photo from Colorado Springs. He was walking elegantly around the house, waiting for a moment to stay alone with Morgan. Nick is so special these days. It is as if he sensed something big, he could feel he will soon get the big money he has been expecting for a long time. His footsteps are longer. Nick and Anne are enchanted by one another, they converse and exchange magic, while Morgan was waiting to see if he will catch his words, and Nick was in fact preparing to hunt. The atmosphere was cheeky and glittery. He finally got to have a conversation with the magnate.

§

My face is tiny. I refer to my cheeks, lips, and glance, among other things. I would like it to stay that way. I look younger, more relieved, and more childish than Anne Morgan.

In Robert's poem "In November", the orchards are trembling, spurge is dry, loneliness in an overcrowded city, the wind is blowing.

Oh, my wife, whose loyal hand I am holding.

What does it mean, Robert, when you ask me in your poem to back away before the New or the Old? Why did you write that my eyes tightly hold silence? Whom are you writing about? Who are you asking this? Robert, what are you looking for?

§

At first he asks secretly, all wrapped up, maybe he is asking what do I back away from, and then tomorrow he says: "My dear, dearest wife of mine," and then, as always, I lead the dance.

DECEMBER

Sarah Bernhardt too published an article in *Bazaar*. She is writing about male roles played by actresses. She is mannish, pretentious, and full of herself; it is no wonder she is playing male parts too. I do not know why even *Bazaar* loves her so much. She is back to New York, again, and everything is happening again. Everything Sarah does is for her own publicity. She is vain. She cannot stand it if she is not in the newspapers. She is completely opposite to the lovely Duse lady, who is dignified and rarely gives interviews. It is no wonder they are rivals.

§

Henry and Lilian visited us this Christmas. They are, however going back to Richmond, where Henry is going to keep his attorney practice.

1901

JANUARY

I imagine what would happen if I had only one day to spend with Nick and he would take me, and I know he would have never do it again. Is that also too much? One day... I could sell all my power for that one day.

I imagine him opening our door, telling me what I need to hear, and putting his hand on my bare shoulder. Desire is biting my eyes. He recently told me I should visualize my desires. I create images, but they do not seem to bite his ribbed light cloak—not even a nip. No rules or other people's powers apply to him.

§

Katherine de Forest agrees with me. She is wondering, there in Paris, how did New York find Sarah Bernhardt? Because she is already declared boring in Paris. Her voice is old and no longer golden, as they used to say. Though, she says Sarah knows no obstacles and her energy is inexhaustible.

FEBRUARY

This year started sensationally for Nick. He received a promise from Morgan, his projects are finally going to come to life, and he looks like he is at the beginning, as if he had not done anything so far, he is preoccupied. Where does that energy come from: it is as if his life depends on every big idea, he is so consumed by them, and on the other hand, he has limitless willingness and imagination for everyone and is ready to take it till the end, to do anything, to write to everyone, to ask a million times.... Every day he is getting up with more and more elan. He does not even sleep. I am tired.

§

I keep looking at an engraving published in *Men's Magazine*. It portrays Nick swinging, with his hands high above his head, controlling the lightnings with the points of his fingers. He is wearing a tailcoat and a top hat. The ends of his tailcoat are whirling. He looks magnificent in his pants reaching as high as his chest. Any woman could fall in love with him by merely watching that orchestration. I cannot stand it anymore.

§

When we would really set our feet and bodies into his universe, we would perish.

§

There was a premiere of *Tosca* in the Met, and the lead diva was Milka Ternina. She comes from Nick's country, they exchanged letters, and we are going to meet her. Sarah Bernhardt already portrayed Tosca in the theater, and I would not like to watch it.

§

We watched the opera. We are thrilled. Then the company came to our salon, and we were most honored by the presence of the diva herself. That woman is not beautiful neither at first nor second glance, but she is captivating, she managed to conquer her own space and now she is dominating it. Nick spent the whole night with her. There is something in women from the stage that fascinates him. They are powerful and intriguing. I cannot even stand writing about it, not to mention thinking of it. However, I know jealousy is going to give me nightmares until the morning. For days, in fact.

§

Now Nick is in *Bazaar,* too. They mentioned him in an article about interesting people. It reads he has been attracting a lot of attention lately because he published it was possible to communicate with the Martians. He is proud of his Slavic background and his three sisters but the article also mentions Marconi.

§

This year started sensationally for Owen as well! He published his first novel, *Arrows of Almighty.* It was published by Macmillan's Publishing.

MARCH

Owen's image was published in *Bookman* illustrated literary magazine. It looks great, his meaty lips reflect the fullness of his life, there is something Spanish about him, I do not know how, but there is. You can notice his refinement, necessary to contribute to an artist's seriousness, but it cannot, nor would Owen like it to, conceal his sensuality.

§

I want to be intriguing. I want to walk arrogantly, with my nose high up in the sky, with a cloud of mystery around me, with an ermine on my shoulders, and a crown on my head. Oh, dear God, why am I so ordinary?

§

I started reading Owen's *Arrows*. Emilia is a female character opening the novel, looking herself in the mirror and saying she is very pretty. Owen must have seen this scene in me. That rascal! He also wrote she twists her eyebrow when she is in the mirror, just like I do. He writes in a jolly style, the scenes go after one another very quickly, everything is fast – but how else would my jolly boy write?

§

If anyone could bring me to life, then that person would be Nick with his magic. Anything is possible in his East Houston Street lab. It is like in some other planet there. You can feel a terribly beautiful paradise peace there – until the blindingly strong lights from the ceiling come to life, that rub the eyes, flow onto your forehead and pulse beneath it. When I close my eyes and bring that pulsing back to life, I no longer have a feeling I am present here and now, in my body and life. I am floating somewhere, in a pleasant dark location that seems to be above some water surface, because there are reflections in the ceiling, like sporadic reflections of water (i.e. a game of light in it). It is hard to describe it. The reflections are dark purple.

It is warm inside the lab, the air is thick and hot, the colors from the ceiling seem to be melting and dripping, as if you can touch them, they are so thick and bright. It is as if we are in some kind of a timeless warm capsule, displaced, and stunned...

And then, a symbolic gate – thin purple glass married spirals appear in front of us. Those are thin and hissing purple snakes. Nick is glad to enchant us every time, but he keeps standing and is quiet as if everything is normal around him, obsolete, seen, as if the magic itself is a given. The wizard is playing with these shows somehow, and he is thinking about big projects, of the whole world, the humanity, the Earth's energy, the merger of continents, communicating with the universe... What is he thinking about when he appears to be thinking and disinterested at the same time, while we are enjoying the purple beams of light?

Purple beams transform into flashing balls, and I could feel all the bodies and objects around me were vibrating, full of life energy, and my own flashing is being merged with their own, and I am disappearing in happiness.

§

Owen is describing the age of Robert's and my birth. Emily is getting married to Harry, they get a son called John, and he is the protagonist of the novel. He describes John's school days, teachers telling the kids they are dumb, boys' fights. He always loved telling us about his school, teachers, and friends.

Emily is dying and John gives her a promise to keep loving the nature. These sentences are Robert's influence.

Nick signed a contract with Morgan! Finally.

Everything around him is spinning like a tornado, taking Robert and me and everything around us with it. Needless to say we are proud and thrilled; simply, you can feel the happiness, touch it, it is all around us, even in champagne bubbles. You could drink it. He is good, lazy, indifferent, and nonchalant, he is not in a hurry now, he is enjoying himself. The tears are big, heavy, and milky. We were carrying some of Nick's burden in our hearts, and now, when he got the money and his opportunity, the tension bursts out through tears and laughter… I wonder how he might be feeling? How his heart got bigger when we are so relieved and peaceful?

§

Owen's character John is going to Yale. My son described himself best when he said his whole class was enjoying John's recital and his teachers were thrilled by his translations.

§

Everything must be perfect tonight. Robert is hurrying me: Nick told everybody to be in "Waldorf-Astoria" at 7:30 PM sharp. We are going to make it, Robert. We are going to pass by the marble Park Avenue, the street of hope, on time. Robert is always punctual, which means he arrives half an hour earlier wherever he goes. I am not late, but I like to enjoy my preparations. I must be exquisite this evening. Nick is organizing a grand reception because of his contract with Morgan, which is going to be this month's event. The hotel is already shining, Nick checked every single detail in advance.

We are going to make it, Robert. I must check if my hair is perfect once more. I am wearing a new scarlet velvet dress, bought for this occasion, and a sparkly royal lily brooch. My hands are still pretty, even though they are older – they are still elegant, thin, and white.

I hop to my feet, then I sit down, and then look in the mirror, spinning in circles, and then I think... *I am coming, Robert!*

When I get to see Nick, standing upright and proud, when I see him welcoming his guests, enjoying this moment in his life, I will sail next to his guests, hover, enjoy together with him, look for his eyes, enjoy. I am coming, Robert!

§

He was so elegant while he was harmoniously moving his hands to instruct the waiters, supervising every little detail trying to be kind and funny at the same time (and he made it). He was simultaneously keen, demanding, and decent! He tried not to show how intensely he was pleased within.

I was stealing his looks, his words, as much as I could. Anne Morgan and Marguerite Merington were trying to stay close to him – Anne did it a bit intrusively, Marguerite seemingly non-intrusively. Stany was buzzing around, as usual.

§

"What a lovely change in our feelings the sky can make," Owen wrote.

§

He came for a moment. I served him wafers, strawberries, and cream. My heart is full when he is eating from the palm of my hand. I could not eat anything, I have no appetite. When we are alone, I need no food. "I am in a hurry, I am in a hurry," it seemed that was all he was saying, but it did not bother me at all, it is important for me to listen to his tone and dance, in a way. When we are alone, I can forget about the cruel reality.

§

The debt of honor is the most important debt, my son writes.

APRIL

Nick is going to leave us again. His destination is now much closer than Colorado Springs, but his desire to move is now, as it seems, much bigger. He went to Colorado to prove himself and now he wants to show off. He bought a piece of land in Wardenclyffe, Long Island. It is situated in Shoreham, a town in Suffolk County. I already see the dark tower he is building in his eyes. Is it the tower I saw in my dream?

Do I foresee, feel, and dream from reading his eyes? How did I get that ability? It must be from all that time we spend together. Simply, it must be that a tiny part of his perceptive power protruded my being's membrane.

I can clearly see the thin construction in his eyes, burning from impatience. What he was collecting in himself and proving in his experiments, he will now be able to show and tell everybody – when he builds what he is planning in Long Island. In his eyes one can see mature power, willingness to discover the undiscovered, to give knowledge on the palm of his hand, to enjoy it for himself for a moment, and then to be happy because the entire world is enjoying the benefits of his inventions. While seated, seemingly calm, his look is ruling the surroundings, it is mildly rustling and roaring at the same time; while he is seated all polished up, that hardworking and persistent man is working for us all. Are we, who are honored to be at his side, ever going to understand him?

§

"What does it mean to be happy? Not knowing anything?" Owen, this is as if it was written by me!

§

I could not sleep knowing that Nick is going to set off this morning. I was rolling in my bed during the night as if I am the one who is committed, as if I was obliged to get up, open the window, let the fresh dawn inside, and go, having already prepared for the expedition. Nevertheless, he was the one who did it all, I was only looking through the window as the darkness is giving way to the outburst of light. Robert was, needless to say, sleeping tightly beside me. I could hear Nick's abrupt steps, opening his windows, hoping not a single sound would disturb the dawn's feeble silence. Maybe there are a few moments in this city, when the night watch changes, when he is silent. Nick caught it and, all ready, went on with his preparations.

I knew it, I saw it, I heard it, lying under my embroidered cover, as heavy as a shroud. The cover is pretty, but it was holding me back, keeping me trapped in this bed, in this room, in my smelly nightgown, my hair was soft, my pillow tucked in, and I wanted to smell the dawn with him, to get up with him, to travel with him, to set off to adventures together. I was crying without shedding a tear. Ironically, my beauty and softness were holding me aback, as well as the safety of Robert's presence. Now I wonder, *Kate, are you holding your horses?*

I was with Nick early this morning, I wanted to be with him, my look was losing sharpness. He was walking down Fifth Avenue with his head up all the way to the Grand Central station – a being giving himself to his ideas, an exciting man who is truly living his life.

§

Owen's John falls in love with Helen and she leaves him; she only wrote a note she was leaving. Owen says loud and clear John is a victim of hopeless and unrequited passion.

These words burn.

At least John is falling in love again, this time with Marjorie. There are happy endings in his novel.

JUNE

We were sitting at the Player's Club with Nick, he was telling us about Wardenclyffe. It was as if he brought fireflies from the nature and put them on his revers. He melted silver and gold and mixed the two colors together. When he starts working on a project, he does not hear or see anything else. He tried to focus on having a conversation with us and he pretty much made it. However, I got an impression we talked to Nick's sherd or a representative of his, and the real Nikola Tesla was standing in the wind absorbing him.

His shimmering did not emit warmth this time. Gold-silver illusion was poised and cold. He told us he cannot join the party we are preparing in honor of Owen.

§

Our Owen is no longer a boy, he graduated from Yale, and yet, as I was observing him at the party (it seems that we have never had a more joyful company in our home before, his friends, the youth have flooded our home): he was the same, it seemed. Or do the parents never notice when their child grows up? His youth is powerful and lavishing. He brought a girl he likes, they met at Yale. This is the first girl he is serious about, in fact, he tried to be nonchalant even then, but I noticed his heart was moved. She is cute, her name is Mary Galt Stockley and is the daughter of a Cleveland financier. She is tender and short, even shorter than me. He would stop his jolly role of the main entertainer for a moment to look at her. She is a bit shy.

JULY
We visited Wardenclyffe. We were playing. The sand, the sun, water, a moment of relaxation, his smile, I was a child, he was a child (Robert was Robert). Oh, that moment of silence in the sand, the droplets on us, we were finally swimming together, his body…. It is hard to describe happiness, almost impossible. And I would like to describe the trace of the sun on our bodies.

The whole coast could hear me laugh. It is hard to describe the waves of excitement in your belly when you let go and over, when you do not think. Rocking in happiness.

The ocean was. luckily, calmer than usual. It was greyish blue. I was diving, sinking on purpose, and letting it throw me out, or pull me to the cold current. Then I would observe the spillage and rejoining of shining Sun flakes on the surface of water with my eyes half-closed and listen to Nick and Robert chat a bit further away from me. I would get closer to them, they were always on a hotter current. I no longer knew what Nick is to me – a friend, a brother, or a son. But then his look (that for him meant going back to Shoreham, an escape from the beach in his mind, and for me my first encounter with him) would take me a few years back in the past. The ocean and his eyes were the same. And then: hot grey, blue and orange gravel and delicious sandwiches, wet hair and taking a nap in the sun. We ripped him away from worries about the tower, at least for a little while. We were alone at the beach and that is why I could dive in and float on the water. I felt the heat of the sunlight directly on the skin of my arms. I was wearing long lingerie, black stockings, and a woolen knee-high dress. I wanted to feel the sun all over my body, while we were napping in silence.

Moments we spent with Nick have so far been filled with conversation, making plans, teasing, worrying, poetry, music. Moments of warm silence were so precious.

The sky was peach and vanilla colored in the evening.

SEPTEMBER

President McKinley was shot in Buffalo!

Our Colonel, our friend Theodor Roosevelt is now, due to the president's death, the main man in the country. He took his oath.

OCTOBER

Nick is again spasmatic. I do not know why, he wrote us that digging the ground for setting up the foundations is now done; he probably wished the work progresses faster. This is going to be a colossal tower. Maybe purple fire will burn in it.

Nick is always on the move; he is impatient, and he needs to act patient. Long-term state of excitement burns his palate, throat, and lips. He is like a fiery spirit wandering the cliffs and, in the twilight, he trembles above the construction and leave red marks behind him.

§

"My dear Mrs. Johnson." Why does he not write "My dearest"?

"My dear Mrs. Johnson, 13 is my lucky number."[12] I know, Nick.

"[S]o I know you will comply with my wish." He wants me to come! ("[to] come to the Waldorf.") I am flying. "And if you do – when I transmit my wireless messages across seas and

---

[12] Marc Seifer, *Wizard*, p. 288

continents you will get the finest bonnet ever made if it breaks me."[13]

I would fly the seas and the continents, only if he would wait for me alone, mine only on a cliff, somewhere, anywhere. Nick, my love! This is one of the many times you are euphoric again, you have hopes, you create big things, wait for big things, my great being. You reserved "a simple lunch," as you say. "You must all come together," you add, my love. Have I the power to play another game with you, to come with my family to dine with the man I have been longing for, for years. Do I have the strength to be euphoric too, to laugh, and be good? I would think of all that in a moment, and for a second nothing is important anymore, only you, and then I realize who I am, where I am, I must be crazy, I should be happy to have even met you, to be able to watch you eat sometime, while you count the napkins, to be able to be a part of your world... Is it not grand?

I am thankful for having met you, for you being so close to me, for being able to look and listen to you, but it happens, I get lost, I cannot withhold and rebuke myself all the time, so I fall, and stay bent, I cannot move. I have you, but I do not have you; I see you, you write letters to me, I can hear you, but you are not mine; you are polite, gallant, you tell jokes to me, you even give me a cheeky look.

---

[13] Marc Seifer, *Wizard*, p. 288.

I am getting ready for "Waldorf-Astoria", I am poised and calm, I must, I am putting my earrings on, taking my gloves, I have cried all my works, now my heart is washed away. I am going to play a game with myself. With my washed heart.

We had lunch with Hobson.

NOVEMBER

Morgan is a strange behemoth and a very unusual man. He weighs his words, retreats, is not keen on giving, but he takes away your energy. It is as if, alongside all those pieces of art he loves to purchase, he collects other people's energy too. Who knows what he found out and what influence he has on people? He can buy anything, who knows what he has bought so far, perhaps some secrets. I can imagine him sitting isolated in dark, looking for secret messages in his treasure. I got goosebumps.

Our Nick depends on that man, he started a game with him, and such games are exhausting and deceptive, they buy strength and spirit. Morgan is selling and buying, buying and selling. Nick discovers, dreams, creates. A colorful and magical specter is flowing from Nick's fingers; he knows but does not wish to understand the tension, conditioning, questioning, obstacles, greed. Nick, your soul is but fragile, your light is kind although your lightnings are sharp and wicked, your energy is refined, it arrived among us, it seems, from a different pure sky. Nick is in agony, he is finding it hard to deal with Morgan's polite scorning. Morgan sees, but does not want to admit, how grand and revolutionary Nick's ideas and plans are. Morgan is behaving as if Nick's project is one in many, similar or the same as all of his investments. Morgan is cold and reserved, now he is bringing his head out from his diamond armor only when he wants it to, he thinks he can hit sand with his cane as he likes it. Nick is hardworking, impatient, harmless, drunk from passion towards the goodness his thoughts are going to bring; he is blind from the desire to finish the tower as soon as possible. He does not ask to be recognized, but for people to respect the grandiosity of the idea and the future of the tower.

He replied to Robert he will not make it to our Thanksgiving dinner. My agitated, restless being signed it as "Nikola the Distant".

Not a tear in the corner of my eye would help him. Is it frozen? No, it is indecisive. I roam too. I tried sending him positive thoughts, but I know he cannot receive them, he is screaming inside, and that is why he always creates this barb orange membrane around him.

§

A long time ago, Robert wrote fall has a dark view. I am starting to love it more and more.

DECEMBER

The face of the winter is sharp, cruel, and merciless. I stayed in bed a little longer, I did not want to get up; it felt nice to stay in a warm bed, that is to say, tucked in in suspense. That sweet moment of not having to think, the attempt to keep dreaming is when you do not want to move your head, get up, nor dive into your life as if it was the easiest thing in the world (sometimes the temptation is to live your own life, to love it). Robert brought the newspapers and the smell of December. I stayed lying in bed, one with my bed, mute, easy and half-conscious. He was frowning and it got me thinking, but nevertheless I remained silent, waiting for him to say something. It was Nick, his work, plans, the idea of his.

A cruel day in every way, unjust and creepy. Friday the 13th, maybe there is something bad about it.

The newspapers wrote that yesterday, in Newfoundland, Canada, Guglielmo Marconi received a message from England – it was a signal marked by the letter S. Nothing will be the same, there is a revolution going on, the journalists write. Marconi made it all up and managed to do it. Marconi used Nick's ideas! Nick was talking about a cheap and simple device that is to transform signals and sounds, to enlighten the masses. Nikola Tesla was the first man to figure out how it would work.

But he is an unprotected being, he is just moving forward, he does not look back, does not protect himself, does not believe there are thieves, he does not foresee them, he is an inventor who invents and has no time to patent his inventions because there is another giant leap he needs to immediately make. He is a playing child, the one who knows it all and does not know anything, my dear Nick, with eyes as blue as the rocks, with white silken fingers, a giant in a network of mediocre people, how is he going to take the news?

He is angry. We feel bitter, we have no words to say. He did not respond for a long time. How can you even fight the unscrupulous? Do the pure and righteous hearts stand a chance against the audacious and thieves? It seems so hard, because in this world the imitators and halflings make it. Could he have done something earlier? He is rushing and flying without stopping by, he is not protecting himself, he forgives and gives without having first thought of it. I am not like that.

Am I vengeful? Am I selfish? Am I materialistic? In comparison to Nick and his love for the humankind, I am such. I am not like him. Am I in a spasm and do I look out for myself? Do I feel repulsive? Do I not love? I do not love the whole world, I admit it.

Does the fact that I love him help my little soul, even a little?

Where does his strength come from? How can he strive to create for everybody? I admire him. His anger destroys only himself. My anger strives to destroy Marconi, I am disgusted and want to do something, to avenge him, if possible.

§

He is trying to hide he has been hit by the blow, and I feel he is in pain.

Nick is wounded, but on the level of being half-asleep, he is still strong and intact. I was dreaming of his strength last night. I had to write to him about it.

"I woke up, dear Mr. Tesla, in your light. So pure and so white a light that seems to spring out from your lovely soul. It is daytime, but on a holy day.

Last night I was in your light until my eyes closed and I am again in your light this morning."[14]

§

Martin was thrilled when he wrote about Marconi's signal transfer.

§

Owen told us his intentions so abruptly. He is soon to be married with Miss Stockley and they will be off to Paris. My great son with an occasionally wandering look directed towards Robert, but also upright and decisive. We both agreed. Owen always had the right to follow his wishes. Now is the time for him just to tell them to us. He wants to get married as soon as possible, he does not want to plan the ceremony nor a grand event.

§

---

[14] A letter from Katherine Johnson to Nikola Tesla, in: "*Žene koje su volele Teslu* (Women Who Loved Tesla)" (feuilleton). *Večernje novosti*, 15. 6–19. 6. 2006.

The greatest Christmas so far has passed. We have another member, Mrs. Johnson—my new daughter in law, Mary. Nick was with us, I talked to him quietly and joyously.

1902

JANUARY

New York is so grey sometimes, when it decides to be, that your eyes hurt from all that greyness. It can never be so repulsive to make me stop loving it. This gigantic city's toothy atmosphere, this concrete Babylon that rises up into the sky is, ironically, the most open of all. At the same time, New York is a water beast with iron teeth, with a head disproportionately big in comparison to its body, and a light, hypnotic watercraft that accepts all the castaways, a cradle-craft. That is why sometimes its horny greyness with forethought can be easily taken, even though it hurts your sight.

New York listens to all of those who do not want to leave, and lets them go without constricting them. It knows they will sometimes come back.

I am not thinking about whether Owen and Mary are going back. We sent them away. I do not want to think of separation. I want to provide them with freedom.

§

Marconi arrived in New York and Martin made sure to organize a lavishing party for him in "Waldorf-Astoria". My poor Nick had to go through it as well – his thief's radiant face, showing off under the blinking wires in the rhythm of the signal he had sent, a radiant face of the man who spoke he had changed the history of communication, people who applaud and indulge him, his enjoyment of the fame, his big portrait, the murmur, the flattering. That thief!

Nick went away to hide in Wardenclyffe. Thank God he was not around during the announced charade. Martin, however, tried to make the banquet as thundering as it could be.

§

It is so horribly cold. You are looking how your tower is finally growing, while great happiness is mixing your great sorrows. How is your soul?

§

New York Times covered the banquet. There were a lot of leeches in one place. They are now in charge, thinking they defeated Nick. I could not read it. How could Robert have read it?

§

Another skyscraper is going to be built soon, it is going to split the avenues as a ship's prow. It will be triangle-shaped – between Fifth Avenue, Broadway, and East 22nd Street, and the longest will be in 23rd Street. A great wonder!

FEBRUARY

"I want you to write a magnificent letter to me, such as those first letters you had sent, and to tell me you are going to dine with me on Friday, February 28, at 8 PM. The only thing you should remember is you need to dedicate all your attention to me or I will come to your lab and spend the day there."[15]

He solves everything in jokes. I do not want jokes!

APRIL

Last night I dreamt of Nick's tower as if it was a living being. A large pillar was connecting its big, naked, furrowed head with the ground, stopping it from flying freely. Its head was forced to keep calm and be wise, and it accepted with such dignity, observing how its body is slowly being built and filled with pale red metal bars. The thing that was hovering was my blue soul. Now when I call in that dream into reality, I feel certain shivers: I am not afraid, but I am feeling uncomfortable. I dreamt of my soul! It was simply blue, not sparking, but regular blue, like the sky. Can Robert feel what I am feeling – Nick's tower's layers subsiding in my stomach?

I want Nick to do something that would make me happy.

JUNE

Robert wrote to Nick to let him know we will be there.

Back in the day I did not believe middle aged people when they told me their bones are tired. I cannot believe it is happening to me as well, I do not want to believe it. I do not accept getting older as calmly and dignified as Robert does. "Why are you

---

[15] A letter from Katherine Johnson to Nikola Tesla, in: "*Žene koje su volele Teslu* (Women Who Loved Tesla)" feuilleton.

getting angry and frowning, Kate?" It should be the opposite, I should be asking him that, because they say men are more prone to fighting the fact they are growing up and getting older, whereas women mature much earlier, and life itself imposes us to reconcile with maturity. I want to run, jump, enjoy the city, eat ice cream, and drink soda water – and not for my back and bones to hurt! The last thing I need is Robert with his monotonous and calming tone. My poor Robert, trying so hard, he is the wise Mississippi, eternally persistent, wide, having the power not to care and emphasize it. He sat by my side, fondling my hair (it is getting greyer and greyer!) and gasped, hiding his giggles. He often knows how to calm me down. How hard has it been for him all of these years? How did it divert his steady flow?

§

We were with him very briefly. He cordially greeted us and when emptiness started filling with bursts of water, I realized how long it has been since I last saw him. Where is that water with no bubbles coming from? His eyes were watery due to a lack of sleep and being awake. Then I got consumed by fire, when I approached the tower and touched it. It is a mammoth, a proud construction. Robert and Nick got away in their conversation. Nick was explaining in numerous details, his voice became but murmur, all the tones were lower all of a sudden, and I put my cheek and hands onto the construction. It was breathing deeply. At first, my cheeks were burning, and then my whole body from all that breathing. It seemed that the tower was drawing the air and energy from the Earth's depth, that it has roots as an oak tree. The tower is my scientist's gigantic second body, thin and bony, as well as his maker, pulsing in a slow rhythm.

There is a wildfire under that icy water. The tower is going to be a steel-toothed tower with no extra decorations, a black powerful being with a big reddish head, the master of the sea, a beast greater than all sea monsters, a gigantic buckle to connect the continents, the thunderer.

§

I entered the tower. It was the same as in reality – solid from the outside, upright and swollen, with a big semicircular, smooth head, only the inside was covered in black glass. A gigantic phallus shape at the beach, full of shattered glass particles. The inside of the tower smelled a bit sour. I was barefoot. I was not afraid, I only knew I want to enter it no matter the cost. I did not stand long, Nick came along very quickly, he skillfully felt me, I smelled of red hair, as always. My smell was stronger than the mixture of insipid glass and the ever stronger, disgusting sour wave of the air.

"Turn around!" he ordered angrily. I turned around.

He drew me near him and started ripping my dress. It felt good. I licked his ear with my tongue, and it made him even crazier. He joined my hands on my back, bound me, and put his big hand palm on my mouth. I caught a layered look, that contained waiting, liberation, and audacity. I put my lips on his fingers and he accepted it and penetrated my mouth deeper. Then he was rough putting me down on the floor, still

243

jointly holding my hands on my back and penetrated me sharply. His revenge was sweet because I wanted it. He broke all of my multiannual games and provocations. I wanted it as well. A rough punishment is his response, I was teasing him for year, and this was his response. I felt his teeth on my intact back. It felt good. My breasts were squashed. He did not stop, he started moving quickly, my hair was wet and smelled even heavier, I was all wet. There was no pain in his last move, when he penetrated as deep as he could, as if he plunged a hot sword in me. On the contrary, I felt the delight because I finally sucked him into my body, he reached the last pulsating point. "Turn around," he said angrily one more time, letting my hands freely and I turned by bare belly towards him. His lips were blue and motionless. I did not feel them, they did not reach the furrows from his hastening teeth. I was smiling, he reached for my lips with his hand once again, to cover them, but he put his hand on my belly. He could not ignore its pulsating, it called upon his hand. I spanned around him with my legs, and he was ready again, stiff, erect, and swollen. He penetrated me again without a kiss. He too was wet now. I was screaming. My eyes stung, my throat was tickling. Maybe my own screams woke me up. I may have been screaming in reality.

JULY

Swami Vivekananda has died, the man who claimed to see the light before he falls asleep. Nick told us about the deepest conversations they have had, about the discussions on the existence of a universal mind that produces the life force and ether.

AUGUST

Flatiron is a building of gasps. Its nose is high. It looks like a rearing horse.

I imagined different scenes that happen in it, every and each one of them on a different floor. In the first, Robert and Nick are talking about me openly. Robert has known for a long time that I love Nick, and he tells it to him. In the second one, Nick and I are hugging tightly. In the third one, the three of us are sitting at a fancy dinner. In the fourth one, Robert and I are in the same room, but very distant, like strangers, like two people who no longer want to look at each other's eyes ever again.

SEPTEMBER

Agnes enjoyed when she took over Thanksgiving Day's dinner preparations. This is glorious for two reasons. I am happy my daughter is very organized, happy to commit, so mature. She is twenty-two, not in a hurry, patiently waiting for her perfect man, and everything is right for her.

I was staring at wet and moist leaves on the grass in Lexington Avenue. I wanted to spend the eternity by the window. And then Agnes got worried, so she approached, as if she was scolding me for looking through the window and asked me whether Nick is going to join us at Thanksgiving dinner.

Lexington Avenue leaves were wrinkled and soft, as if it joined due to moist, as if someone tailored and sew them together.

Will he come? He was not here last year. Weary, exhausted, shaking from excitement, negotiations, plans. I felt he would not join us. Then I realized I must not let it happen.

It was as if a window was broken. I jumped up and quickly wrote him a letter. He must come, I beg him to come, he must come, it is going to be empty without him. My hand was shaking, and the words were getting bigger and bigger near the end of the letter. Then I made a remark it is urgent on the back of the letter and called for a special messenger.

Agnes was silent, surprised by me jumping up, my fast reaction, acting so crazy all of a sudden. It was getting dark, Robert entered the house silently, and the two of us sat and silently waited for Nick to reply. Robert looked at us not realizing what was going on. Everything stopped again. The time seems to stop on certain occasions. I think Robert was surprised by our still movements and dead silence. We seemed to be in a similar position, whereas in Agnes a paralyzing sorrow was developing, in me everything was dancing.

I could hear the messenger knocking feverishly on Nick's door, because the message *is* urgent. My burning energy, unexpectedly born after a lazy and aimless looking through the window, has spread around the city, on the path of that crazy letter; I did not regret the fact that Nick would be upset and think something has happened to one of us, I did not feel anything besides that urge, an incredible urge to tell him something immediately, that urge that splits your limbs, streaming through the body, and burns.

Agnes claims Nick's response arrived quickly, but I cannot tell; I do not know, I only heard Robert going in and out a few times. It seemed he was whispering about something with

Agnes. She says I talked to them as well, but I do not remember it. He signed "Nikola" only.

"Someday I will tell you just what I think of people who mark their letters 'important' or send dispatches at night"[16] – this is how he started his letter.

I was ashamed. *That crazy Kate,* he must have thought, *impulsive, stubborn, adamant Kate.* I interrupted him, got him upset, and scared him. I often wonder how dare I be so bold as to make such moves, but only when I make them, not before that. When I decide about something, nothing can stop me from doing it. I do not think twice, I just make the decision, and it leads me with an invisible hand. Must everything be as I say? I got Nick upset, he wrote he will spend the holiday in quiet meditation. That crazy Kate, calling him up, demanding, asking, expecting, pleading, begging, not resting. Is that bad? He is feeling bad, he did not comfortable now, although he had said he would travel 1000 miles if need be to afford such a great treat as my dinner.

"Mrs. Filipov's dinner."

Only I am Mrs. Filipov, there is no other, and the one who got him upset while he was collecting strength to combat. With windmills? No, with visible and tangible giants whose money

---

[16] Nikola Tesla's letter to Katharine Johnson, in: Marc Seifer, *Wizard,* p. 304.

he depends on. He is in pain, they are torturing him, my poor one, he is desperate.

"I have a great many hard nuts to crack,"[17] he wrote.

He is sitting alone in his dark room, focusing on and thinking up strategies to raise more money from new investors. How can it be that Nikola Tesla is asking for help, writing letters, explaining for God knows how many times why they need to invest in his projects?

I fear for him. I feel as if, without his will, his energy is shrinking, he is sick of convincing people, he is overflooded and misunderstood.

I told Agnes to send him a reply, I did not dare to write again. I was even afraid of myself. Then Robert stepped in. I was selfishly unaware of his sorrow. His face showed a mixture of being angry at the powerful people who make Nikola Tesla suffer and defeat because he is unable to help him. My dear Robert could not see his sorrow right away because he is calm, because he is trying not to hurt anyone around him with his feelings. He told me, in a subdued tone, to leave Nick alone, not to respond. Dear Robert can control his own pain, I cannot. I made a grimace of helplessness, I bit my tongue so hard, pressed my fists and went to the boudoir.

---

[17] Nikola Tesla's letter to Katharine Johnson, in: Marc Seifer, *Wizard*, p. 304.

I have been sitting for hours. The night is dry. When I am at the boudoir, I seem to transform into real Katherine, it is as if I take everything off. I let go of my own bites, I lick my wounds, and my tissue seems to regenerate. My passion breaks free in it, it flows from me, and I let it go. Nick too is awake in this dry night, still and with his mind away from his body. He is now in a wavy reality, where human forms are silent statues and babbling, wrinkled shadows.

In this dry night, I mix my sorrow and desperation because of Nick's suffering, and red passion.

Robert is reading a book in our bedroom.

"Never mind my absence in body," Nick wrote in his today's letter.

One part of his rocky spirit might return to the city, I call upon it while writing this.

§

The Johnsons' line is alive! Mary gave birth to Robert Underwood Johnson Junior! We are so happy we are crying. Is there greater happiness than this? Our line is continued. Robert is in ecstasy, he cried. He hugged me like never before.

We got a letter that little Robert is independent, as if he is already a big boy. That child is going to be a somebody. Owen wrote he has never seen a baby have such a look.

OCTOBER

I saw a blue velvet dress for a tea party. It resembles turtle shell.

NOVEMBER

Cruel winds blow and clash around the Flatiron Building. The New Yorkers gather in front of it to watch the women's and girls' ankles because the wind blows away their skirts the most in that location.

I exist with my family, we are holding hands. A part of our merry little circle. I am thankful to God, I do not want to take credit for anything, my wise, direct, and cultured children are simply there.

We hold hands and give thanks. Nick did not arrive. I sent him the warmth from the palms of our hands, our separate peace, the sparks from my children's eyes, a touch, a hug, and a kiss. I enjoyed taking the food, completely aware of the beauty of the moment I was in. I know Nick is curing himself in loneliness. I was overjoyed with life during the Thanksgiving dinner. I felt the absence of thoughts. It was as if someone's hand collected tiredness off of my shoulders. It was as if my heart rested.

DECEMBER

Christmas without Nick. I wish him all the happiness in this world. He already has my unchanged love.

1903

JANUARY

Agnes got a letter from Nick. He still cannot find the time for all of us, but there is a lot of love and friendship. He would like to see us, but that is not possible.

"Love and friendship."

He wants to spare us from seeing him tired. His word "love" has a wide definition; it relates to the Johnsons family, but also to me. He almost never uses it.

§

We are travelling to Rome tomorrow. Mark Twain is already in Genoa and maybe we will meet again in Italy.

FEBRUARY

We kissed at the beginning of the Spanish Steps, on the cheek.

When we went down the stairs, Robert noticed the house where Keats used to live (and died in) was in a very bad condition. It is almost certain he is going to do something about it tomorrow.

I am not afraid of dying. I am afraid of the pain. After us, just like after Keats, some rooms and libraries are going to remain, full of light or not, quiet or not, and some other people are going to walk in them.

Robert scheduled a meeting with all the American writers currently residing in Rome. Only men always go to meetings. I organize parties.

He has a very important task here in Rome. Eight years ago, he received a medal from King Umberto, *Cavaliere of Coronad d'Italia,* for his activity in the International Copyright Protection Campaign. Before we even set off, Robert had mentioned it to the Italian Ambassador in Washington, and he detailed in return all the procedures he is going to be honored with – to put our names and address in the Queen Mother's Registry, since King Umberto is no longer alive. Tomorrow we are going to visit the Margherita Palace; we have already appointed the audience, via the Embassy. Count De Gubernatis trained us about the rules of the procedure and now we are ready.

I sent Nick a postcard. It shows two short trees in the front, with an antique temple and an aqueduct in the back.

§

The Queen Mother has an interesting face, maybe the most intriguing face I have ever seen in a woman.

Robert read his poem about Italy and the Queen Mother made a remark, I have no idea what about, because I wandered in fear, and without thinking and with no consideration of the protocol I immediately asked: "Your Highness, is it too long?"

Everybody looked at me laughing, and she was all motherly, whereas Robert, thank God, did not take notice of my big mouth, and continued reading.

Kate, who always has to say what she thinks, the impulsive, irresponsible, unrestrained, wild Kate!

APRIL

We are in Florence. Little Robert Underwood Johnson is the prettiest boy we have ever seen. We call him Robbie. Our dear Owen is a father, and he is all so serious now. He is now the head of his little family. He can always count on us.

He gained a lot of acquaintances and friends. Paris is now his city just like New York is. He says it feels like home, he knows its soul, enjoys the commitments. He has created a life he had always wanted and has moved on. My child-father got up at one point, took me by the hand and started dancing with me following a silent tact, holding me firmly and smiling at me.

My closeness with Robert had brought us to this merry-go-round, to this happy and healthy children and their offspring, all these new roads and new blood. I was happy.

Owen is ready to try it all, but of course, only the wild things that do not put anyone else at risk. His soul is as restless as mine.

§

Twain's gentle Olivia died in Genoa. This is another blow on the man whose mission is to make people smile. And even worse, Gene's health is getting worse. She's been suffering from pneumonia for a long time now.

SEPTEMBER

The beauty that surrounds us seems to be mocking Nikola Tesla. His creditors want their money back, he will not be able to finish his tower, he is in debt, and Morgan is silent.

Nick probably thinks everybody besides him is happy. Maybe he is standing in a pleasant breeze around his tower, feeling the lazy waves bend around him.

§

There was a thunderstorm while I was reading Owen's letter. I went outside to the balcony and looked at the sky, it was so evenly blue that my eyes hurt. I went back into the room, but an even stranger thing happened: a white and yellow stain shone in the middle of my forehead.

I knew those symbols and signals have something to do with Nick. I felt the ground slipping my feet and ran inside. I nestled Owen's letter onto my chest. It helped me calm down, but I still did not know what happened to Nick.

§

Morgan wrote to him that he can no longer invest in Wardenclyffe. Wanting to express his power and impotence, Nikola Tesla sent him an angry response in the form of incredible fireworks he had arranged in the tower, addressed directly to Morgan.

My last week's white and yellow forehead stain is a scar from that fireworks, I am sure of it.

My thwarted creature, now frowning, raises his arms above the black ocean and conquer its blackness with his streams of light. Gigantic light tongues lick the sky, silver and gold flashes mirror the polished, scared ocean. He raises his arms and laughs in panic to his own flashes' ability to calm the eternal black panel. Then he puts his hands on his face because he does not understand why Morgan no longer wants to send him money. Power and impotence. I know that juncture very well.

§

Still no letters from Nick from Wardenclyffe. Robert is upset too. I did not tell him of the strange thunder, he would comment I overreact again.

§

He is back to New York all broken. Martin wrote to us what had happened.

I was right: that thunderstorm was connected to him; only I could hear it from Long Island. The tower was on for a moment, and it made horrendous sounds and blinding light.

His creditors barged in the other day and confiscated some of his equipment. The tower's maker is sitting and not leaving "Waldorf-Astoria".

OCTOBER

Everyone is playing a game. But when great players think of their next move, thwarted one in particular, the whole city trembles. A feeling from the inside tells me Morgan is hiding something.

Robert is organizing a party in "Waldorf-Astoria" tomorrow regarding fundraising for buying Keats' home in Rome. Twain is going to read a poem of Shelley's, there will be music and dancing, and some more reciting, and Shelley's portrait is going to be exhibited, as well as Keats- and Shelley-inspired illustrations.

NOVEMBER

New York is not lazy. It is a beehive, a living thing, a sedate organism, intertwining words. a composition of melodies, a swollen center of the world.

Nick informed us he will be with us for the holiday. Now this is joyous news.

§

If only I had a device that would memorize images! Without it, they are left with my memory and impressions and my ability to turn them into words. It is not enough. It is hard to describe how glad we all were to see progress in his efforts to keep the tower, that he has risen, that he is again our old Nick. He jokingly demanded I cut off a piece of turkey. How could one describe time? I am no writer like Robert, and I convulse over this paper. I do not know how to transmit images from my memory just the way they were. I do not even know how to transmit them as they are for me now. I processed them in my soul, I added some more sparks to them. They became priceless. Nick was telling us how he is after other rich people – John Davison Rockefeller, Edward Henry Harriman, and Thomas Fortune Ryan. The latter one gave him a check to mark the start of their cooperation.

He is enjoying rich people's company. Robert noticed it too and made a joke about it.

I did not have a good feeling about that check and that Ryan. While Nick was talking, in my mind I saw a cold, frozen image. Let us hope my feeling is wrong.

§

Robert saw Mr. President, our Theodore Roosevelt, in the flesh. He was telling him about his Yosemite travels, lead my John Moore.

DECEMBER

Nick has decided to personally go to Morgan again. At least he has an inside helper – Anne Morgan. He tells her a lot of things. He made a great achievement by founding the Colony Club, the first one to be founded for women by women, and their building is going to be built in Madison Avenue. There is a word that Anne is a lesbian and is in a relationship with the girls with whom she had founded the club—that they are living together. Her decisiveness is male and sometimes her face made of stone. If the word is true, than it is so funny I was once jealous of her. Although her relationship with Nick is still special, ever stronger, it seems they both are eccentrics who found a solid interlocutor. Do similar minds like each other more? She is different, exclusive, a woman who initiates things, she is solid, her ideas are unusual. I am an honest and impulsive girl. Anne is smart, but cold. I am perceptive and ardent. He must love me more as a friend! My impulsiveness gives him woes, but I hope I am sweeter too. I am Mrs. Filipov!

At least for a while, I aroused indulgence and burlesque in him.

§

Anne really helped Nick when he entered Morgan's home.

He is avoiding us, just before Christmas. The conversation must have made a wrong turn, not as he hoped for.

§

Nick went to *The Century*'s Editorial Office for a few times, he is interested in a scientific paper Robert is supposed to publish. I only know the author is a European scientist, I did not ask around more than that.

The Wright brothers' aircraft successfully flew a few times in Northern California!

§

How can he be so senseless? He knows I am suffering without his company. What worth is it to greet me over Robert, from the editorial office? Today it seems I cannot stand heat nor cold, electric bangs, my own crashes, and unquenched desires.

What am I? A sparkling little ball drawn by the current from one side to the other? Irregularly, too, to make it even more difficult for me. It takes me to a certain place, it manages to calm me down, and then it shakes me up, so I hit my head against a wall.

I wrote the following to him: "How can you be indifferent to such devotion? If you are unhappy and disappointed and down on you luck, then all the more reason why you should seek the companionship and support of your loyal friends."[18] I also wrote he is most unkind for not coming to see me. If Robert would ever read it....

Nick is really unkind! Nobody will ever love him as I do.

§

I wrote to him today I was at home last Saturday and all of Sunday because I was expecting him to come. He did not come. I also wrote how I am tired of waiting for a reply.

§

Christmas was calm, but it was silence before the storm. We were not wearing masks, but we were all silent about important matters. This is not new to me, I must be quiet. It seemed everybody knew what I was silent about.

---

[18] A letter from Katherine Johnson to Nikola Tesla, in: Marc Seifer, *Wizard*, p. 322.

1904

JANUARY

Nick is losing his senses. Morgan did not approve funds for him just yet, although Nick often writes asking him to, sincerely and openly, but it is no use. He no longer knows what to do. He was never in a similar situation before, not being able to influence anything. His biggest project is at risk. The tower is still silent, instead of speaking up and talking to the other continents with its deep voice.

I still often dream of it; it changes colors, from yellow to dark purple. I am often afraid of the tower in my dreams, I do not know why. What I am also afraid of is that sometimes I see the tower crashing in my dreams, with horrid sounds, that wake me up without fail. I also wake Robert because I scream between sleep and reality.

How long does it last to be between sleep and reality? For how long does that bliss of being half-asleep and half-alive last?

Robert then consoles me, telling me I am afraid without a cause, Morgan cannot let it not be finished or, God forbid, tear down the object he had personally invested in.

Is Nick afraid? Has he ever felt fear?

He has changed, he started writing his letters with a pencil instead of a pen. The smoothness of a pen trail made his tangled handwriting so special. His words written with a pencil are now smudged and crooked. He swallows them; he no longer likes what he has to write down. He is still isolated. I must save him somehow!

§

How has it been for him so that he needed to ask for a loan from us? We have him all our savings at that moment. That poor man, he signed as "Nikola the Poor". He is kind of joking about it, and we all know the situation is grave.

He is changing, losing focus; Robert says it is impossible, but I see it. Women notice people's distractedness better than men. Robert says his mind will not let him get deranged. I believe, when one's soul is being torn, his mind loses a battle. At least I know it well. I have never even thought of it happening to Nick, the master of self-control and a persistent plan implementer, but I feel the sensitive changes in his waves that reach us; it is as if they whisper to me that he is losing control.

§

For a few nights in a row I have been feeling fire between my legs. A light bulb. It is a pulsating hank of yarn whose golden threads, as they unroll, connect with my veins.

FEBRUARY
Agnes' time has come. She has been waiting patiently, like a silkworm in a cocoon, and how the time has come for her to get what she has been meekly building in her thoughts. I admire her. Everything has always been so simple for her. She is dazzled by something and enjoys the tiny details, and in the evening she goes back to her knowledge cocoon.

French H. Holden, a physician she met at the New Year's celebration, is the right man for her. There are no negotiations nor play between them, they found each other, both so meek and stable, without unnecessary illusions. Their encounter was not like Owen and Mary's, full of movement and mutual inspiration; it was thought of in advance, they just approached one another, and the circle closed. Agnes is not euphoric, now she is making even greater plans. I am glad she is finding her happiness. No one has ever even questioned that.

MARCH
Milka Ternina has arrived to the Met as their lead soprano. There has been a lot of word about her last successful performance in Wagner's *Parsifal*. We are going to invite her to pay us a visit.

APRIL
Nick still has not gotten his money from Ryan nor Morgan. The negotiations with Ryan are even over.

MAY
We got another grandchild! Olivia Johnson was born in Paris.

§

Inevitability. Birth and death stand hand in hand, looking one another in the eye. Robert's mother has died.

§

I started looking at Ellen differently; we are sisters, close but distant. Her skin is drier and her eyes aback. It is as if she is made of silent clay. She told me fires have toughened me, that they do not bring ash on my skin nor hair, because they are still aflame, and I am still alive. What breaks me gives me strength at the same time. It is easier to feel broken, it is more visible and obvious. When it erases my thoughts, it seems to be stronger, and it is expected to be strong – I do not stop and feel it in my whole body. I am chasing something else.

SEPTEMBER
Mark Twain moved back to New York again. He lost Gene, too. He is only left with Clara, but he is not bitter, he does not seek pity, he is not lost. He is bearing his sorrows proudly on his back, they are his only, and does not reveal them to others. He rents a Gothic house on Fifth Avenue, three blocks north of Washington Square.

Marguerite Merington published another text in *Bazaar*. It is a report from her boat travels. Who is going to read my writing?

DECEMBER
Agony never ends. In October Morgan wrote to Nick there is nothing he can do regarding Wardenclyffe. Nick kept writing to him. Nikola Tesla is begging. His pleas worry me, I cannot stand what he is facing, but I know this: he is fighting for a cause greater than all human empires, he is fighting for it as if he is to save his own child, and you are not ashamed of anything in such situations. Other people's arrogance cannot touch Nikola Tesla. Morgan is a senseless hydra. Nick described him his torn soul and his rose water tears. He is a man who can observe the entire planet from a distance, as a

gigantic patient ghost, he is simultaneously in our and in other worlds, and who has discovered so many secrets, that man is forced, half-insane and without stopping or quitting, to send pleas to that Madison Avenue hydra, sitting all serious on its throne and pretending to be wise.

All of Nick's letters are barely legible, his words are crammed and tiny; it is as if he considers them worthless, as if he is in a cramp while he is holding the pencil. There is no more elegance and power in his papers, words that would bring about that the tip of his pen was sparkling while he was writing. The grey energy from his current letters has only one power – to take away the will of its readers. I am weak when I read them, I get tired and exhausted. How can I help you?

1905

MARCH

I noticed a car model, Robert says it is called, "Franklin A". I fell in love with it. It is dark green and so elegant, in a nutshell, it is the most modern and most beautiful car of all. I wrote to Nick about it.

§

I told Robert to invite Nick for dinner, hoping his rationality would seem more appealing than my childishness. I do not know whether one should be realistic and keep one's head cool in the hardest of times, which could lead to pessimism, or let everything go and deal with crazy things. I am more inclined to the latter, although mostly when it comes to counselling others. It is easy to be a jester when you are referring to other people's problems. Nobody can help anyone and that is the scariest of all things. No matter how much I understood other people's suffering, I cannot accept them because they are not mine.

§

He responded he is not coming to us for dinner. He is working hard to provide me with that car I like. It is but a joke, a little star fading away in a dark forest full of wolves. My friend is thinking of me; how much strength did it require to look back in his bitterness towards my little wishes?

Owen and Mary cannot wait until we come, which is why they are going to come and visit us.

MAY

Hobson got married, I am so happy for him! His Gizelda is a spitting image of refinement, it is as if she is made of lace. Nick was also a guest at their relatively modest wedding; he tried so hard so no one would notice his half-heartedness. He was standing elegantly erect, as always, silent when needed, talkative when someone asked to be entertained, all sparkly, but wounded, he was hiding behind the compliments he gave.

I would like to help him, but there is nothing I can do. I can only ask Morgan for help on his behalf, and that would have to remain a secret. How am I going to do that?

§

I keep sending him invitations, but all in vain. He firsts lures me with his visits, and then comes draft.

§

"We are soon going to be very far away but you are never going to find that out. You no longer need anybody, being so inhuman. It is so strange we cannot do without you."[19] I wrote

---

[19]   Reworked   from http://www.novosti.rs/dodatni_sadrzaj/clanci.119.html:277840-Zagrlila-svetlost-duse.

this to him because a man without a heart deserves to learn the truth of himself. He is merciless. He is an inhuman creature.

§

I have no mercy! He must be in Long Island, his heart draws him there. It is no one's fault I give my heart to someone who has not asked it from me. That someone loves his strange construction that is now roaring over the ocean.

§

Robert is to be in Washington for days now, I am alone and free. Nikola Tesla is in Long Island. Does he also feel the need for closeness? Or at least for warmth, moaning? How is it that he never feels a need for sharing what lies on his soul with someone? I am free as a bird on this indigo-colored night. I would risk anything if he were here. I would regret nothing. And if I knew there would be no tomorrow for my acting, I would be with him. Why all this torture? One night with him would be enough to leave happy.

§

"I will be here this evening, but suppose you are throughout the week at your country residence in the remote wilds of Long Island. However, if you happen to be rusticated at your favorite resort, the Waldorf, send me a line when you receive this and let me know when I may expect you... But whatever you may be you may always find me the same."[20]

The night is intimate, and I am free. I feel my words and our close "you" I want to send him are down in my throat, as if I am gobbling the ink I used for writing them. What could be worse than the longing that is even stronger when free? This will be a long night.

§

I want his manly skin to scratch against my own. I want him to thrust his beard under my neck, and to put my head onto his naked stomach.

AUGUST

We have been looking at Owen's, Mary's, Robbie's, and Olivia's merry eyes for two months now. We took them to Cony Island to see the Luna Park and Dreamland. Robbie told us, confidentially, that they are not going back to Paris, but to Africa.

Robbie calls me bon mamman. Today after lunch he told me, quietly, that we all hear voices, and we must always talk back to them. If we do not get a response, it is the devil's voice (that is exactly what he said), and if we do, then it is our guardian angel.

---

[20] A letter from Katherine Johnson to Nikola Tesla, in: Margaret Cheney, *Tesla: Man out of Time*, p. 214.

Robbie told me yesterday he is trying to forget about the bad things. Kids know more than we do. Robert gave him our old *Ivanhoe* to browse through.

SEPTEMBER
Now we can breathe a sigh of relief. Agnes got married. We organized a modest wedding, just like she wanted. Nick brought her unrealistic violet roses. Even though she knew what she wanted, and she clearly and precisely made her plans, she was sad for a few days before the wedding, as if she was saying goodbye to our brown house. Robert's favorite and a spitting image of his, our Agnes was as beautiful as a dove on her wedding day. Nick told that to her and he was truly right. That is Nikola Tesla: when you least expect it, he shows he monitors and feels everything in only one word. He is the soul of this world.

§

Nick was kidding me. He told me to resent millionaires less, because he is soon going to become one of them.

NOVEMBER
Mark Twain is also writing for *Bazaar*.

DECEMBER
What is this state called? Uneasiness comes all of a sudden and out of nowhere. Is that sorrow? Dissatisfaction? Resentment? Unfulfillment? Crankiness? Senselessness? Anger? Weakness?

I do not know what to do with myself and I am a little afraid of the night that is soon to come. Nothing can console me.

Why am I cursed? How can I make those few steps to close a circle? There is oh so little I need to be fulfilled and happy. A little or a lot? It depends, from time to time. I have it all, but I have nothing. I no longer fight for life as I used to. This means I no longer hope. Why am I the only one who cannot make those few steps? Why must everything be perfect? It must be!

I asked Nick to come, for my sakes, because he is the only person capable of cheering me up. He is not even thinking of it.

§

Mornings are usually magical. The dawns burst with sense above our heads. When they make their bang, they leave a colorful semicircle of possibilities in the sky, florid sparks we can pick from – only if we are ready.

But what if a gloomy dream flashes before our eyes in the dawn? Then the morning also gets gloomy. I dreamt of Nick thinking above a steaming lake. It was breath coming from monstrous grinning mouth, floating on the lake's surface like ditch water. I know he is moody. I must write to him immediately and ask what the matter is.

§

No response, again. I begged him to come. I cannot stand listening and expecting anymore.

He came, the circle is round again.

He was serious and cheerful. We were confused because of our imminent trip to Italy.

1906

JANUARY

Can one run away from oneself in Florence? I no longer feel a noose around my neck, am I becoming more free? Is the noose even gone or will it pinch me forever? Do people who put a rope around their neck decide to do so because they want to chase away the imaginary noose with it?

§

"Kate, you are in Florence, why are you feeling down now?"

Robert is right.

Meeting Tomaso Salvini again made a few steps faster.

FEBRUARY

I am crushed. I feel so tired. I am losing the ground beneath me.

This is not me, a person lying down in her bed, especially not now when the sky above Florence is so purple. Something is seriously not right.

§

For two weeks I have been an immovable, weak being, bloated and with high fever, within a moment. I am now a little bit fresher, although still weak. Robert had discovered that in the vicinity of a Fiesolo Cathedral, in the old San Girolamo monastery, in one of the Medici family's property, there is a home of the Blue Nun Sisterhood (i.e. "the little Merry's troupe"). He wants to take me to, as he says, a charming shelter on a divine slope, so I can recover there.

§

It is so wonderful here. I feel protected. The sisters are the kindest creatures I have ever met. They were born so gentle, and they wish to help others. Self-sacrifice cannot be attained, people are born with it. You can feel at peace even in the courtyard.

I am not thinking of anything. I walk around the courtyard, I go to the gardens, I observe the fountain and oleander and cypress trees, and I look down the slope – you can see Florence from up here like it is on the palm of your hand.

I open my hand and then close it again and it seems my whole life is on it. There is nothing bleak in that thought, nor any other color or further questions. I talk to the sisters only about the ordinary things during that day, nothing else.

For the first time in my life, thousands of thoughts do not come to my mind, and I feel absolutely happy.

I was photographed by a famous Florentine photographer Scemboque. I like the photo, I am going to keep it as a real souvenir. I look sad and classy.

MAY
Paris is different. It now has a monstrous Eiffel Tower, visible from all around the city.

Mary is pregnant again and soon to deliver. I cannot recognize Robert with our grandchildren, he was never like that when Owen and Agnes were little.

JUNE

He sent us in a short note that he is not capable of seeing anyone.

I must do something, I must go to see Morgan alone!

§

I beat myself, because of him, because of that open blackness that is now like a nightmare (for Nick it is probably a nightmare in reality). I humiliated myself and am not sorry for it. I called for a carriage and went to Wall Street. I was a woman among businessmen, a skirt among suits. They gave me strange looks as I was getting off the carriage, I was afraid, uncomfortable, but spite and love guided me. I entered 23 Wall Street and demanded to personally see Morgan. What audacity, what an adventure, nobody knew, and nobody will ever find out. Who am I in that busy world, in a city within a city, full of people, in a city with no emotions? A trembling woman whom John Pierpont Morgan refused to receive. What else can I do? I did not even manage to ask him, to kneel before that powerful man with a strange, sick, malformed nose. Everybody is scared of him, and no one dares to mention his red swollen nose. Everyone first thinks about what to tell him and then do they speak to him. I did not think through or plan because of Nick, I just abruptly went outside and went there. I am now both blind and deaf and defeated without a struggle, and I no longer know anything.

§

Why are we being so humiliated in this world when the only thing we want to do is good?

§

I met him, he was like a ghost. I wanted to meet him so badly, because I do not even remember when the last time I saw him was. It was as if he was trying to perish from our thoughts, as if he wanted us to forget about him. I was calling out to him, in my thoughts and aloud, in moments of solitude, and my calls returned like an echo. He did not receive them, he did not even want to hear them.

And then I met him at the Flatiron Building, everything was so alive around us, and his face sick and dead. He barely greeted me, did not even want to keep talking, just said hi.

He crushed me. He is finally disappointed, defeated, tears have dried his eyes. He went away. He was so unpleasant for acquainting with me, he did not ask any questions. I do not know how long it has been since I gathered my strength and moved on to Lexington Avenue.

My dear Nick, you cannot fight a hydra with its tentacles thrusted in every part of this city you tried to take a peek of, fighting for Wardenclyffe. It hurts seeing you so crushed and pale, your eyes were so blue, and your face seemed rough.

I dreamt of him crying, and every tear he dropped made his face melt. He was alone and abandoned, did not care about anything, he was as stiff as a wooden puppet.

Morgan's face with no worries is silent in darkness, orchestrating.

§

I feel as if the city itself was attacked and murdered. Stany was its builder-spirit, its initiator and cornerstone, there are so many buildings he had built... And not to mention the horror of silence, nobody even wants to talk about it, everybody is just reading, nobody is feeling a thing...

Robert's rationality managed to calm me down a bit. "You need to understand them," he said, "this is the life Stanford was having in the past years, what he drank, what crisis he was in, whom he slept with, everything was being talked about – a puritan spirit is running away from such things without thinking." Whatever he may be like in the past years, he was the pillar and arch of this city, its triumphal arch. And now everybody is ashamed of him, even Robert is hesitant to comment.

I wonder how Nick is doing, they were going out so much together. Nick knew of all his adulterous secrets and hid them wisely, and there was a lot to rumor about. Now everything is in the open, Stany's eccentricissism, obsessions, an incredible lover's nest with mirrored ceilings and heavy red velvet curtains....

All the details from that fatal night are being revealed: Stany's former lover, Evelyn Naisbitt was there when her jealous husband shot him between the eyes in the "Rue Garden" restaurant in Madison Square Garden. Stany was murdered by a gun decorated in pearls – what morbid elegance and extravagance, all the way to his miserable ending.

When Stany got shot in the face, there was hysteria in the restaurant.

Oh, God, take me first, before everybody, before Robert and Nick!

§

We were among the people who hid on his funeral day – going to the funeral of a man accused of minor rape can ruin one's reputation. We were silent in our house, separated from one another in order not to get into a fight. Nick went to the funeral. Nick's heart is brave.

JULY

It is Nick's fiftieth birthday tomorrow. That creature managed to stay young. What is inside of him? A mechanism that renews his energy? A cup full of light? A grail? Mercy? What is he made of? His hair is not grey, it is still thick and black. It has not changed at all. He is not worn down. He is resilient and ready to sacrifice even more. When I see myself in his eyes, I see my glow is slowly fading away. Robert now looks older, but elderly age has made him look more dignified and sure of himself. Nikola Tesla is not getting older. Only I have changed for the worse, losing my battles. And am none the wiser.

AUGUST

He now signs his letters (when he manages to send them) as "N. Tesla". He is no longer Nick or Nikola for us. Now I am probably Mrs. Johnson, a stranger, an unimportant woman from Lexington Avenue. Indeed, who am I in comparison to the apparent doom of Wardenclyffe, that did not even get to open its fiery purple eyes? Who are Robert and I now, in his madness? Some caring, boring shadows. And when we get such cold and official letters from him, we cannot even read his handwriting, it is so illegible.

I am now one in a thousand Katherine Johnson who is not allowed to enter his thoughts and dreams. He wants to be alone, and he is unwell, he is sick, crucified, he lost his balance.

Whenever I can, I pass by "Waldorf-Astoria". I look at his closed window. I no longer feel sorrow nor resentment. Nothing. He did that. He deleted us, he used magic to replace his smiles and words with holes in our bodies that neither bleed nor eat us up; we are only aware of their disgusting presence, and tired of everything. But hope dies last. And hope is energy.

SEPTEMBER

We got another granddaughter. Owen's daughter is going to be called Katherine, like me.

DECEMBER

Another granddaughter, Leticia! Our dear Agnes gave birth to a lovely daughter and gave her an unexpected name.

1907

MARCH

Mary got married to an antique furniture manufacturer, how nice. I am so sorry she is no longer going to stay with us. All of our servants are the witnesses of our lives, our family.

SEPTEMBER

While he was away for such a long time in Colorado Springs, I thought that is the worst thing of all. But this dry year unfortunately surpassed even that period of separation. Nikola Tesla is here, or is it only a shadow of his? He is here, but wants to stay separated, silent, and dead to us all.

OCTOBER

I know he is not feeling really better, it cannot be, considering the fact that his biggest problem is not solved, but maybe his heart wanted to melt, maybe he wants us to get near him again. Should I get closer? He wrote to me: "I am getting in deeper and deeper trouble." Finally, some words that express closeness, he is finally talking to Katherine, again with honesty and openness. Does that mean he is still fighting or giving up? What is he thinking of, how can he look when he does not let the light reach his eyes, does he even want to get out? Rumors are coming from "Waldorf" that he turned into a starving, thin, and pathetic figure with an indifferent look. The staff just approached his door, and he would sit in the darkness, as a statue, hiding his impatience and waiting for them to get lost. For months. Wake up!

I heard that people in "Waldorf-Astoria" are saying he has found a pigeon in front of the Public Library and is taking care of it in his room. A pigeon, Nick? And what about other people? You are so cruel to the people who love you.

§

Marguerite Merington wrote to me that she invited him to see her play, *Love Finds a Way*. Her efforts are now turning into success. It is so wonderful to be a female writer.

§

Is he waking up? He does not want to see us, but at least he left his room. He wrote to Robert of going to Wardenclyffe by a night train. What could he be doing over there? The night must be moist and heavy, there is no one there. I will not be able to sleep.

§

Robert brought a copy of *New York Times* where Nikola Tesla is giving a public address, after quite some time. An interview, as a matter of fact. He reports he went there alone, to let a strong current through his head, connected to a device.

Is he waking up? Is he dazzled? Is he thinking? Is he forgetting? Is he returning? Leaving? Getting lost?

NOVEMBER

I have not seen him yet, but I feel Nick is turning his new face to the world. No wonder, since he has so many hidden drawers in his body, and now he simply decided to open one of them and take out a character that was lying assembled neatly in it. That character is grinning, he is angry and mad, though even that is better than the deadness.

He started writing for magazines again, so bristly, feisty, and with self-praise. I read some of those articles and a contour of this new character started appearing between the lines, like a thin mask of a strange, smooth, shiny paper. That paper face is perfectly sitting on top of Nick's and now is quizzically giggling. Can anyone else see this or does everyone read the prophetic, scientific words?

DECEMBER
Owen and Mary dared to take a giant leap with little Katherine. We are having more and more people over for Christmas. Katherine, with her tiny face, does not look like me at all, but resembles Mary perfectly. Nick arrived, but he did not stay for long. He was not feeling pleasant in our tumultuous home. He is happy for us, but he is drawn by the ludicrous currents and his face was petrified for a moment.

§

Children grow, years go by, music is getting faster and perkier, tones are shorter, it is getting shorter.

WATER

1908

JANUARY

Robert gave me embroidered, silky stockings. My feet are still refined.

FEBRUARY

Nikola Tesla came again, Twain brought him to us. It was a quiet encounter, but it seemed not a day went by since we last met. It was full of silence, but not the cranky kind of silence, full of subaudition and understanding. Even Twain was not childish. Diamond pride smoldered in Tesla's eyes.. Worries have made his body tired, but not his spirit. He is thinner, more serious, silent, distant, but that is our Nick; our bodies are but shells, although they speak a lot and talk to each other, and God knows how I wanted my body to talk to him, but our voice is important too, and the look, and I shall take them with me forever, I will be able to take them with me to the afterlife. We are but waves, our inner rustlings speak the most and conquer other people by flooding their eyes with water.

§

Twain said the greatest disappointment in his life would be to die in the year of the next Halley's comet return, since it brought him in the last time. He is passionate about astronomy and calls it the greatest foolishness of all.

Wise old Twain, a storyteller, a joker, a gentleman, a child, an unreal and real being at the same time, the one who warns when you need to be silly. Hardy and brave, no matter what. He cannot die.

The comet is to return in 1910.

MARCH
Fifth Avenue is changing. Sidewalks in its southern part are being sacrificed due to an extension. All things new are better than the old, they say.

APRIL
Dead peace is ruling over the cemeteries; everything is dead in them, nothing is there.

MAY
Mary came to pay us a visit. I was alone, arranging books at the library. She has changed, put on some weight; she looks nice and happy.

Robert's poems about Italy are going to be published in the *Italian Skies* anthology, and we are so happy about the new edition of his poems. There is not much else that brings us joy.

SEPTEMBER
I have been thinking about the afterlife for quite some time now. I think there is something when we die, and I think we can communicate with ghosts. There are so many examples of mediums that talked to them in their sessions, everybody is talking about them, there are witnesses too. Robert says spiritualism is a new fraudulent thing of the moment and women are naive; they are the ones who are usually prone to

believing in such things. This is true, there are more female mediums, as I heard. The famous Fox sisters allegedly talked to ghosts.

I am reading Charles Elliot's *Mysteries*.

If we are but statues made of compressed wet sand and if we only melt into the ground after death....

§

Ghosts of the deceased can and want to talk to the living, it is possible. Ghosts have their own world where they advance, like we climb the stairs, open doors, enter. Every person's spark – is never gone. A person who wants to hear its crackling movements when it passes our reality is going to hear it. Maybe the voices are all around us, only we do not know how to pick them, we do not pay attention to them, we do not leave our cocoons. Tesla must be able to hear them. He wants to join the body and the breath, the Earth and the stars, the visible and the dreams. He is shimmering differently than us, he can feel low frequencies and their electromagnetic oscillations. He speaks that way too: he uses known words, but he can join the Earth with the stars. For a long time he does not want to discuss his work, he is getting more mysterious, and that only means he stepped deeper into the truth.

I could feed on his kisses for an eternity, sweet dark honey would run from his lips.

He just laughed when I mentioned spiritualism.

§

"Dear Katherine," he told me today when he was mildly looking at me, "everything can be explained with scientific facts." I insisted on spiritualist theories and reminded him what he once told us about seeing an angel-shaped cloud before his mother's death.

 "But you forget I realized this image was only a reflection of an icon I had already seen at a church."

In London, Nick met William Crooks, who believes in supernatural phenomena and the connection of this world and the other. He admitted he was intrigued and under a strong impression for a short time, but nevertheless he realized science can explain everything.

I am not convinced. Knowledge is one thing, a feeling but another. I believe the dead can send us messages, the only thing we need to do is listen closely. Maybe a message from a dead person is a sentence a passenger in a train sitting by us?

NOVEMBER
It is nice to have a family.

1909

JANUARY
Owen keeps publishing, he is going to become a real writer. His second book is very important to us and to those who are observing. *The Eternal Boy.* Absolutely true.

MARCH

Duse is no longer an actress, and the word is she is in a lesbian relationship with a feminist.

NOVEMBER

Gilder died. Robert was telling me this almost grunting. The main thing about Gilder's character was his fidelity, Robert claims.

§

If there is the worst weather one can imagine in November, then those are these days. One cannot stand only heavy rain, wind, and greyness, but misery is also screaming from around the corner, it is as if it curled away to press one's soul. Or do I feel that way only because Robert is depressive? Or am I not good at getting older? I am tired of blunt pain in my knees, sometimes I wish they are stronger and sharper, instead of being silent and persistent, and it seems I will never be free of them. Robert is as grey as the city, great responsibility awaits him, because of the death of someone dear to him. Helena seems calm, she knew, she could feel it, she has reconciled with it, it seems, but no one can even suppose another person's pain. Dear Lord, please take me before everyone else, before my children, Robert and Nick. I beg this of you.

Do we feel the weight of tiredness and fear on our shoulders or has imminent sorrow possessed us? I know what Robert must be thinking and we both know what lies before him. It is going to be good news, but how can he be happy in such circumstances?

He is still responsible, stable, and organized, but he does not let people see he is overwhelmed. I, however, see everything – he is going to overcome it and quickly fit into what are to be his new roles. Robert is persistent and a great fighter. His job is also an escape and a reality. Robert does not let anything permanently break him. My sorrow is going to last, it creeped in like a parasite into my body. The worst thing is that it is unspecified, I do not know what is wrong with me. It is best for me to close myself in my room and write in solitude. The greyness still hangs around, but at least I am doing something meaningful.

Robert believes you can always go forward. He believes his own strength as well: first, he is going to act as if desperation has not taken over him, and then he will suppress and defeat it with work. I do not know how to act or suppress, greyness gets ahold of me by the neck and suffocates me. Nothing is wrong with me, and yet everything is wrong with me. All is good and nothing is good. Everything is grey, just like that, neither black nor white. I am floating in greyness, not doing a thing. Twain is coming to Gilder's funeral. He will not be able to cheer me up either.

§

Robert Underwood Johnson has been promoted to *The Century*'s Editor in Chief.

DECEMBER
Sometimes it seems to me I have had enough of my life. This is new to me; I have never felt this way before.

I started reading Oliver Lodge's *The Survival of Man*. He believes there is life after death and one can communicate with the dead. His deceased associates have spoken to him through a famous medium, Mrs. Piper from Boston. It must be true, why would he lie? Our soul lives on after death and wants to communicate with the dead.

§

I feel sleepy, I cannot get up so easily in the morning, no matter how long I have slept.

§

If Sir Lodge's writing is true, then we should not fear death. Death is only the beginning of the new learning process the soul enjoys.

Where are such voices? Where do the voices of the dead live? If anyone here, on Earth, can hear them, why cannot we hear them all? If one can hear them, then they must be around? What is closeness? Who are the people dear to us?

Would I want to say something? Would I want to visit or touch someone dear?

§

I speak the truth only to this paper, and nobody is ever going to read it. My truth is my burden. I had to hide the most from the people I would like to talk to. I keep hiding it. Am I living a lie or am I protecting someone?

Fire is now permanently black, as heavy as resin. It no longer burns, now it is a part of me, it is an abyss where dark coal tingles and stirs. Coal is like a cracked scar. Fiery lava, thick fire crawls from the cracks.

§

Another Christmas dinner has passed. Robert was down and he transferred his feelings to us as well. Most of the evening was calmer than the usual.

Kids are now used to leaving us alone with Nick, by the fireplace, when tiny hours come. They are now the age I was when I started waking up. Am I asleep again? The three of us were sitting quietly by the fireplace, the night has already passed, our conversation was not smooth, but no one was feeling unpleasant, we were all slow. Or tired? Or old? Nick was also more silent. Robert had an obvious reason for feeling down – it is rumored he needs to increase the circulation of *The Century*... nonetheless by introducing low-brow content and vocabulary. The time has come now for ordinary magazines to sell better, the daily life and sensational stories, the extreme things that are in collision with elegance and art. What is this time now? Of course ordinary stories nor sensational headlines are fit for *The Century*. Is anyone still interested in wise, scientific, informative, expressive, inspirational stories? What do people buy today?

Those questions are too heavy a burden for my shoulders. Robert carries them on his back, and it is hard for him. I do not know how to help him.

We were sitting down, listening to the silence disturbed only by crackling. The night too was old and silent as death.

I mentioned Sir Oliver Lodge and his ideas to Nick.

"Kate, you are still the greatest child in this house," he said. "Such means of communication do not exist."

1910

JANUARY

Oliver Lodge says he ascertained our soul is an emanation of electricity and in the moment of death the energy of 11 to 25 grams in weight is being liberated. We are energy and energy cannot disappear.

FEBRUARY

John and Ava Astor got divorced. He already has a potential second wife on the horizon, but she is not even eighteen. New York is going to be talking about this divorce for months.

Owen has a new piece, he wrote about his Lawrenceville schooldays, about his childish games and parties. A boy can do anything only if he wants to.

MARCH

Twain is feeling very bad. Clara is with him. She is a strong, successful young woman.

APRIL

I could not dare to write about the comet yesterday because I feared Twain's prophecy was going to come true. And it did, he had a heart attack. He died just like he had foreseen. If this is really true, if the brightest spirit of all has died, then death truly exists.

Nick came to be silent with us. Twain's death took a part of all of our hearts, and the reddest one. We are like birds, but without a voice. We would sing black spiritual songs, any songs, Twain used to love them all, and sing too, but we cannot, we simply cannot sing in such great misery.

§

We were all at the funeral in Elmira. His Olivia's family tomb is situated there. I do not even have to believe one can talk with the spirits of the dead, I know Twain's giggling soul is going to stay with us forever.

MAY

Another tragedy hit us, this time in our family. Owen's Mary has died! My dear child needs me now, and I am not around. I cannot deal with the fact my grandchildren are now practically orphans.

AUGUST

I write to Owen all the time, and he keeps responding to us. He is fine, for a person in his situation, trying to move on, he must. Robert recognized worry on my face, and I on his. Owen is a fighter, we both know it, he will land on his feet, but I cannot neglect what he does not have, it is my child's pain.

SEPTEMBER

In his book *My Inventions*, Nick revealed his ability to visit other worlds. He lies down, settles his breathing and bodily juices, and travels to them with his inner eyes. He sees a blue sky where heavy green sails unfurl, he catches any of them, positions himself, the sail accepts him, gently. He sits down comfortably like a grain of pea in a peapod, it is warm for him, his blinking yellow traces color the greenery and tease him, luring his eyelids. Yet, he remains faithful. He opens himself up only when he arrives to a parallel world. Those are the worlds where different present occur. Or: he can travel to different parts of the planet without moving a finger from his hotel room.

We do not know how to do that, but I am sure – dreams, signs, and voices I see and hear are definitely messages from parallel worlds, they blink like fire tongues on smooth stages of the visible reality. We cannot fully understand it either. But I can imitate Nick. I am going to wear a white dress. The summer is still here. I am still the same Kate who loved wearing white clothes when I was young. I am going to take a white parasol that resembles a mushroom, its inner side is darker. It is green. I am going to step into the trembling city, so white, and merge with it.

§

Maybe we are in a different dimension? In some kind of a bandage of its circle the two of us are a couple, maybe we are one.

DECEMBER

I can finally see my son's and grandchildren's eyes. I do not want them to go back to Paris.

§

I was sitting down with my grandchildren on the floor, playing all day long. It seemed I forgot about everything, as if nothing before today had ever happened. I did not even hear them at one moment, although they tried to pull me by the arms.

<u>1911</u>

JANUARY

Kipling wrote us. He is happy about our arrival to the Old World.

MARCH

Robert gave me a goodbye kiss. He needs me, he wants me no matter what I do. He opens his mouth so wide as never before, with all the power he has, he breathes in both the present and the future. He was kissing me as if he had been waiting for me for years, and I am not his at all, not even now. I am not even Tesla's. I am no one's. What can one do with the love one is offered on the palm of another's hand when one wishes for something else, wishing to leave? He hugs me and my body stepped into the empty uncertainty, hugging my sorrow too. Does he alleviate it? I cannot kiss him, but I return the kiss in order to at least alleviate his thirst. Is that duty, old, encrusted, bordeaux love?

JUNE

London can show its traditionality, sharpness, imperial power and glory.

Europe is different than us, its soul's layers are tightly glued to one another. We have wide and long areas one cannot even perceive; those are vast areas between the cities, good and simple areas, glorious in its simplicity. I am not talking about what is better, only different. Everything is tightly close here, especially now that the processions parade every day, they must prove with their clatter and heavy steps how powerful and ancient they are. Europe is serious, people are smiling less. The United States are practical and frivolous, more daring, one can breathe easily in it, energy keeps moving in it. Europe has knots. It is wise, but those knots sometimes restrain it. It is all entertaining to me – we live to see the coronation of King George V and his wife, Queen Mary. Robert is a bit upset we get up so late, because the hotel is the only imitation of American skyscrapers London can offer, and because it is overcrowded everywhere. He is not a hater, only a bit cranky and nervous. Or is he getting older? He looked at my face and asked me how I managed to keep my eyes so innocent. Eyes do not get old, my dear Robert. Maybe my look is older, my forehead, cheeks, but not my eyes, no. I look at him: his moustache and beard are even longer now, his brows thicker, he looks more serious. A poet, an editor in chief, a serious man, respectable, honest, and devoted. I am no poet, nor editor in chief, nor a serious person. Among the numerous observers of what was going on in the city, that are to end up in Buckingham palace, I am the red Kate, Irish born, grown up in a wide and broad-minded America, an ordinary woman, unusual, found, lost, I observe a parade of people in uniforms, they are all trying to present the British power. How did I get here, what am I doing, what do I love, where will I return to, will I return, who am I – nobody knows.

§

We were standing by Westminster Abbey on coronation day.

King George V's look is stable and intelligent. Queen Mary's lips are tight, and eyes almost shut. The atmosphere in the hotel this evening is very formal as well.

§

Robert is admitted to the Atheneum Club and is going to visit it during our stay in London, as he says, to enjoy the peace and being alone. Gentlemen go to clubs in England to have some privacy, which is quite understandable, having in mind the English mentality. In the US, gentlemen go to clubs for conversation.

§

How small we are in comparison to the sky!

§

When Robert was at the club, he wrote to Kipling, so we are both invited to visit him at his Burwash home.

§

Kipling greeted us with a smile. He showed us his wonderful garden. You can feel the English spirit of orderliness, and the craziness that eradiates from the old tree's cracks. Robert believes there is no finer gentlemen than the Englishmen, because they are generous, loyal, modest, and true friends. He got the impression the Americans are considered to be too unrestrained. We agree there is something weird about the Englishmen's reserved attitude.

§

We visited Oxford, wandering around the city, walking closely to one another, I was calm and peaceful. My dear husband walks down the middle of his life's road, fairly and surely, I love his kindness, I want to kneel before it, to regret, to cry. Tears would cure me. He calms all of my woes, guides me, taking care of me, he does not ask for anything, he only gives. He gives his hand and heart and will continue to do so until death does us part. I am a wrong person, I am the one with a fault.

In Oxford, in my most loyal friend's embrace, the one who understands me best and forgives me everything (I hope he understands and forgives everything), I was happy. We were wandering, carried no travel guide, wandering but we have found each other.

JULY
Owen adores France and we are now going to visit together. My beautiful son, a handsome man, has the refinement of a French gentleman and Tom Sawyer's lucidity. He has joy in his look, despite everything. He is hardworking, but not melancholic, he writes, but does not separate himself from the world, he is devoted, but he can easily respond to an invitation to an adventure. He is writing a novel about a Yale student, his name is Stover. He is very skilled at transmitting his experience and thoughts into text, but to play and distance from himself at the same time. Little Robert is a story of his own! Robert, Olivia, and Katherine are like curious puppies—an inseparable threesome running around without stopping, being tireless

and loud. I love the way they are, they want to know everything and want to get everywhere.

§

Robert is going to visit the French Academy *(L'Académie Française)* and will enter the meeting auditorium. I will not be able to enter it, but an academic, Robert's acquaintance, an old gentleman, got me a card for the upcoming reception at Edmond Rostand's in the Academy. Owen too participated in getting a ticket for me.

§

It was touching and glorious. Traditional ceremony at the Academy reception is always being held in a church across the Academy's paved courtyard. It seemed like rose petals were falling down from the dome.

§

We visited Nemours near Fontainebleau, to meet the Morvelle family. Robert is delighted how they treat old people in France. "It is the atmosphere of French sophistication," he later noticed. I agree.

§

Bretagne is also delicious. We have visited Carnac. I fell onto the ground. Something induced and invited me while we were walking along the vastness where menhirs lie. Robert told me "menhir" is a Celtic word, meaning "standing stone".

§

When I touch my face with my fingers and feel the presence, it is rougher, but I often see what used to be. Did I stop, deep inside, or am I just hoping I did? In fact, it would be stupid if I did, because it is wise to change. But it is also wise not to change.

OCTOBER

Thank God, Nikola Tesla has crossed our doorstep again. He too is dressed in a new shell, there is another layer of wisdom on his face.

NOVEMBER

Owen arrived in New York for the promotion of his book, *Stover on Yale*. Owen McMahon Johnson knows how to attract the attention, he is a dignified wolf and a melancholic bohemian, just like New York, cruel and soft. There were a lot of young people in the reading. They all felt Owen is a new literary star. He does not have the unnecessary modesty like Robert, he knows how to present his strongest points and emit them directly to the audience, flat-out. Robert is a high-quality artist, but he keeps questioning himself whether he could have done something better, thinking how it will get better, and then he overthinks it, he gets skittish, although deep down inside he knows his actual worth. My child of the new age seems to be saying: "I am good and not afraid to prove it right now."

Nick was present and delighted by Owen's appearance. He congratulated to us as well. He passed by people like an invisible count wearing a long cloak. He was talking to Agnes the most.

I should indeed be grateful for everything.

§

I started reading *Stover on Yale*, I enjoy the well-rounded text when everything is done, even though he had already sent us short fragments. He published some parts of the novel in *McClure's Magazine*. He shows special sympathy for his generation and the days of his youth, one can feel he wrote it with a lot of love. He is cheeky, but simple. It is a new American writing style, which I like even though I come from a different era. There is no pathetic writing, nor contemplation that can sometimes have no purpose, as well as hypersensitivity. He writes directly, in a simple manner. As clear as day.

Owen uses Stover to describe a secret society in Yale—Skull and Bones. While reading, I remember the shifty stories our son was telling us about in real life, as well as many of his anecdotes described in his college letters.

§

I made Nick take a large piece of pumpkin pie. I was holding it in my hand until it got warm again. He involuntarily took the little package, but I insisted, as always. Pumpkin pie is a small but very powerful orange sun, summer joy transmitted into fruit of the fall. He left our Thanksgiving dinner earlier than usual. We stayed by the fireplace with Agnes, French, Owen, and all of their children. The little ones ate too much pie and they lay down on the sofa, all curled up, again like fatty puppies.

Stover is making friends with McCarthy and McNabb, but also he has a rival called Hunter. That secret society plays a significant role at Yale. Is my son a part of it? Stover applied for a cruel wrestling match although he is not a wrestler. Is my son, in fact, a fighter, a belligerent person? Stover attains his popularity. Owen was popular in Yale, I know that. Owen likes to prove himself, although he does it in a smarter, more subtle way.

Owen still writes about his growing up and his boyishness. It is not possible to always stay by your child, but you cannot influence everything what happens to it, and it is not necessary to do so either because boys need to learn to fight for themselves, when you prepare them for life. Boys need to face many situations in life.

My boy did and he proved to have enjoyed his boyhood.

§

Owen McMahon Johnson wrote Stover is finally his own master, free to leave and come back, free to set off to an adventure and live different things, free to let go and live the unknown and guarded mystery called life. I am happy Owen understands.

My child is a creator, and I enter big secret tunnels with him, and I get to know his thoughts about life. Life is a battle in the open, Owen says, where courage and a thinking mind need to win. My child writes fast, short, and cleverly—just the same as he is. He is living his life as I wanted to, he inherited my aspirations, and managed to accomplish them. I am happy.

Owen writes as he speaks – he interrupts people, but only the closest, jolly as a child, harmlessly, without an introduction and description. He is describing himself all the time – he is fearlessly crazy, friendly, adventurous, and talkative. He is not scared of criticizing the human spirit, racing for success, and secret societies. He is not a member after all? Do I know it all?

1912

JANUARY

Owen got married again, this time to an American woman, Esther Ellen Cobb. She is an intellectual and a very clever woman. She is cute, but I think she will pose a great challenge for Owen. Nevertheless, he knows what is best for him, and who is to quench his solace. I worry about the children the most.

APRIL

The greatest ship of all time, the Titanic, has sunk. How terrible. The icy ocean has swallowed the cleft ship with a great amount of its passengers.

John Jacob Astor was among the deceased. His second wife Madelyn has survived. I think I never want to travel over the ocean again.

MAY

My sight is getting worse, as if I cannot manage to do anything. On the other hand, everything seems to be settled inside of me.

JUNE

Nick purchased Sarah Bernhardt's biography and added it to his library.

DECEMBER

Robert got an unpleasant letter from *The Century*'s trustees. His restlessness is different, he never raises his voice, and he always tries not to transfer it to other, to us. His restlessness is rare and quiet, it plays only in his mind. His face is even more serious.

The letter states the fact that three years since Gilder's death have passed, and the circulation has decreased despite all of his efforts. Trustees wanted him to suggest some venturesome people who could profile the magazine's special features. So Robert is capable, but insufficiently.

He works in accordance with the old era's rules, but publishing now demands sensationalism, less studies, they want a modern approach. Robert was never good at that. He does not want to compete, he is what he is. He believes quality will win. Maybe quality wins in the long term, but trustees want it to improve right now.

Does he know it? Did he not want to compete because he knew his steadiness is something he cannot abandon? Did he not want to compete because he knew I have nothing to look for in our friend's heart? Was he, perhaps, competing? How can he still love me if he knows it? Oh, that intact attachment of his! Does he know it and is he letting go of me? Does he love me that much? If so, then it is more difficult for him than me! Could he let me go to the better man? He loves me so much that he could give me freedom even though it would break his heart. I could not give him freedom, I am not such a person, I am possessive and vain. I would accept my freedom, but I would not give it to him.

Would I accept it? I would rush to it. Would I feel guilty?

What we keep silent about are most frequently the real truths.
What is Robert silent about? And why is he staying silent?

<u>1913</u>

JANUARY

I would like to feel the touch of an electric hand on my belly, into which my old feelings go, like tree rings. It would be a rough bark to protect them.

FEBRUARY

Owen published a new book, called *The Salamander*. He dedicated it to Esther. It is a novel about the modern New York and a girl named Dore. He starts his story again by looking at a mirror. His writing is now more serious, more detailed – golden stockings, rust-colored shoes, legs, neck, and the modern girls of the today he knows. I cannot be that woman looking herself in the mirror. Everything is different. Dresses, decorations, hair. The girl looks at herself at the beginning of the novel and the phone rings. We live in this new time. This is my time too, I live in it, but it is as if I merely observe it.

Girls want excitement, like Dore herself says: she is bored, she is going to fall in love every day, and she would do anything to change her life. How are they so smarter, more mature, and decisive than my generation? They can and want to go wild and are free to say when in company: "I am crazy, I got crazy." Owen is not making up, he faithfully describes the atmosphere: girls go to parties alone, they fight, run away, drive cars, are happy about conquests, big and small, they wait, nobody gives them advice to marry young, they can completely get lost in their adventures. Dore dines alone in our Lexington Avenue.

She orders a cup of coffee, snacks, milk, and baked potatoes. She goes to the cabaret for fun and is scandalously flirting. Characters use Broadway slang. Everything is so fast. You can read the novel as quick as lightning.

§

Owen's heroine wonders what a woman's life is. She says it is a change of illusions.

In the very end she says she will always keep being a child. Owen, we know whom you heard this from. However, you use the omniscient writer's words to say the rebellious Dore turned into a conventional member of the society.

MARCH

The great Morgan has died. News are like an empty glass on a table – nobody needs them, there is nothing in them. Nick sent a letter of condolences as a cultivated person. He is always dignified.

The coffin with Morgan's body was open in his famous library, covered with flowers. Four carriages followed the hearse down New York streets, the police secured their passage. New York Stock Exchange was closed until noon, to pay him respect.

Nikola Tesla and Robert Underwood Johnson were at the dead office.

Both Astor and Morgan are gone, a whole era ends. Does time have an ending? It does. An era dies and then is immediately replaced by another one.

APRIL

We were radiant again, like we used to be. Billion lights have been lit, again, in front of our eyes; they illuminated our faces, like they used to, the three of us were at the top of the city, Nick got his elan back, everything was like it used to be. He took us to the opening of the Woolworth Building, the tallest in the world. Only New York can have such a thing. Nick is also planning to move there. It was marvelous last night.

It was being built for three years. It was hidden behind dark metal scaffolding. It was opened tonight. It resembles a Gothic cathedral. And the sphynx.

Nick was walking in front of us so quickly, he was in fact running. His energy was fluttery again. He is still like a boy. There is no sluggishness whatsoever in the way he walks. We went to the gigantic lobby breathless. We were standing in semi-darkness, with New York's crème de la crème; quiet murmurs turned into whispers, while everyone was wearing their best suits and dresses. Nick whispered we are waiting for President Wilson to press the button in Washington, and then a miracle is to happen. We were standing in darkness, waiting. I heard Nick breathing with excitement, by breasts were like an armor that wanted to fall off.

Then all the light bulbs and spotlights lit up, so we found ourselves in a sea of billion blinding lights, and imitations of Medieval mosaics were in front of us. We bathed in the light, the gold, and the yellow marble.

311

"Let us fly!" I shouted and drew my men towards the elevator that lead to the building's rooftop. We were first there to land, and we flew! It is 792 feet high!

The building was shimmering! We were at the top of the modern golden cathedral, and beneath us, New York, the center of the world, was breathing. I leaned my two men's cheeks onto my face, we were connected. I surprised Nick. The nocturnal wind was crazy, it undid our hair, we were all so close to the sky. I could reach it! This was a good night. Nick made the cities light up. His cheek was next to my face for a brief moment, on top of the world, in the wind, between darkness and light, between the sky and the earth. We were standing on a golden building's rooftop. I touched the sky.

MAY

Robert resigned as Editor in Chief at *The Century* and is to retire. I cannot believe it is all over. They accepted his resignation.

JUNE

Nick is back to Wardenclyffe, nostalgia and chipped hope took him there. We are close to desperation, too. Robert is depressive, and every worry of his is mine too. Something is up, something that is destroying everything, since for the sake of popularity people seek star dust and mists. It seems a great misfortune is to come.

Robert's sorrow is dignified, although you can read defeat on his face, it brings something more – a financial crisis for us. We were never in such financial problems before. 327 Lexington Avenue house has never seen such imminent silence.

AUGUST
The world around us is crazy. Everybody else seems to have more hope than us. Faces are radiated, they do not feel a disaster coming. They make chiffon dresses, resembling an Oriental style, short, with a feather in your hair, everybody is perfectly ready to have their wishes come true.

NOVEMBER
Our kids are in one place, and everything is easier now.

§

Robert became the American Academy of Arts and Letters Secretary.

DECEMBER
Last night *The Century* organized a dinner party at the Cherry in Robert's honor. Nick, Robert, and I were perhaps tired, exhausted, people whose only hope was taken away from. Are we alike? I do not know it, but we had a condensed glow in our eyes. Agnes and Owen, thank God, had pale yellow glow of the East in their eyes.

1914

JANUARY

Paderewski had arrived. This time with his second wife, Baroness De Rosen. He is going to California to buy an estate. He plans to make wine.

MARCH

George Westinghouse, the man who had first recognized Nikola Tesla's vision, has died today. It was a long time ago. And now death is coming for the rest....

MAY

New fashion is starting to entertain me now, big stripes on baggy short dresses no longer surprise me, everything is so quirky and peculiar, women put strong makeup around their eyes and lips, like masks, they wear turbans, squared blazers, and pointy tight hats. An entertaining circus. Carelessness? Freedom? Probably.

SEPTEMBER

The war started off in Europe. I feel scared for all of our children in Paris.

DECEMBER

Christmas is coming and we are still deep in financial problems. I am really scared we are going to lose the house. When Robert is around, I try to be as brave as he is, but when I am alone, fear surrounds me; I have never felt so cold in our house, I get the chills.

Nick started giving Robert back the money we had lent a long time ago. If we were in a better situation, Robert would have never accepted, but now he is forced to, so he gets all confused when he receives the money. Nick encouraged him to write poetry because he is going to earn lots of money. He told me not to worry and sleep tight. In the meantime, he is going to solve our problems.

§

John Moore has died today. We feel broken. Nick is going to join us in mourning. I cannot even think.

§

Nick is a nocturnal man, it does not make him fall into bedsheets; he does not know the state between sleep and reality because reality is sleep for him, and sleep – a reality.

He loves going to Grand Central Station by night, he hears an angelic, crackling sound that belongs to the stars and the cosmos, it is a silent and seductive music. Turquoise sky and constellations are painted with thin yellow lines on the Grand Central Station's ceiling. There is no time in it. Breathing gets less frequent and more shallow.

In the wake of the dawn, when some of us are still getting up, he goes to his hotel room and hang around with his pigeons. He counts his steps on the way to the park.

I've missed him, for years now.

1915

MARCH

We are reading Owen's new book, *The Spirit of France*. It is not a polished book, on the contrary – Owen is writing about the war and heroism of the French people.

SEPTEMBER

Kipling's son John was killed in war. He was only eighteen.

OCTOBER

The newspapers are writing that Nick's Wardenclyffe tower is a million-dollar folly!

NOVEMBER

I must rewrite these sentences from Nick's letter to Robert because they contain timelessness:

"In a thousand years there will be many thousand recipients of the Nobel Prize. But I have not less than four dozen of my creations identified with my name in technical literature. These are honors real and permanent which are bestowed not by a few who are apt to err, but by the whole world which seldom makes a mistake, and for any of these I would give all the Nobel Prizes which will be distributed during the next thousand years."[21]

---

[21] A letter from Nikola Tesla addressed to Robert Underwood Johnson, in: Marc Seifer, *Wizard*, p. 408.

The same silent rule applies – Robert lets me read Nick's letters, he offers them to me, but he never asks to read those on my name, nor do I offer them to him. It has been like this forever.

DECEMBER

What is going on with all of us? Where is that golden powder? Did this new age bring us fear of poverty and worries? To us and Tesla as well?

The end of the year is nigh, and I do not see any opportunities with regard to finances. Not to mention all the stories that go about the city, how they close me into a miniature shell! I would stand Robert's and my worries more easily only if I knew Nick is safe. News about him angrily close one door after another every other day, right in front of my nose; I feel I am in a nightmare, I keep searching for light in a hall, I go and the blackness closes, with a terrible whizz.

Nick has not been paying his "Waldorf-Astoria" bills. *The World* has published he has not got a cent left, chambermaids say that pigeon excrement stench from his sims is unbearable.

What old ruins' toothless jaws are eating you up? They are swallowing us as well.

<u>1916</u>

MARCH

Nick's portrait was revealed yesterday, done in complete secrecy, even we did not know of it; he always spoke posing is a waste of time. He is portrayed under strong light filtered through real glass. He told us we posed under the same light. He felt unpleasant when people observed the portrait, but he sustained not to fidget or say anything. Besides accepting such a thing, it is so strange whom he had been posing for – he was painted by an eccentric Hungarian princess, Vilma Lwoff-Parlaghy, who lives in the "Plaza Hotel" with innumerous dogs. I saw her, the portrait is exhibited in her studio. I was indifferent towards her although Nick gave her something exclusive, in his own way. I have not tried to learn why and how. At one point you realize you should draw a line in your desire to learn things and step only into the warm waves of feelings. At least I felt that way last night. I was only looking at a dry shape in the portrait, I did not fight anything, I was floating in the blue.

§

We are in big trouble! Robert keeps insisting that we sell the house. It is unthinkable, but very likely to happen. It is not important that I am not capable of imagining it, what is important is that it can happen. Will it even happen? They would take away our lives together with the house! This is our golden city and number 327 Lexington Avenue is our holy place. I have been living here and have lived it all. I am going to defend our house with positive thoughts. Maybe that horrible thing cannot happen after all if you are not able to imagine it?

I will defend our house like those big, lazy snakes that guard houses, that Washington residents used to find under their home foundations. They are the good kind of snakes. My thoughts are going to be our snake's body, full of sunlight. I must find the sun, although rain is falling down my face.

§

Robert wrote Nick a letter. He is quite desperate and direct – he asks him to remember us if he ever gets to receive the Nobel Prize, because we barely get to keep the house. A lot of woes bestow upon Robert. The burden has clung to his forehead. His sorrow hurts me even more. We have been silent for days again.

SEPTEMBER
Gilder's wife, Helen, has died as well. She had just turned seventy, she was what she was all the way to the end – a sophisticated artist, a woman full of business enthusiasm, the one who does not fear anything and welcomes any situation with a calm reflection in the mirror.

1917

FEBRUARY

Owen, my dear child, it seems you are destined to have many turns in your life. First you told us your new book, *Virtuous Wives*, is published, and then you told us you are getting a divorce. You told us that you cannot stand it anymore, that you have found a new love, and that you are going to marry as soon as you get a divorce. You say she is lovely, enchanting, tender, an artistic soul, you say she is refined, that the whole France is in the eyes of Cecile Denise de la Garde.

Cecile Denise's father was a member of the Chamber of Deputies, and her mother a Spaniard. She is volunteering as a nurse for the Red Cross at a Tonon hospital.

APRIL

Today the US Congress officially declared we are entering the Great War, at the request of President Wilson.

My dear Lord, what is happening to this world?

MAY

Nick is convinced. He was almost blackmailed into receiving the Edison Medal he has been awarded with. He invited us and Miss Merington to the ceremony. I had been observing him for a long time. He was seemingly distant, but in his thoughts, as always, he is a fiery blacksmith. His skin is not glowing anymore, and his cheeks have gone inside, which adds depth to his eyes even more. His light is now black and purple and thick. What am I like in his mirror? If he ever caught a glimpse of me. I know he did. He did not want to receive that medal. The atmosphere was disdainful and artificial, with exceptions of course. I swear I did not notice when he had disappeared, even though I was observing him with patience. He was gone, like from a touch of a magic wand! The speeches went on and we were sitting until the very end, applauding.

When we wanted to leave, it seemed the city was absolutely empty, although I do not remember there has ever been more people in the streets. There are more and more residents in New York day by day. People, cars, everything was abuzz around us, the blocks spoke differently, more modern and relaxed than in our early times. Everything was faster, shorter, more exciting, louder. I wanted to stand still and not to go back home, thinking Nick would pass by in his wandering. He did not wander. They found him behind the Bryant Park library, feeding the pigeons.

§

He became a pillar, a monument in a park, onto which the pigeons land, and I am still a restless being, still fighting herself only, wondering and not finding any answers. Questions are deep inside of me, and I smile for everybody on the outside. This creates an imbalance in my body, so I cannot stand still like him. Will my older age fight the power of my volcanoes?

JULY
This is what old age is – you cannot even write anymore. I have been trying and when I look at my handwriting – it is not like

it used to be. This is because I have been lying down in my bed for two days now, not being able to lift my head alone. I hold my notebook under my throat...

What kind of a flu is this in the midst of the summer?

§

Only I feel weak, everybody else is vivacious. Only I lack strength.

Have I ever been brave? Have I ever done, say something important? Speaking is courageous.

§

Robert says another two days have passed. Two suns and moons have passed between these few winding lines?

§

I am really c

§

Robert says another two days have passed. Or is the same scene going over and over again?

§

Maybe I am brave. I was feeling a little better this morning, but last night... my knees tottered, I was dying. I no longer feel cold this morning, and for the first time my bedsheets are not wet.

§

Yesterday afternoon Robert told me Nick is going to come over to say goodbye to us because he is moving to Chicago. At first I thought I did not hear it well. Nothing seems real these days. The only real thing was the fire that was pressing my body and it was as if I was melting into the scarlet hotspots, I felt I was being swallowed by them.

§

Yesterday afternoon I decided I must fight the fire. Nick is leaving and who knows when we are to see him again. Robert informed he is going to tell him I am sick and cannot go downstairs. That was true, I felt I could not get down. But I had to be brave. I had to turn "I cannot" into "I can" — no matter the cost. I thought if I did not see him, I would really die. This morning too I have been asking myself whether anything makes sense anymore, but it is easier to know you show a little courage, while you were resisting and getting up. It is easier to go that way.

§

I heard voices and my knight entering our home. I was lying still. He came to say goodbye, nothing will ever be the same, my thoughts have been in a whirlpool inside of me, waking up and lifting my sluggish body, piece by piece. I do not know even how I got dressed, I only know I was dry, and my skin hurt. It almost cracked, and a wet spot was left on my bed. Fire and water inside of me, at the same time, draught and flood. I felt bitterness in my throat and the pain made my head explode. I wore my prettiest bordeaux dress. I went slowly down the stairs, as a petrified child. I was never that slow in my life, I held the railing, Nick's voice was giving me strength and pulling me. My trace was no longer wet on the staircase, it became brittle. I entered the light.

§

I entered the light of the past, the days of our youth, when Nikola Tesla only started frequenting with us, the salon was the same again, we were the same, and I was laughing. He accepted my hand on his elongated arm. Or did he just hold me? Did I ask it from him? Has he touched me? I do not know, I do not know, I think he did! The touch of my superior being probably invigorated me, and I am feeling better this morning! Did he give it to me? His hands were in white gloves, he was wearing a straw hat, and there was escape in his eyes.

§

His flowers are next to my bed. He is gone. Does anything make sense anymore? I am as dry as this morning. I have had enough of this life.

AUGUST
Nikola Tesla's Wardenclyffe Tower was torn down. The US Army used explosive to tear it down. Masked under worry and fear of having it overtaken by the enemy, Nick's true enemies' grinning faces have given the last blow on the pride that stood above their own powers. I would say envy has won. Some secret forces, some secret agreements. I do not know it, I just feel it.

These are the times when I keep dying, in waves. Like I have been hit by them when I was young, they proudly stop and weaken me now. I turned down for a few times now. It is terrible. The good thing is that Nick did not see his tower's doom.

§

I purposefully wanted to keep being half-asleep because I am neither asleep nor awake, and both states are cruel. Being half-asleep is safe, I do not know where I am. However, I was still blown by the image of Nikola Tesla's helpless notes taken by the wind around the crippled tower.

§

How can he withhold himself, how can he not wish to seek revenge? He could cause a devastating earthquake, like the one that hit New York a long time ago. Where does he find the strength to prevent revenge?

SEPTEMBER

I have good news: Cecile gave us our fourth grandson. His name is Owen Denise. Somewhere far away my child lives his own exciting life, laughing, and crying, holding his new baby in his arms.

§

Robbie wrote us a letter. He calls Cecile *mammette*. He says she laughs even when she speaks.

DECEMBER

I got a letter from Owen containing a lot of leftovers, its edges
are torn with pain, I know him, I know how he writes, I know
when he is trying to hide when something is not right.

1918

JANUARY

Everything is tight.

MAY

Cecile died early in the morning. My dear Owen, my dear children!

APRIL

I love our friends' faces, for a moment they take away nervousness that makes me bite everything around me. Paderewski is in New York. He is still young and messy, years do not have power over him.

DECEMBER

I went through deathly agony, one of the first to get the great fever that is now called the Spanish flu. I think my body was all wet and I lost my consciousness, I had been recovering during the whole of fall and now I am back on my feet. My ears bled and I had had red spots all over my body. My body was so close to the border, but there was indifferent silence on the other side, dear Robert was with me all the time, which I now know because he had told me so, and I felt and saw only the reflections of his worry and strength. He seemed to be but a ghost, that I am a ghost, I do not even know what I was like during the past few months. I only know I shall never be the same, I am different now, my blood is weaker.

§

He finally came back from Chicago. I was waiting for him in a calmer way now. It was not just about my illness, but I did not even get used to it. I sort of mutely accept the fact that he is not around. A spasm in my belly remained, lust is still foaming, but I was happy for even thinking he is alive and healthy somewhere, that he exists. It is enough just to know Nikola Tesla exists, even if he is far away from me. I have memories.

He gave me wings when he arrived, and of course I prefer him being closer, but I have no right to try to control anything, to call and lure him, nor to flirtatiously demand or send letters every day. I calmed down.

His eyes were the same as they used to be. Our hair is now greyer and our faces rougher, but we are still that magnificent circle sitting around our Christmas dinner table. Our friendship is now our halo. Peace is happiness.

We could not open all doors in Nick's thoughts. He is different. He is hiding something. Solitude has changed him. He is not unpleasant, only quieter. It is not that he does not want to speak, I can see he cannot, he shut the door himself, and now, even if he wanted to, he would not be able to open them.

1919

JANUARY

On the cover of the new *Century* magazine is a lonely soldier of the Great War looking up at a star in the sky from a grim, waste land. Almost the entire issue has been dedicated to the Great War.

§

Paderewski became the Minister of the Exterior and the Prime Minister of Poland.

FEBRUARY

Robert keeps changing little notebooks in which he jots down first impressions and thoughts that cannot wait. The covers of the newest one are watery green.

MARCH

Owen remarried, this time with someone of my namesake, Catherine Sayre Burton.

APRIL

I have one word for this new era – nonchalance.

Robert is in his thoughts. Henry sent him a letter reminding him of their father's death 50 years ago. Death is terrible! I do not want to think it is the end.

MAY

Poor Robert. He is right to say the city and everything that surrounds us is in full force, all the juices are woken, spring tiredness has passed and now you can enjoy the warm ripeness of the streets. He puts everything so nicely. Unfortunately, he described himself nicely as well – an elderly poet in bed. He is sick, I have been taking care of him the entire day. I was his shadow. Just like he was mine.

I have always been a shadow. That is me. He managed to write a letter to Nick, to remind him of an old $2000 debt. He barely managed to do it, but not so much because of the exhaustion, but because he felt uneasy for doing it. We have always been helping Nick, without planning and wishing to have the money back. We now do not even have money to pay our taxes. No wonder Robert was sick. He got sick from worrying and humiliation.

He immediately sent us $500.

The night is completely black and calm. I know he is sitting by the window like me, tired and exhausted like I am. However, purple lightnings are in his thoughts. Like a strong love of red and purple, from a bang of light, a lightning spread around the roofs. It is followed by a thunder of inevitability, after which there is no rain. His call is blurry.

§

Nick sent us another $500, because Robert begged him for money again. I cannot stand it anymore!

NOVEMBER

I am weak, exhausted and have no will.

Yesterday Robert found me lying on the salon's floor. Thank God he was there on time, because I had lost consciousness. I do not remember anything, I just felt sick, started sweating and everything turned black all of a sudden.

§

Sometimes Robert and I read Nick's letters as if they are fairy tales – we need to use our imagination. Nick's words often demand a lot of imagination. I know he speaks of the future, it is already present and real in his thoughts (he does not ignore memories nor visions, both dimensions are equal in his world, and vibrate passionately). This time he wrote to Robert how we could see images from the world at our home, on some kind of a device. We had to imagine nine machines with wings at the height of hundreds of miles, taking negatives and unwrapping image rolls when they land, that we see on a camera. He called this process the television. I will not be able to sleep. Or I will dream of those flying machines. Or of the shrieks of dangerous fairytale dragons. I do not know; Nick's visions sometimes frighten me. Having devices in the atmosphere, above our heads, taking photos of people? Transmitting such images? Devices with wings? I do not know.

§

Last night I lost consciousness again, I fell off of the bed in our bedroom. Robert put pledges on my forehead, counted my heartbeats, and did everything in his power to make me feel

331

better, but I cannot help the fear. The blackness I am falling in is terrible, voiceless, senseless. I do not want to believe in it!

DECEMBER

Today we have only $19.41 left on our bank account. If a miracle does not save us soon, we are doomed. Robert is going to have to beg Nick for money again.

§

Traces of winter mark our back, and traces of spring our face. In any case, we are getting older. You can see how old you are best in the faces of your peers.

§

I have never seen Robert prouder than right now. He marched into the room. If you did not know him, you could think he was proud always, but no, this was just Robert being happy. He rarely expresses euphoric feelings and is clumsy when he is flooded with emotions. To cover his clumsiness, he becomes official. I have never seen him like today before.

He is always indulgent and weak towards me, always polite, always a true gentleman, always respectful and giving nice words.

"I am going to become the US Ambassador in Italy!"

He stood on his knees by my bed and kissed my hand.

"How are you going to go there without your wife? That is impossible," I said it with seriousness. "I cannot travel."

"I know you are going to feel better in time," he solemnly promised and foretold, and I believed his words.

I shared his pride and cried from happiness. I do not feel like traveling, I would not like to move, but I must follow my husband, the Ambassador. I am going to feel better!

§

Tesla, who is now officially declared to be a weirdo – in New York salons and newspapers – came to spend Christmas with us. He is weirder. He is petty, asocial, keeps running away. He does not eat meat nor solid food, he spends time only with pigeons, summons them by night, all the pigeons of New York fly to him, he does not talk, he does not make gestures, he is acting like an apparition, communicating with hem in purple tones. He no longer needs luxury, he changed everything. He crushed everything. And he does not wish to get back to us. He is not unpleasant towards us but is getting more distant. Besides, we might be off to Europe soon. He is going to remain completely alone. I do not want to travel, but I must, because of love and duty. Those are the two most important things in life. Nick promised I will get better. He advised me to walk more, to eat better food (I must) and read only light and comic literature.

People do not change easily, but Nick can do it, he had decided that a long time ago and now he just let himself go.

1920

JANUARY

We got another granddaughter; Owen's Catherine gave birth to Patricia. Happiness is being rebuilt, it always wins misfortune.

§

I took a walk. This morning Robert got an official letter from President Wilson appointing him as the Ambassador. I was not there when it had arrived, but it seems Robert has not moved from that same pose ever since he read it and me getting inside. He is sitting at his writing desk, happily in thoughts and proud, but perhaps a little worried how he is going to fulfill his duty. Regardless, he is perfectly decisive and unremitting, ready to answer the call. I have been collecting all the pieces of my stained glass and looking for a source of light to revive the colors of the glass. This morning's frost helped me do it. It froze my cheeks and blood rushed to my heart. However, this all still seems to be but a dream, even a joke – Robert holding an official presidential letter in his hand. He fits into the picture. I hope I will too.

I run away from the blackness.

§

"Dear Mr. Tesla,

Would you give me the pleasure of seeing you among my guests next Saturday evening? Some old friends of your are going to be here as well... [...]

Oh, just leave millionaires aside, those with bashful titles from Waldorf and Fifth Avenue, and come visit the far Lexington Avenue one more time, to see simple people who are different only according to great weakness. I really think it is so refreshing, like when you go out from a greenhouse into a fresh, open garden full of morning dew. I have heard about you so much. I am sure you do not even know it yourself and I am dying to tell it to you. But, of course, you do not even care to hear it. Do you know I will be abroad early in spring. And who knows, maybe these friendly scenes will not even know of me anymore? So, if you have not forgotten about me completely or if you did not forget you loved me – I forgot to forget – you better come.

Oh, how fast the days fly. So few days I have left. [...] Be human, be kind and come."[22]

§

"Have a nice trip, dear Katherine," he said blurrily looking at me. I did not manage to tell him anything in private. I did not dare, in fact – as usual. He did not let me, in fact – as usual. The wine we served was dark purple, I have never tasted better

---

[22] A letter from Katherine Johnson to Nikola Tesla, retrieved from: www.tesla.big-forum.net.

wine in my life, you could drink it like water, without a voice. Everybody toasted his excellency, Robert. Nick seemed to have always known such a journey would happen and everything would be alright. He sensed Robert's happiness. He knows everything, just does not give it all away. He did not touch the wine. He is testing himself, testing his will.

Everything is different.

FEBRUARY

We are leaving the house today. I am writing and Robert is going about the house. Everything has been neatly packed for a long time now, he never seems to forget about anything, and now he does not know what to do with himself so is making up little tasks. Maybe he unpacked smaller suitcases to inspect. I can hear him walking about. I can hear his elderly walk, however persistent and assured. How can I take my whole house with me? How can I move all things dear to me? I have been sitting for a few hours before we depart, seemingly calm, writing. Robert is obviously bothered by that. I do not wish to leave these few hours before our departure. I do not want to move. The weather is bright and cold. The sun is deceptive.

Our home is silent, it does not foresee anything. Everything is as usual. When we leave, everything is going to be the same in the city. I cannot even imagine it. I can, but I do not want to. Now, when our departure is imminent, I do not want to leave the ordinary, our routines and the known, established everyday rituals.

Robert is peeking out and warning me with his look. My serious Robert. Pedant, as well. His beard is now as white as the snow. It is still thick.

I am looking at my reflection in the mirror. I am tenderly smiling at myself. I wore a simple black dress. My hands are small. I like that. I like my soft long black leather gloves, too. I am dressed like an elderly woman. My silhouette is bigger than it used to be, my waist is a bit wider. But the prettiest is my smile. I do not flatter myself.

§

Boarding the ship was pompous. Many journalists came, Robert and I were posing in front of the French ocean liner for some time. Agnes brought me a bouquet of tiny wildflowers. We are going to Europe again, but this is neither an ordinary journey nor an adventure. We are going to live in a different location permanently. The journalists were shouting: "Mister ambassador, mister ambassador!" Robert obliged them with decisive dignity, he really seems like a man who is destined for that position. He is not pretending at all. Simply, he is the new US ambassador in Italy, as if that position was made for him only. He is not insecure at all. When they called him out, he immediately became what he is supposed to represent, and is playing his role easily and naturally. And I was his little bee. "Mrs. Johnson," they told me, officially; I gave him my sweet little smile with a nod on the right, I love my sweet little smile, and I looked at the reporters notably and mysteriously. Robert stood upright, with his lips decisively pinched together, with his snow shite beard, clean, solemn, and important. I was a tiny bee flying over wildflowers. I nevertheless trembled from excitement, although nobody noticed. New York remained in its white and yellow glow. Wherever you go, that mighty city will remain in the same location, unaware of your personal little departure.

The air in the liner is cruel, the water is crystal clear, as if it is calling you into its cold depth. I was looking at it so sunny as New York panorama remained for long. He stayed over there, in that moorland. Is he now alone in that anthill? Who is going to help him? Who is he going to meet?

§

A salty tear quickly dropped over my wrinkles and became one with the deep. I still do not have that device Nick had mentioned to help me send messages across the ocean to someone on the land who has the same device. Cold sun's whiteness covered the blue crust of the water and won.

§

What was I even doing this whole time? Nobody would even notice me being gone. If I have not been born, everything would be completely the same on this deck, only without me. Robert is reading and doing his papers.

My children are my work, through and through. They have the tamest eyes in the world. I know they miss me. I exaggerate when I speak of nonsense.

I am going on a mission for the benefit of the United States of America, to be a dignified official support to the Ambassador, the father of my children. It is about time a slap hurts me and warn me the time of longing has long passed.

MARCH

Prostitutes in Paris are wearing short dresses above their knees and white stockings visible in big boots. Everything changes, just like in New York, only everything seems to be both decadent and new. Everything keeps being only new in New York, always new. It is covered and uncovered here. Robert and I are no longer people who like social unusualness. Robert was never that person. I am now the old Mrs. Johnson. Paris is a city reborn after the war and you can feel the spirit of freedom everywhere, especially in women.

The most important thing is to hug Owen and his Catherine, our little Robert, Olivia, Owen Denise, and the little Patricia.

Owen has changed. Strange life has made him settle. He is not pale, his blood cannot go dim, but he is calmer. He is going to wake up.

Children are one's treasure.

APRIL

Rome is going to be different to us now because we are no longer tourists. I like the Roman yellow light, coral colors around us, the brightness, everybody is wearing coral colors. The city and the people in it are guarded by the old walls. The steps of the time are obvious, dusty, and full of earth here. We were choosing postcards. Many have a pink-orange patina.

The one with the Saturn's temple we have sent to our family in New York. And the same one to Nick.

§

Since all the Embassy employees greeted our arrival, respecting the rules, at the train station, and brought us to our Grand Hotel, our official commitments have commenced. Mostly Robert's. Since he took his credentials to the Ministry of the Exterior and since the royal carriage came to pick us up in a few days to take us to a reception by King Vittorio Emanuele III (very friendly), I too can officially receive other ambassadors' wives. We were introduced to Queen Elena and the Queen Mother, Margherita of Savoy. Time is returning, it seems, only everything is now serious and official. I was dignified.

§

Today I visited the Pantheon. I promised to be alone, but I was waiting to have a day off. Robert went to San Remo to a conference.

Entering the Pantheon is like entering your own death, but it is not scary at all, because in that reflection one feels completely safe and secure. The shaft through which God's attention comes in is connected to our eyes and forehead.

§

I have numerous obligations. Private dinners, tea parties, arrangements, invitations, flowers, orders, requests....

Olivia is with us. She is going to continue her education in Rome. Little Robert is attending a French boarding school.

We met Mr. Vesnić, the Ambassador of Yugoslavia in Italy. I carefully listened to what he was saying. He is such a caring and decent man, a true gentleman.

AUGUST
Robbie wants to blow away the Moon from his window.

NOVEMBER
We are sending letters and postcards, but some replies seldomly arrive.

DECEMBER
We were at a dinner in the Quirinale Palace, used by the King for state affairs. This time he organized a party in the honor of the Danish royal couple. Robert was comparing his impressions all night long. He says this is the most luxurious event in this palace. The King's guard shone in their scarlet and white uniforms with brass helmets. They stand upright. But their hard work, humanity, thoughts, looks do not shine.

1921

JANUARY

We were at a New Year's party with Mr. Vesnić and agreed to travel to Belgrade with him.

FEBRUARY

We were standing up on a hill above the mouth of two rivers. We stayed at the Europa Hotel. Sharp energy coming from the mouth of the river's heart cut my view. The feeling was not unpleasant because greatness comes from it. The greatest power is for a grand one to allow the tiny one to flow into him with love, and then for them to join together. That is called sufferance. I was talking about Nick all the time, probably his ears were burning. His salty power never allowed the sweet water to flow into him. No matter how much I have tried, there was always a stony bastion that was surrounding him, just like this one in Belgrade, above the two rivers. Paradoxically, we are away from Rome, thereby away from New York, but in Belgrade I feel I am again close to Nick. All the silence about him is now open and unraveled, all the words that have been pushed aside.

For decades I have been on watch in front of that strange man's bastion in order to find a secret way in. I sleep, I fall, he rejects me, I give up, dream, get tired.

We sent him a postcard from Belgrade. It is so nice here, an interesting compound of the old and the new.

I am trying to find his past. It is nice to crouch in a nutshell. They can lie me down onto the frozen ground, I would not feel a thing, tucked into this tiny, voiceless space.

§

I want to go back home and never return. I no longer want to travel anywhere, I want to be at home and relax. I am tired. Of everything.

MARCH

Robert, Owen, and Olivia drove an airship above Rome and the Albano Lake! They begged me to join them, but I stayed at the hotel. I feel terribly weak. Or have I no courage?

§

He again drove from Rome to Naples yesterday. He told me he had seen almond blossoms, white roads, Vesuvius crater, the Capri island, and how the sky was clean. He sent a radio message from the airship to the Department of War in Washington. And another to Robbie, who is back to his Ramsay Hall school.

The new era has truly come. Aircrafts are flying above our heads, messages traveling mysterious ways, all of this was foreseen by Nikola Tesla a long time ago. Everything is coming true. He sees even what is to happen in a few years, only the thing is that no one can follow him. He hears holy words from the space nobody else hears. He still did not tell us everything he had heard. The new world is coming, clamoring like a hurricane, storming like a volcano, the new world is going to replace this tired old one.

§

Owen brought us a manuscript of his new novel called *The Wasted Generation*. He is writing about an American who applied for the French Foreign Legion in the dawning of the war.

We also had dinner at the Embassy of Brazil.

MAY

Owen is great at golf. He loves painting and running around the Roman galleries.

JULY

It is over. Robert is no longer the Ambassador. We are going back home, completely opposite to the many Americans who bought castles and villas in Europe. I was dignified, nobody could notice how tired I am. I was the way I used to be, a person who kindly greets and sends off many famous and important people, I was smiling, I gave my hand, I bowed, bridged, I provided home, bread... Now I can retire and be only a tired old lady.

I cannot wait until we set off, I would like to leave now, right away, from this spot, and wait for any means of transport to take me home. I no longer want other cities, I want my city whose every corner I know like the palm of my hand.

There are no more mood swings, playing with oneself, fooling myself with imagination, laughing out loud, no thrills nor heat. I am tired of everything. I shall return to introduce a flat tone, a smooth surface of a lake people have not yet discovered. I do not want to travel anywhere anymore. I want my home.

NOVEMBER

When you enter New York, your truly start crying from happiness. It is a ghost always in motion.

It is more vibrant now, faster, crazier. Jazz is the new music. I do not completely understand it, but young people are crazy about it. Everybody is drinking dry martini and it seems they are stunned from the booze and gusts of positive energy that bursts from every corner. I have never been more tired from a journey. It is devastating, but it accepted me—I am its. New York still has that transparent, almost metal air, as *The Century* described it a long time ago. Back in the last century.

§

He came to our Thanksgiving dinner yesterday. It seemed as if he was forced to, but not in his heart, he loved us with his eyes, and was distant in his body.

DECEMBER

Christmas was the same. Ordinary words. Unordinary feelings. Just the way it must be, it must.

§

My dear Owen, what is going on with your life? You have just told us that your fourth wife, Catherine, has died. I cannot even express what feelings of transiency and senselessness I am currently experiencing. I got such terrible chills. I cannot help you at all. Childhood images keep reminiscing and the sounds I have forgotten about. They are nice, but so powerful that they give me the shakes. Horrible beauty that kills.

1922

JANUARY

The greatest light I have ever seen was the revelation and a passage to brokenness.

His face does not show years. Sometimes he looks at me like he used to, almost passionately, but that look usually vanishes. He is still orderly and perfectly polished, but now he seems a bit old-fashioned. Still, his soul remains the same.

MARCH

Robert started writing his memoirs. He is going to depict our family and all the great people that visited our home, our travels, all of his activities.... It is going to be a big serious intellectual memory book.

APRIL

Nikola Tesla is talking to himself. The blinds are down. He is not talking about his work, not even to us. He publicly speaks only about restraining from everything, about asceticism. He no longer eats boiled fish, only vegetarian food. He is turning into a ghost.

Everything is different, everything is darker. We hear no words from him, we only have feelings and dreams. Last night I dreamt of him showing me intersected skies, layers of different colors. He made a hand gesture and the sky immediately cleared up. It became clearer to inspect. Then he said he wants to catch the vibrations from the purple layer, to take them to us and turn them into electricity we already know of.

We are not seeing him again.

MAY

He was seen going out from St. Patrick's Cathedral. He always loved going there.

Is he still flying in his dreams, as he frequently used to paraphrase it to us? Does he still visit the distant places while he is half-asleep?

JUNE

Jazz is a miracle. I envy those who are young with it. Girls are now showing their ankles and knees, they smoke cigarettes from a cigarette holder, they wear tiny hats with tight rims, long pearl necklaces, their dresses are flat, there are no rough taft wrinkles, everything is easy, everything so simple.

NOVEMBER

Silver is falling down from the sky.

DECEMBER

I am looking at old photos. They portray my youth and fire. A smooth face, glossy eyes, fresh audaciousness.

1923

JANUARY

Owen finally moved back to America. He said he is never going abroad again. Now he lives in Stockbridge, Massachusetts, and he intends to stay there.

MARCH

Robert asked Nick in a letter to send him some of the photos from his lab from the old days to put them in his memoirs. It seems as if we are so official, not close friends. He does not visit us, we do not share meals together, we do not laugh, nor listen to music, nor do we read poetry.

MAY

I want to go to Maine. I would like to go there alone. Who knows what awaits me, I am both physically and mentally weak. Next year I may not be able to move. Even now I feel tiredness in my bones and legs. I do not want to burden anyone with my slow walking and grey clouds.

Robert wrote an introduction to his memoirs that are soon to be published.

JUNE

I am in Maine, staying in a hotel. I am trying to arrange my thoughts. The journey itself was difficult for me, but it was worth it, my lungs already absorb the freshness. While I sit facing the ocean, for moments it seems nothing has ever happened. I get completely empty. I no longer know anyone nor remember anything. The great sea forcefully erases all the tensions. I am happy. I am alone and no to belong to anyone.

JULY

"I came here a month ago, quite alone, to this hotel full, but empty for me, since it is a strange world. Here, I am as detached as if nothing belonged to me but memory. At times I am filled with sadness and long for that which is not – just as intensely as I did when a young girl and I listened to the waves of the sea, which is still unknown, and still beating about me. And you? What are you doing? I wish I could have news of you my ever dear and ever silent friend, be it good or bad. But if you will not send me a line, then send me a thought and it will be received by a finely attuned instrument.

I do not know why I am so sad, but I feel as if everything in life had slipped from me. Perhaps I am too much alone and only need companionship. I think I would be happier if I knew something about you. You, who are unconscious of everything but your work and who have no human needs. This is not what I want to say and so I am Faithfully yours.

P. S. Do you remember the gold dollar that passed between you and Robert? I am wearing it this summer as a talisman for all of us."[23]

---

[23] A letter from Katherine Johnson to Nikola Tesla, in: Margaret Cheney, *Tesla: Man out of Time*, p. 273–274.

Has he ever been with a woman? He claims he has not. I do not believe him. When I catch a flaming piece of his look, I do not trust him at all. His hands are sensual when they want to reveal themselves. He is skillfully hiding. In his gloves. In science.

§

Memories are like gunshot wounds.

NOVEMBER

Robert's memoirs were published in Boston. He dedicated them to me. He put the book in my lap once he received a copy. "To Katherine McMahon Johnson." I am his eternal dream, a wish, and a friend. He has no dilemmas, he is holding me only while he puts treasure into my lap. Robert Underwood Johnson is hardworking and diligent, he does not miss anything, he treasures all of his memories. Thanks to his efforts, we are always going to be alive, the people he loves and whom he remembers with respect. My feelings are inconsistent, and I managed to mix them up. They intertwine and argue, I push them away and then search for them, I give them back their dignity. It is as if they are a pile of sand from the coasts of the Atlantic, the wind takes away them layer by layer, erasing them.

§

I randomly flipped the pages of *Remembered Yesterdays*, devouring Robert's sentences about our sophisticated orderly life.

Robert's merit is grand – he wrote his memoirs only from his recollections, he never had the time to write a journal.

He is the moon. Dignified and calm, pale yellow. He is not the fire that creates the whole world, but he skillfully receives light from it, and steadily gives it to us. The moon is only seemingly a flat disc that feeds from the sun's energy. Without the moon, we would not be able to live the nights nor see the road in darkness. Robert is a guide, always at your service, powerful in his quiet empire.

Nikola Tesla is the sun, he creates, and without him there would be no world, but he can burn you, so you feel your own burnt flesh. He can make you blind, so you do not see during the day or night, so you do not feel the noble Moon's cold glow. But he can also stir your blood, so you feel the heat for days.

I was looking at both the yellow and platinum light, they used to guide me. And what light am I?

§

Robert knows.

1924

JANUARY

It is New Year's Eve, and I am sick and exhausted. These are the words of an old lady. But I am not old! The cutlery is clinging in the salons. People are full of hope. Rivers of smiles run down the city, winter gusts cannot harm them. My mouth is dry and tight. I am weak, although I do not want to get up. Is my body even listening to my thoughts? Indubitably. I have no desires, therefore no life juices. I always asked myself what it would be to have no desires. I am now in that state, completely consciously. Or has fate brought me to this state? Nevertheless, this is a state of pleasant desperation. A flat line. Indifference. I do not have to, and I will not. I want not to want. I love being sick.

True and false optimism, visits, socializing… I do not want any of those things. I had times of glow, it was all over me. Bright and piercing lumps of light I used to make tiaras of. I never bought them. Where is that glow now? What did it serve for anyway? Where is my smile described by Robert, the one I used to share with everybody like a rose that shares its scent?

§

We are living in a world of vibrations. We are the energy. We are vibrations. We are electricity. We are lightbulbs. When you emit your own waves and let them go, they find their alike and return to you. Why could I not then be with him? He turns the sky into purple and rejects all the waves he does not want. He used to say a man progresses towards his goal as if he was wearing magic boots – if his desire is strong. I used to have it. And it did not come true. My inessential passion confronted all of his and was beaten up in the very beginning.

§

Am I crazy? Am I ungrateful? I have been selfish these days, not thinking of anyone but myself.

What did I live to see? What did I build? I do not know whose life I have been living. It seems the one I have experienced is not mine.

Kate, a child, who does not wish to mature, who likes melancholy and does things out of spite even more because of it. How can one change one's own nature?

FEBRUARY
Owen found a new partner—a widow, Gertrude Bovee Le Boutillier. He fell in love, and is writing to us to let us know he is searching for happiness once again.

MARCH
Do memories have a value? It seems their force is valuable when they scorch our skin. I start thinking that the fact that I loved someone was worth it, it counts, my fascination, my effort, my giving. Or is it false strength? Can we really have them? Can they fulfill us? Here they are, climbing up the stairs, sneaking around, and entering my room. It is springtime, but I ordered to have all the blinds down. I do not want beams of light. I do not want light and glare, I do not want to see myself.

This house is a treasury of memories, wherever I look, they burst out. I want darkness.

Robert is compassionate. I do not need pity!

§

It is hard to live two lives.

§

I did not say it, I did not show it, I did not play it, I did not perform, I was not used, I did not use. I am nothing.

§

All those parties and socializing I used to organize were nice.... Nice? They were my job, obligation, pleasure, sense. But I was not the protagonist, I did not spill anything, all of them who came, they all spilled beauty, I enjoyed it, but I could have spilled more of my beauty. I am tired of all those parties and fun, organizing, I am tired of all the voices and steps, other people's goals. I was looking for fun, I wanted to create it around me. I never had it in me, nor did I provide it. I did not provide anything. Nothing excites me. I did not generate excitement, I did not graze anyone, the sun did not scorch me enough, as if I was living in shadows. Robert would have fallen in love with any other cheerful and unusual girl had he met her before me. Oh, God, I am so cruel. I do not do him justice. This is it – there is no coming back.

§

I chose an idea and put it on the pedestal of my life, I used to think about it all the time, I sacrificed my other thoughts. Where is my success? Where is my peace of mind?

Who knows me really? I was losing myself in all those faces.

§

How many times did I give and send to Nick a pinch of my soul or my entire soul? I cannot determine it. When I compare myself with his devotion, mine is small. When I was capriciously young, everything I had was the greatest.

§

Who is going to read about me? Why am I writing this? I am going to tell Robert to burn this notebook down. He should read it and burn it.

§

Agnes and Leticia are frequently in our home. Agnes is caring, as if she was my mother. I get upset about everything and cannot stand neither the sounds nor footsteps. Leticia is even staying away from me.

APRIL

Have I made even one step outside of the ordinary? Other people around me have fought, they lived. They all knew what they wanted. I did not do anything right. I thought I was burning out. Not enough, Katherine McMahon! The beginnings were frivolous and not serious. You have never reached the endings. You have lived a protected and comfortable life. You wanted that. Did you put your hand in the fire for anything? Even Owen and Agnes have lived more than you have. You are a fine pearl protected by mother shell that has now rolled under the bed. And it is going to stay there. A pearl that was rejected by the person you loved.

Have I lived my life just when it was happening or after, slowly, thinking of the events that passed? Who am I in a sea of real and imaginary kisses?

The only woman in New York who wrote her name instead of her husbands on her visiting card. Is that it?

Katherine McMahon, you, simply, were not good enough for anything.

AUGUST

Nick sent me a letter with a recommendation for my diet so I can recover and gather my strength as soon as possible. What should I return to? To live other people's lives, to look how they parade beside me and accomplish all of their wishes, to greet and take care of them, to celebrate other people's success?

No wonders can no longer satisfy me.

Robert told me he is going to pray bitterness leaves me, and then weakness would go away too. Bitterness is killing me slowly, like poison. It came from the stomach, all the way up to my throat. Why am I being like this? I am going to be punished in an even worse way.

§

Robert was never an idle person, a false idealist, a pathetic man wallowing in his insecurity and doom. He always had a firm hand and stable thoughts and was always a source of security. Such people deserve to live a long life. I will pray for him. It is not his fault. He lives a noble life – just the way he is, always maturely accepting his role and responsibility. I cannot know how much he suffocated his premonitions and small defeats caused my me, took them off of his face as soon as I showed up—wanting to always please me, even when I rejected him. If it were not for him, I would have sunk a long time ago. He was a shield that enabled me to fly. Never consciously, never on purpose. My face was wrinkled on our pillow, but what would become of me had he not bring that pillow? Who knows?

Dear Robert, I wounded him, and he accepted it—loving me just the way I was. He never showed me his wounds. He was whole for me always, even though he knew everything.

Nevertheless, I do not regret anything. My life was a strange phenomenon, a complex movement, just like Nick used to say. I was moved and so I moved myself, and wherever I went away from myself, that was always me.

I am proud. I kept him in my thoughts, creating images in different worlds, we were connected. What used to take away my breath also kept me alive. Black holes in my body shine away. Now I see them, and I am ready. I realize it. He is the Beautiful that was born inside of me after all those years of longing for him. The waves from the depth of my forehead appear, I can feel them now, thinking like this. Love was and is inside me, it does not even depend on whether he returns it or not. Love is spilled inside of me, I swim in it, at this moment, and forever.

The clouds are huge. I do not want to forget his beauty even when I die.

§

I give this notebook to Robert, so he can read it from the very beginning. When he comes back to my room, he returns it. I always ask him whether he is really reading it. He honestly replies: "I am," and then he puts his hand on my forehead.

I told him, "Forgive me everything there is to forgive. I also forgive you everything."

SEPTEMBER

I think I dreamt of flying in my sleep, just like Nick used to say it often happens to him.

NOVEMBER

Dreams are reality, and life is but a dream.

§

Who is going to take care of him when I am gone? Who can stay up like I do? He is unprotected. Lonely. He left us all. Everybody left him.

§

My children… the warmth above my sick bed.

§

Now I have no questions, I am finally mature, like the fall, with a robe colored in old gold.

§

Thank you.

Thank you, all y'all.

§

Who is going to do it?

DECEMBER

[Added by Robert Underwood Johnson personally]

KATHERINE MACMAHON JOHNSON DIED ON DECEMBER 31, 1924 IN NEW YORK. SHE WAS BURIED IN STOCKBRIDGE.

HER LAST WISH WAS CONCERNING NIKOLA TESLA.

"Dear Tesla,

It was Mrs. Johnson's injunction that last night of her life that I should keep in touch with Tesla. This is a pretty hard thing to do, but it will not be my fault if it is not done.

Yours faithfully,

Luka"[24]

---

[24] A letter from Robert Underwood Johnson to Nikola Tesla, in: Marc Seifer, *Wizard*, p. 440.

1936

DECEMBER

[Added by Robert Underwood Johnson personally]

"Oh, if I could only help you with something in your illness. On this night twenty years ago my dearest wife, who tenderly loved you, has died. One of the last things she had said was: 'Keep in touch with Tesla and look after him.' You know how much I intended to do so, and how hard it was to maintain our relationship. Do not let me lose it in the forthcoming year, my dear friend. Besides us and the Hobsons, you have very few friends left to look after you. You should invite Agnes to visit you, because I am unable… Agnes is going to be very helpful to you. All you need is to pick up the phone. Go on, do it in memory of late Mrs. Johnson.

Yours faithfully and forever loyal, R. U. Johnson, alias Luka Filipov."[25]

---

[25] A letter from Robert Underwood Johnson to Nikola Tesla, in: Special Addendum to "*Nepoznati Tesla* (The Unknown Tesla)". *Galaksija*, No. 86, June 1979.

ETHER

1937

Where are you, Nick? I see you! Your cheeks are dry and your hair completely white, you are old and thin, but still incredibly vital! I assumed it would be so. You are tough, you tall man!

You must hear me but will not admit it to yourself. Can you hear me, my love? I am free and on my own. I let my voice go, I found a clue in the living reality's crust. My love! My soul! My light! You are the meekness. You are the kindness. You are everything.

I will observe you for eternity. My eternity is a moment of yours. Grand birds fly above me, they pass by me, calling me loudly.

You are in New York. It is even more beautiful and bigger now than it once was. It is decorated with Chrysler and Empire State building, the modern cathedrals, a powerful stairway to heaven. You dine alone, have no friends. You do not like the sunshine, you draw the curtains on. You spend your last few bucks on pigeon seeds. Are you taking care of yourself?

You still walk down the streets, not looking at anyone. You wear an old suit, always the same, that famous Fifth Avenue dandy is gone. Where are your extravagant deep green shoes made of capsized leather?

You dream as you walk, you do not mind the traffic. You are barely recognized by anyone, and you do not recognize them either. You feel good about it. Are you looking at big window shafts? Can you see my face? I used to look at my reflection in them. When we do it, our reflection remains on the glass, the light does not go out. It remains like a layer of frost in the corner of a window.

When I was leaving, I passed through thick fog high above the ground, where my former thoughts have been chatting, all so orderly and alive. Everything is alive, everything is flashing, nothing is ever dead. You once told me we are a part of a reservoir of inexhaustible energy that renews itself.

Can you hear me, my love? I know you can. Transferring thoughts is possible. Especially now, when I am in a different world, you talk to even better. You should only close your eyes. You are sensitive to low pitches other people cannot hear. You can get down even lower, into the greener reality. You know where eternal energy sources lie, you know where to find them, you know people are going to understand it one day. You understand the curvy spines of time. Things from the other side are not foreign.

You can touch all the waves if you want to, they turn into bronze waterfalls under your skin. They go through you.

Watch out, do not go out today, mind the cars! If you decide to go out anyway, pay attention to a young mother saying "Stop!" to her child! You should also stop! It is a sign!

The air is ribbed. The sky is white. The water is burning here. The fire sounds like water. I see the droplets, transparent eyes in which red heat is aflame. Here you can walk on the winds.

I speak without my lips. I live without my body. I observe many things: everything is round, and all is one. The universe is a big machine that is never to vanish, you said it.

I know you are going to remember me right at this moment. The breath of my words is reaching you. I am not gone. I am young. I am calm. I still love you. Everything is alright. The end of everything is the beginning of everything else. I learn. I enjoy myself.

I will keep posting. Pay attention to the dedicated rustle of the Grand Central Station's hallways. Listen to what the people sitting behind you on a train are saying.

I am waiting for you, you are the purest soul of all. Long time ago I put you onto my life's pedestal, I have lived for you. When our two worlds and our two times finally meet, you will be mine only in the light in which silver and gold are balanced out. You are going to touch me, kiss me, penetrate me, we are going to become one. I am going to feel your nakedness, even whiter before fiery looks that roam free. Your former and present dreams of me, full of moisture and sweat, are alive for eternity, in this world behind doors ajar they are going to be open widely and real. I am going to tremble from all the little deaths that are to follow one another, a myriad of climaxes. Your male strength, however, is never going to go away, I will put it in my mouth and drink it until my sweet exhaustion. To eternity, in fact. There is time for everything here, the events roll out simultaneously, in parallels, there are no priorities, no sacrifice, I do not have to be the second because the science is the first. Swami said long time ago that all events exist in a vibrating state in Akasha, can you remember? Of course, you do.

I am keeping all of your New York looks full of hidden zeal. You were keeping yourself from showing to me, but you could not manage to do it every time. You did not want to tell me so many things, you had no time, but all those words are alive and are going to be mine in this starry freedom where there is no before nor afterwards, no behind and no fronts.

I am waiting for you. I am happy.

ABOUT THE AUTHOR

Ana Atanasković (b. in 1973 in Kruševac, Serbia) is an author, journalist, and a copywriter. She is a graduated Philologist – English major, with an MA in Publishing Marketing.

So far she published: a collection of short stories *Beogradske majske priče* (2006), a novel *Duet duša* (2008), a novel *Jelena Anžujska* (2009. i 2010), a novel *Moja ljubav Nikola Tesla* (2013), a collection of short stories *Beograd je ljubav* (2017), a novel *Kraljica jorgovana* (unabridged version of *Jelena Anžujska*, 2019) and a novel *Davorjanka Paunović* (2020).

She worked as a journalist for ELLE magazine, VipTripDiplomatic, Vodič za život, Sensa, Lepota & Zdravlje, Esquire, Ilustrovana Politika and numerous other services.

She is a laureate of the best lavender story prizes (*Bonux* and *Sofia*) and best book review (*Lisa* and *Laguna*).

She has given her "Tesla and Women" lecture in Philadelphia and, on numerous occasions, in Serbia.

She is currently living and working in Belgrade.